BROOKLYN SUMMER

MAGGIE CUMMINGS

Praise for Ma...
Perfect

"If you like friends-to-lovers romances, you will enjoy this book. If you are a fan of books about dogs, you will love this book. I enjoyed it, and I fit into both categories."—*Rainbow Reflections*

"Maggie Cummings has an amazing talent for writing characters I easily fall for, and she brings them to life with such panache... This is a feel-good tale that left me with a smile on my face. Highly recommended."—*Kitty Kat's Book Review Blog*

Against All Odds

"I started reading the book trying to dissect the writing and ended up forgetting all about the fact that three people were involved in writing it because the story just grabbed me by the ears and dragged me along for the ride...[A] really great romantic suspense that manages both parts of the equation perfectly. This is a book you won't be able to put down."—*C-Spot Reviews*

Definite Possibility

"I enjoyed this book, well written with well-developed characters, including some familiar faces from the previous book in the series. The leads had good chemistry and the angst level was just right. It was an enjoyable read for a quiet afternoon."—*Melina Bickard, Librarian, Waterloo Library (UK)*

"[T]wo parallel romances give a quick pace to the book with more drama and romance...But what I really liked is that the story goes beyond both romances and is a tale of friendship, family and love. Overall, a heartwarming and feel-good story with a bit of drama on the side."—*Lez Review Books*

Totally Worth It

"[I]t was...really nice reading about people going through the same transitory period in their lives that I, and many other twenty-somethings, also are...By the end of the book, I was a little jealous that I didn't live in Bay West like the characters. Needless to say, I was pretty pleased when I found out that this was going to be a series because Bay West has so much potential...I can't wait to see where Cummings takes us next."—*Read All About Queer Lit*

By the Author

Totally Worth It

Serious Potential

Definite Possibility

Perfect Partners

Against All Odds (with Kris Bryant and M. Ullrich)

Brooklyn Summer

BROOKLYN SUMMER

by

Maggie Cummings

2020

ISBN 13: 978-1-63555-578-3

This Trade Paperback Original Is Published By
Bold Strokes Books, Inc.
P.O. Box 249
Valley Falls, NY 12185

First Edition: February 2020

Credits
Editor: Ruth Sternglantz
Production Design: Stacia Seaman
Cover Design by Tammy Seidick

Acknowledgments

With each book, the network of support seems to grow wider and stronger. For starters, I'd like to thank Rad, Sandy, and the entire team at BSB for creating such a great place to work. Thank you also to Ruth Sternglantz, my amazing editor, for always keeping me on point, for guiding me, teaching me, and for never growing tired of my endless questions. To my fellow writers, who are both friends and colleagues, thank you for making this journey so much fun.

I am so grateful for my tribe—my chosen family, my given family. I truly could not accomplish anything without the support of Kat, Caleb, and Abby, who are my whole heart and the most important part of my life. Without their encouragement, love, and continual supply of hugs and Hershey's kisses, I'd be truly lost. I also feel incredibly fortunate for Nush, who always pushes me to keep going and keeps me laughing along the way. Thank you to all my friends who are consistently supportive. I am just so lucky to have such a wonderful group of people who feel more like family than anything else. To Sheila, Matt, Lucy, and Lizzie, thanks for always cheering me on. I'm so thankful to all my relatives for their encouragement, especially my parents and grandparents, who spent so many hours telling stories about Brooklyn and Ireland that somehow sank in and made their way into the backstory of the characters on these pages. I'm grateful for the rich history, the culture, the entertainment value, but most importantly for having a family so willing and ready to share it all.

For Peggy Buckley,
the original Brooklyn girl

Chapter One

I need a vacation from my life."

Ashleigh McAllister flopped on a sturdy barstool as she sized up her friend's overhauled Brooklyn pub.

"Soon enough. School's over in what, two days?" Liam asked as he looked over his domain.

"It's basically over now. Today was the last full day. Tomorrow is twelve o'clock dismissal."

"See that. Relief, right around the corner."

"From work, at least." She fidgeted with the edge of a napkin. In the past, summer break meant free time, lazy days, mini vacations. Since her divorce was final, the weeks ahead felt like a series of empty days lying in wait. "The classroom has been my saving grace this whole year."

"Speaking of, you're still bringing your teacher friends by, right? They drink like fish, and honestly, I could use the business."

"It's all set up. Everyone's pumped."

"Awesome. It's supposed to be gorgeous. It's going to be my first night opening up the back. I'm hoping to tap into that summer energy."

"That sounds fun. Can I go see how it looks back there?"

"Not yet."

Ashleigh frowned.

"Don't be mad. I just want it to be perfect when you see it."

"Fine. But the only reason I'm not mad is because I love you." Ashleigh tried to bring some spirit into her voice even though her mood was in the gutter. "I'm a sucker for a good reveal. I bet it's going to change the vibe of this whole place."

"That's the plan." He crossed his fingers to the sky. "So what's the matter?" he asked. "Why the glum face? Bill and Peg driving you crazy at home?"

"I wish. In fact, the opposite's true." Ashleigh had zero reasons to complain, but she was sorry for herself today. "My parents are amazing. Mom makes my lunch every day. My dad folds my laundry. They'll regret this when I never move out again."

"Stop. They love you. We all do."

"Not all." She glanced out the open bay window hoping the sun glare would obscure the emotions that still felt fresh. "Clearly."

He filled a pint glass to the brim with ice, gunned in some seltzer, and hit it with a splash of OJ. "Here you go, my dear." He placed the drink directly in front of her and egged her on with a nod of his chin. "Tell the old whiskey slinger here what's wrong."

She eyed the drink suspiciously. "There's no alcohol in this, is there?"

"And violate your strict weekday prohibition?" He teased her openly. "Of course not."

"Just making sure." She stirred the drink with a paper straw, watching the ice form a tiny whirlpool. "Quit making me sound so uptight. I'm just not that big a fan of day drinking."

"You are a nerd." He winked at her. "It's part of your charm." He leaned on the bar across from where she was sitting. "So, talk to me. I *am* a bartender, you know."

"Don't act like this is all in your genetic makeup. You've been a bartender for exactly nine months."

"Ten," he corrected. "And this was my parents' place, and my grandfather's before that. So, technically, it is in my blood." His smile was endearing and it struck Ashleigh how much she'd missed him over the years. "But that's not the point. I've been your best friend since birth. In all seriousness, I'm here for you. Out with it," he ordered.

She pulled a long sip from her straw, searching for courage in her virgin cocktail. "I saw them again. Reagan and Josh."

He groaned. "When?"

"Just now. After I walked Granny to her tai chi class at the senior center. They were leaving CrossFit on Fifth and Sackett. Holding hands."

"Gross."

"Right?"

"Who holds hands on the way out of the gym? All sweaty and salty? Blech." He shivered in dramatic disgust.

"Not what I meant. But I'll take it."

"How'd it go when you saw them? The convo, I mean."

"Oh my God, I didn't talk to them. I turned the corner and hightailed it here." Ashleigh saw them too often in the neighborhood, and usually she swallowed her pride and engaged them. Today she didn't have it in her. She held her chin high in the air. "That's when I decided that I'm just going to spend the whole summer right here. This way I'm sure to avoid them." She forced a smile and coupled it with a defiant nod.

"I'm a fan of this decision." He did an impromptu celebratory dance raising the roof with both hands. "Ash, you can come here every day. Honestly, I would love it. Because I love you and I missed your face and I love spending time with you." He reached for a bar rag from his back pocket. "But—"

"Here it comes."

"Don't with the woe-is-me tone. I'm not going to lecture you." He leaned over and took her face in his strong hands and kissed her forehead. "But I ain't gonna coddle you either." Liam reached for a lime and tossed it to himself before grabbing a bar knife to start breaking it down. "It wouldn't hurt you to get back out there."

Ashleigh felt a smidge of betrayal and she wanted him to know it. She folded her arms across her chest and pouted.

"Come on. Don't give me that look. You and Reagan have been over for ages. You even told me so. Eons ago. You sent me emails saying you were growing apart. And that was back when I was in Asia, I believe."

Her look of confusion must have revealed she didn't follow his timeline.

"My point is, I was stationed there, let me think…" He paused for a second, doing the calculation in his head. "Seven years ago. Seven years," he added for emphasis. "It's actually insane that you stayed married this long. When you knew—you knew—almost a decade ago, that it was over."

"I don't know if I really knew."

"You knew. You told me you had doubts. You said you and Reagan were more like friends than anything else. That you'd slipped into the dreaded lesbian bed death." He widened his eyes for dramatic emphasis before he suddenly stopped slicing the lime and looked right at her. "Please don't tell me you haven't gotten any action in seven years."

"Shut up." She was embarrassed and worried it showed. It hadn't been quite that long, but while the demise of her marriage had been amicable, it had not been amorous. She grabbed a handful of cardboard coasters and threw them at him like Frisbees to break the tension.

"Hey. I'm trying to keep this place clean!" He bent down to pick up the mess immediately. "I'm not making fun of you," he said. He walked over to her and leaned on the spotless bar top. "Ashleigh, your divorce has been final since September. It's June. The entire year it was one thing after another. First it was the beginning of the school year, then running the math club, helping the AP students get ready for college entrance exams, helping the non-AP kids get ready for college entrance exams." His smile was sweet and supportive as he enumerated her excuses on his fingertips. "It's summer. You live in downtown Brooklyn, the unofficial capital of the lesbian universe. Christ, you can't throw a rock without hitting a pair of women pushing a repurposed, handcrafted, organic stroller together."

"Or my ex-wife and her new boy toy."

"It sucks that Reagan's with someone else. And that you all live within a three-block radius of each other." He touched her forearm. "I feel you." He pushed off the bar. "But it's time you get back out there too. You're thirty-seven. Not ninety-seven."

"I can't even imagine being in another relationship."

"Hold up. Problem number one. Who said anything about a relationship? I said get back out there. Play the field. Date."

"Easy for you to say. Guys practically throw themselves at you. Women too, I bet."

"Even if that was the case, I've never had any interest, and you know it." He snapped the bar rag in her direction with a laugh. "As far as guys go"—he shrugged in submission—"I've been in the Army for the last twenty years, so even though I was surrounded by guys, it was not exploding with opportunity."

"Now that you're home, I bet you find the perfect guy in no time."

"No worries." His smile was impish. "I'm rather enjoying myself assessing the options."

"I wish I had one ounce of your confidence."

"I don't know why you don't." He dropped his rag and reached for more fruit to prep the bar for the dinner crowd he hoped would begin to filter in. Working on a lemon, he snuck a sideways glance. "Look at you. Long blond hair, blue eyes, adorable dork factor. I can't believe women aren't lining up for you. Oh, wait"—he held his knife in the air—"I can. Because you never leave the house. And you refuse dating apps. So how the fuck are they supposed to find you?"

"I leave the house." Okay, it was mostly to go to work, but technically it was the truth.

"Work doesn't count. But only because you're not interested in any of your colleagues."

"They're all straight. Or men. Or straight men."

"The worst offenders of our society."

"You're telling me." Her sigh was heavy and filled with defeat.

"Yikes." He winced. "I wasn't even meaning to reference Josh."

She wiped the condensation off the glass of her unfinished drink, unable to block out the image of Reagan and how happy she'd looked today, even from afar.

"Hey." Liam brought her back to the present. "Forget her. You're going to find someone. I promise. You're gorgeous, and smart, and sweet. If Reagan couldn't see that in all the years you were together, she's definitely not worth your time right now."

"Thanks, Liam."

"I love ya, Ash. You deserve to be happy. I want that for you."

"I do too." She reached for her phone and zipped in her passcode. "And I have a plan for that."

"Good. Whatcha got cooking?" Liam nodded at her phone.

"You're going to like it. It involves leaving my parents' house. A lot."

He waved his hands excitedly, not having to dig deep to find his inner queen. "Praise be."

"I decided that instead of hanging around Park Slope all summer where I am apparently bound to continuously run into Reagan and her boyfriend"—it was still difficult to say those words out loud—"I'm going to live it up."

"I'm listening."

She pulled up a calendar on her phone. "I'm—correction, we're— going to do New York City." Reading his confusion, she held up a hand.

"Stay with me. All the things that tourists do: museums, the Statue of Liberty, Chinatown, Roosevelt Island, Broadway, all that stuff is at our fingertips. But how often do we really take advantage of it? Hardly at all," she said, answering her own question. "This is going to be our summer of spontaneity. We'll do something different each day." She'd crafted her agenda for weeks and couldn't help but feel a surge of pleasure at seeing it displayed in all its color-coded glory on the screen. With the tip of her finger she panned back and forth so he could get a good look. "All the fun of being tourists, but we get to sleep in our own beds at night. Well, you get to sleep in your own bed. I get to sleep in the twin bed of my youth. I'm blocking that part out."

"I love it. Only one problem." He fanned his hand over the bar. "I'm kind of stuck here, trying desperately to turn this place into a sustainable future."

Ashleigh smiled in commiseration. "I thought you might say that. I do have a backup plan."

"Shauna?" He sounded hopeful.

"As if." Ashleigh fake frowned. "She and Mike are in full blown wedding prep."

"Is that hard for you?" He sounded so sincere that she wanted to reach over the bar and hug him.

"Eh. Not really. I'm happy for Shauna. She's waited a long time for this. And Mike's a sweetheart."

"Sorry, tell me your plan," he said, getting them back on track.

"It's not as much fun as exploring with you. And I'm sure I can drag Shauna and Mike with me here and there. But in the meantime, I'll live the dream on my own, day-tripping through the city. You promise to join me whenever you can spare a day away from here. I'll save anything you're really into for when you can make it. The other stuff"— she took a deep breath—"I'll just have to be brave and go it alone. I'll take a million pics, and then I'll head straight here after and we can deconstruct the day together." She'd known his ability to participate might be limited. It had been worth asking anyway. His expression told her if things were different, he wouldn't hesitate to join her. In a way, that was enough. "This works too," she said with a happy shrug. "It will keep me out of my parents' way, and I'll get some quality time with you. Liam, I missed you. I'm so happy you're finally home."

"I fully support this plan. One condition."

"What?" She heard optimism creeping into her tone, and she smiled at her old friend knowing he was helping her out of her slump. "Anything for you."

"Promise me you'll flirt on your adventures."

"I was married for twelve years. I don't remember how to flirt."

"Ashleigh." His voice was stern.

"I promise to try."

"I'll take it." He fiddled with the levers of his on-tap offerings. "So, tomorrow is the official start of summer."

"Technically, the start of summer was last week."

"I meant summer *vacation*."

"Sorry, yes. Why?"

"No reason. Just a lot riding on the season to bring this place back to where it needs to be." He seemed nervous and Ashleigh wanted to comfort him.

"It's going to be great. The secret outdoor area"—she pointed at the back with her chin—"that's going to be a game changer. People love to chill outside. I've got practically the whole staff coming tomorrow. There's been a group text going on for days because it's all anyone can talk about. Half of them already spread the word in their own friend circles to meet up here too. Everyone's down to party. It'll be great exposure for this place. Add in some beautiful weather, banging drinks, good food, and a hot bartender, *pshh*." She threw in a dismissive wave to make her point. "This place will be a gold mine in no time."

"Thanks, Ash."

She winked. "I gotta go scoop up Granny. See you tomorrow."

"Come early."

She answered him with a furrowed brow, surprised at the forcefulness of his request.

"I'm just saying—I know tomorrow's a half day for you. Instead of sitting on your parents' couch until party time, come hang with me."

"Okay."

"That was easy."

"What can I say? I love leaving the house." Her shrug was playful and matched the spirit she felt shifting her entire outlook. "It's my new thing."

CHAPTER TWO

K ellan flopped on the bed and the fabric of her T-shirt immediately stuck to the sweat on her stomach. In a post-workout daze, she watched the blades of the ceiling fan rotate above her. She propped up on her elbows and surveyed the luxurious apartment that she'd call home for the next two months. Aunt Holly might work for a nonprofit, but dang, this place was fancy. Sure it was only a studio, but it was modern and sleek, with high-end appliances and a fucking fab king size bed she was melting into.

"Blue?" she called. With her gaze alone, she searched for the cat she'd been summoned across the country to babysit. "*Blu-ue.*" She let his name linger, almost dragging it into two syllables, hoping some lyricism would cover the natural huskiness of her voice. "Come on, little guy, it's you and me the rest of the summer. We'd better get to know each other." She patted the bed gently, extending an invitation of sorts. She couldn't help but smile when he peeked his tiny head out from behind a tall plant in the corner. "There you are."

Kellan kicked one shoe off and winced when Blue scampered away at the sound of the New Balance hitting the hardwood floor. "Sorry, man. I need a learning curve. This is new for me too." She made sure to take more care in removing her other sneaker and, seeming to appreciate it, the cat cautiously reemerged from behind the kitchen island. "Give it time, bro. We'll be besties before you know it."

She sat upright, respecting his distance as she peeled off her no-show socks. Her sweaty shirt was next. She stood up, appreciating the light breeze from the open window on her bare abs. She scanned the room for a place to store her dirty clothes before remembering the laundry closet Aunt Holly had showed off as part of the lightning tour this morning. Kellan walked to the door and opened it. Jackpot. To the side of the stackable washer-dryer was a rectangular mesh basket perfectly sized for the space. She nodded in a kind of respect. New Yorkers might not have a lot of space, but they sure knew how to leverage every inch.

"I'm thinking about a shower, Blue." She tossed her clothes in the hamper. "It was hot out there," she said, mostly to herself. Hot, but gorgeous.

After a hurried good-bye, her aunt headed off to Europe, leaving Kellan alone in the apartment. She had no plans, no schedule. It took her all of five minutes to unpack her suitcase into the space Aunt Holly had cleared out for her. A routine inventory check confirmed the kitchen was stocked with essentials, some decent snacks, quality beer. It was cute that her aunt had obviously attempted to make her feel at home. And it saved her the trouble of grocery shopping on her first day.

With no chores on her agenda, she had time to do anything she wanted, which certainly included looking up Dara. She could kid herself all she wanted—the fact that her former best friend lived in New York's most populated borough factored in to her decision to accept this summer gig. But now that she was here, the thought of making contact terrified her. So rather than face those fears, she pushed them right out of her mind, same as she'd done for years. Instead, she reached for her workout gear. In virtually no time she'd changed into shorts and a dry-fit tee and fired up her running app. With the help of a few key addresses, Strava had a route calculated that was just over two miles and delivered her directly to Liam's bar.

Once she'd decided on a run it seemed like a no-brainer to head to her old buddy's place and say hi, even though she hadn't yet contacted him to let him know she was in town. Honestly, it all happened so quickly that her head was still spinning. But her good intentions fell by the wayside when she exited the apartment building via the lobby's side entrance, depositing her squarely in Brooklyn Bridge Park. The waterfront practically called to her, beckoning her to explore its footpaths surrounded in lush greenery, the Manhattan skyline nothing but a Hail Mary pass away.

On autopilot, she jogged the concrete trails, keeping a steady pace. The area seemed trendy but chill at the same time, with its mixed makeup of millennials and hipsters, even some boomers hanging out. She imagined them talking politics and culture as she cruised along, Slipknot blasting through her headphones. She continued running, ignoring the navigation, letting the flow of pedestrian traffic guide her past picnic tables and park benches, restaurants and coffee shops littered along the route. A path down to the water's edge showcased a playground and a dog run. Trees, shrubs, and wild grasses were perfectly manicured and situated to bring some green to the landscape, while still maintaining the urban vibe. It blew her mind that the highway was a stone's throw from the front of Aunt Holly's posh building and yet a freaking garden oasis existed virtually in the backyard.

Her calves burned when she came to a section of the park with some small hills, but she welcomed the challenge. At the top, she was rewarded with a lovely view of the converted piers, bursting with activity. A soccer match being played on a makeshift pitch. Pickup basketball and beach volleyball, complete with sand, set up on another. She strode by two women in bikini tops and shorts, resisting the urge to crane her neck and check them out as they passed her and entered the area demarcated as the Pop-up Pool. What was this place?

She smiled to herself and cranked her music higher, completely unsure what she'd signed on for. This summer hiatus might not have been on her agenda, but she was here for it. By the time she looked at her watch, she'd already clocked five miles and she was nowhere near Liam's Place in Park Slope. Out of steam, she returned to the comfort of her summer digs. Tomorrow was another day.

Under the stream of perfectly scalding water, she assessed her options for the evening. On the one hand, her run had piqued her interest to explore the nightlife here in downtown Brooklyn. But at the same time, she was exhausted from her late-night arrival the previous evening, and her energy was dwindling.

She toweled off her short hair and threw on a soft tee and cozy sweats. Padding through the apartment, she explored the local map on her cell as she searched for nearby takeout options. Her roommate watched from a kitchen stool, and she walked over, gently stroking his soft gray head. "What do you think, Blue? Netflix and chill?"

The cat pushed his face right into Kellan's knuckles, rubbing his jawline and purring loudly. "That's what I'm talking about."

Three slices of pizza later, she flopped on the couch, and Blue hopped up beside her, seeming to exercise mild caution as he settled in next to her. Kellan thought he wanted to be friends and was taking some time to make sure she was trustworthy. She knew it was cheating when she gifted him a few pieces of cheese and pepperoni. She didn't want to overdo it, but she needed him to know she had his back. He didn't know her from Adam, and she imagined the little guy was experiencing some confusion over the sudden absence of his regular person.

"That guy's trouble." She pointed at the screen as she voiced her opinion on the plot of the bank heist movie they were watching. It wasn't necessary to entertain Blue with conversation, but she hoped getting used to her voice might help him adjust to the arrangement. True to feline sensibility, he was thoroughly unaffected by the news of the villain's presence, but he sprawled out on the couch, mashing his jaw into the raised seam of the cushion. Kellan took it as an invitation to pet him, and when he didn't recoil, she counted it as success.

"Now, for the next order of business." She reached for her phone and found Liam Connolly in her contacts. She opened a text but really had no idea what to say. In fact, she had no idea what his life or schedule was like. It occurred to her she hadn't communicated with him at all since she'd seen him about two years ago, stationed together on the other side of the world. For all she knew, his plan to reboot his family's once thriving restaurant never materialized, and he'd moved on to his next venture by now. But her airport Google search had confirmed Connolly's Public House on Fifth Avenue between Sackett and Union was open for business under new management. Her gut told her she knew exactly who was calling the shots.

Kellan opened a text thread but immediately faltered over what to say. She wanted him to know she was here but didn't want to drop her whole saga on him without even checking in on how he was doing. Plus he could be busy at work, or on vacation, or preoccupied with any number of things. A loud car chase in the movie distracted her, and drawn back into the storyline, she quit overthinking her message and typed simply: *Hey buddy. How's life in the real world?*

A few minutes passed. Long enough for the noble thieves to make off with their loot, when her phone vibrated with a response from Liam.

Kellan! How the eff are you?

She grinned, hearing his spirited affect in the words.

I'm good, bro. How are you?

Fantastic. What's new? You out yet?

Yes, sir. Actually, I'm on a different kind of assignment at the moment. In Brooklyn.

GTFO!!

She loved how excited he was. *Truth*, she responded.

Where? Why? How? Wait, do I need clearance for this intel? Did you pick up a government gig?

Ha! Not even close. I'm apartment sitting for my aunt who had to go out of town for work.

Excellent. I'm working at the bar my parents used to own. I'm running the place these days. I'll shoot you the address. It might be far from where you're staying, but I'd love to see you, if you're up to it.

She remembered all about his dream to take over his family's bar, from the quality talks about their plans for the afterlife, as they called it. *I remember, dude. So happy to hear you are making your dream a reality.*

Yup.

I'm completely shot tonight. Would tomorrow work?

His response was an immediate and enthusiastic *Absolutely!* followed by more bubbles. She waited it out to hear what else he had to say. *Actually tomorrow is a thousand times better. I'm doing a summer launch tomorrow, I'll explain when I see you. My point is, at the moment I'm running around like crazy to make sure I'm all squared away.* She started to type a response, but another message came through before she hit send. *Tomorrow will be fun. I'm hoping to be busy but I'll make sure we get to hang.*

No worries. I'm here for the whole summer.

No way, really?

Yep. I was kind of hoping you might show me around NYC a bit. On your days off or whatever.

I'm sure we can arrange something.

Awesome. I'll come by tomorrow.

The earlier, the better. I can't wait to see your face!

10-4, buddy!

Kellan was grinning from ear to ear. She loved that they could slip right back into friendship as though no time had passed between them. In a perfect world, reconnecting would be this smooth with Dara. Logic dictated it should. She and Dara had been inseparable once, a thousand times closer than she'd ever been with Liam. But that was before Dara left the military and had the baby. Their lives were so different now, and with so much time gone by, she second-guessed everything that once connected them.

She reached over and petted Blue right between his ears, abandoning the thought on the spot. "All right, Blue." She rolled her shoulders and her neck, stretching out the kinks from her heady thoughts, the previous day's travel, and more miles than she'd planned to cover on foot today. "It's been a day. But I'm excited to see my friend tomorrow, so it's a wrap for me. Not sure where you normally lay your head, but that bed is definitely big enough for the two of us." She shrugged. "No pressure. Just letting you know I'm cool if you are."

She stood and brushed her teeth, stripping down to boxers before she slid between the sheets. She was halfway to dreamland but still managed half a smile when she felt Blue settle at the foot of the mattress. Not bad for day one.

CHAPTER THREE

Right before first period, Ashleigh made a big announcement in the teacher's lounge that the festivities at Liam's place were kicking off at three o'clock sharp, and any late arrivals would pay the price with extra shots. She only said it because the younger staff were huge partiers, and she knew it would get a reaction. Even though she wasn't much of a drinker, she'd still be the first one there. She had promised Liam one-on-one time. He was nervous about the overhaul of Connolly's being a success, and she wanted to help him feel at ease. This one afternoon might not make a dent in the summer, but thirsty teachers on the last day of school were a sure thing. At least he'd have a crowd tonight.

At two fifteen she sauntered down the steps into the backyard of Connolly's Public House, her jaw falling open wider with each step.

"Oh my God, Li, this looks amazing."

"Not bad, right?" Liam said from behind the bar where he was loading the coolers full of ice.

"Not bad?" She did a full three-sixty to get the full effect of his handiwork, her summer dress twirling as she spun around. "It's absolutely gorgeous. I love it." She nodded in appreciation of his efforts. "I get why you didn't want me to see it until now." Ashleigh ran her hand across the top of a wooden picnic table, the tan wood contrasting nicely with the dark red of her manicured fingernails. "It's insane that this is the same place that was so overgrown we could hide from our parents, back in the day."

"Remember the time you dragged me back here to tell me Courtney Polinski kissed you at Shauna's sleepover?"

"Shh!" She looked over her shoulder. "Shauna doesn't even know that."

"Shauna doesn't know about you and Courtney Polinksi?" His tone called bullshit.

Ashleigh didn't know why she was embarrassed over a kiss that happened two decades ago, but she felt herself blushing just the same. "She knows. Just not, you know, the details."

He rolled his eyes at her delayed discretion.

"She knows we kissed. I may have left out the part that it was at her house, while she was asleep in the other room." She waved him off. "You know Shauna—she's a drama queen. She'd be mad that she was left out somehow."

"That is true."

Ashleigh twisted to look at the sconces along the edges of the property and draped over the center of the yard. This place was going to look fabulous when the sun went down. She swiveled to ask him a question about the renovation process but was immediately drawn to the rear of the service bar set up at the back of the courtyard. There was an Irish flag displayed on one side of the bar's support wall, the rainbow flag on the other side. In between, genuine military regalia from Liam's time in the US Army. Ashleigh choked up.

"Really nice touch, Liam."

He shrugged. "That's me." He ticked his head toward the décor. "That's exactly who I am up there. I'm not hiding anything. I'm proud of every part of my life."

"Cheers to that."

"Speaking of, let me make you a drink. I'll use a light hand, I promise. I know it's going to be a long night."

"Why not?"

Ashleigh watched him whip up a fruity concoction that was mostly ice and juice with some rum. His phone buzzed as he placed the cocktail in front of her. He read the message quickly.

"Damn. Hang on, Ash. There's an issue downstairs with one of the draft lines. I'll be right back. Watch the bar for me?" He was gone instantly, slipping out the side of the bar and taking in twos the steps that led inside.

"Under control," she called after him as she raised her glass in testimony.

The day was bright and warm and she tilted her head back to revel in the sun. She was ready for this. Ready for summer. She loved teaching, but the year had taken its toll. Sure, a lot of her anxiety could be attributed to her freshly divorced status and her less than ideal living situation. As a result, she had poured everything into work, even more than usual. Right now, she could think of no better way to release the tension than a stress-free celebration with her colleagues at her oldest friend's revamped bar—a spot her ex-wife wouldn't dare show her face with the new beau.

A wave of music from inside broke her train of thought, and Ashleigh looked up at the back door, expecting to see Liam returning from his task. But instead there was a person hovering at the top step seeming to survey the courtyard. She peeked her head in the back door, releasing the music once more, before slowly descending the stairs and ambling over to the bar. She looked around the space expectantly before retrieving her phone, alternating between texting and checking over her shoulders.

Ashleigh sipped her drink and tried not to stare, but it was hard to ignore the person completely since it was just the two of them. She pretended to focus on her own phone but even in her periphery, her attention was drawn to the stranger, a scant few feet away. She had a look Ashleigh found intriguing. Tall and muscular, she was attractive in a handsome sort of a way. Her brown hair was buzzed into a fade on the sides but longer on top, and when it flopped forward, Ashleigh wondered if that was the humidity at work or a deliberate part of the look. She wore a dark gray T-shirt that fit perfectly across broad shoulders, a sleeve of tattoos stretching from biceps to wrist along one arm. The thick band of her boxers was slightly visible when she gripped the edge of the bar and leaned over, apparently checking to see if anyone was behind it.

"Are you looking for someone?" Ashleigh asked.

The answer was a killer smile and green eyes that didn't quit.

"Ugh. That's not what I meant," Ashleigh said, not entertaining the come-on for even a second. "Don't even tell me that works?"

"You'd be surprised." A soft, confident chuckle accompanied the answer.

"I was only asking because it seemed like you were looking for someone, and a bunch of the teachers from the school where I work are meeting up here. I thought maybe you were a friend of a friend, that's all."

"Which school is that?"

"Brooklyn Tech," she offered, hearing the lilt in her own tone, as though she was asking a question, rather than stating a fact.

"College?" The response *was* a question.

"High school. Over in Fort Greene."

The woman paused, seeming to think for a second, then squinting one eye for effect. "Mm, nope. Don't know it."

"So that's a no." Ashleigh tried to keep the snark out of her voice, but she was trying to be kind, and this person seemed intent on flirting.

"I'm sorry." Another soft low chuckle slid out. "I was just kidding around. I am actually meeting someone." She ran her hand through her hair, pushing it off her forehead. It fell forward immediately. "Not meeting someone, but…" She checked her phone again as she rubbed the back of her neck. Ashleigh wondered if it was a nervous habit or if this was just another part of her shtick. "Do you know if Liam Connolly is here?"

"He is."

"Oh, cool." She drummed her fingers on the bar top.

"He just went downstairs. He should be back in a second."

The woman nodded, seeming appreciative for the information. "So, do you come here often?"

Ashleigh nearly choked on her drink. "Oh my God, stop. That is the cheesiest line."

A dashing smile spread across the stranger's face, and there was a genuine twinkle in her lively green eyes. "I was actually just making conversation. Wondering if you knew Liam."

"Oh." Ashleigh fidgeted nervously at the hem of her dress. "I just thought—" She was completely embarrassed at her assumption. "I mean, I do. Know Liam, that is. He's my friend." Why was she so flustered at the thought this gorgeous butch might be hitting on her?

"Excellent." Her grin was sexy, and against Ashleigh's will it made her stomach flutter. With a wink, she added, "He's my friend too. I'm Kellan—"

"Dwyer." Liam's shriek was a full octave higher than Ashleigh had ever heard from him. Before she could process what was happening, Liam was there, throwing his arms around Kellan and pulling her into a tight hug that lasted several seconds. Stepping back, Ashleigh saw his real smile. "Kellan *freaking* Dwyer. How the hell are you?"

"Better now."

"My God, it is good to see you stateside." He stepped back to get a good look and Ashleigh felt a twinge of awkwardness to be part of such an emotional moment. "I'm sorry, I still can't believe it. Let me get you a drink." He slipped behind the bar with ease. "Ash, you were supposed to watch the bar. That means get people drinks." His tone was as playful as ever and she knew he wasn't really mad.

"I just got here, Liam. It's all good."

Liam poured an IPA and Kellan raised it in thanks before taking the first sip.

"Did you two meet?" Liam asked waving back and forth between Kellan and Ashleigh.

"We were just getting to that," Kellan said.

"Ashleigh McAllister, Kellan Dwyer." Liam looked at Ashleigh. "Kellan and I were in the Army together."

"Thank you for your service." Ashleigh pulled herself together and extended her hand, finally completing their aborted introduction. Kellan's handshake was the perfect balance of firm and sincere, her soft palm strong and delicate. Out of nowhere, Ashleigh felt a shiver down her spine. What the fuck was happening to her?

"It's nice to meet you, Ashleigh." Without releasing Ashleigh's hand, Kellan turned to Liam. "Is this...*the* Ashleigh?"

"The one and only," he answered.

Her expression turned serious as she spoke. "I'm honored. Liam talked about you. Quite a lot. Your support got him through a lot of rough times. Don't worry—I'm not gonna make him cry right here and ruin his tough-guy soldier rep. Suffice it to say he's lucky to have a friend like you." She raised her glass, toasting the moment.

"Thank you." Ashleigh felt her cheeks flush at the sincerity of Kellan's comment. She hated that she was blushing.

"So, Kellan, what gives? You're really out for good?" Liam asked, interrupting the moment.

"One hundred percent civilian."

"Wow. Retired. How fucking old are we?"

"Young at heart, Liam." She thumped her chest twice and held up her fist for him to pound.

"Also, like, young in age." Ashleigh stuttered out. "He's not even forty. I can't imagine you're not right around that vicinity." Was she fishing? Scratch that, she knew she was—the real question was why?

"I'm thirty-eight." Kellan didn't miss a beat. "Signed up right after high school graduation." She raised her glass. "To the military. If you don't get killed or PTSD, it's a dream career."

"Boo-yah." Liam toasted her with his bottled water. "Anyway, what brings you to Brooklyn? The way you used to talk, I thought for sure you'd never leave Colorado again once you made it home."

"I guess my love for Vail might have slipped out here and there." Her laugh was low and easy.

"Slipped out." Liam laughed out loud. "It's all you talked about for the entire six months we were sweating it out in the desert in Afghanistan." Ashleigh watched Liam lean his weight against the beam supporting the top-shelf booze. "Everything was skiing and the mountains and the trails and how you couldn't wait to get home and start working at your family's resort."

"That is the ultimate plan. It's gorgeous there." Kellan looked momentarily transported, the light in her eye glinting over an obvious memory. "But, alas. Duty called."

Ashleigh was enjoying listening to their back and forth. She liked the deep easy cadence of Kellan's speech and the way her smooth fingers caressed the curve of her beer stein as she spoke.

"My aunt's company transferred her for the summer. Some last-minute thing, I don't really know. She runs a nonprofit that I barely understand. Anyway, normally it'd be no big deal, but she just adopted a cat a few months back. She couldn't take him along, and she didn't want to hire a sitter she wasn't able to vet properly, so my mom asked me if I'd step in for the summer." She shrugged. "How could I say no?"

"All summer." Liam clapped in excitement. "That's fantastic news. What do you have planned?"

Kellan responded with a shrug and a smile. "You're looking at it, bud." She met his high five. "My entire responsibilities are to feed the cat and collect the mail. That's it." She fingered the edges of a cardboard coaster. "I know you're busy with this place, but I was hoping I might steal you here and there to show me some of the sights."

"Sure, sure." He didn't make eye contact, though, and Ashleigh knew it was stress over his time commitment to the bar. She also knew this was where she should step in and offer her services as ambassador to New York.

"Hey, party people!"

Shauna's dramatic entrance saved her. Calling out and striking a pose at the top of the stoop as she arrived, Shauna Williams had a way of commanding an audience, and today was no exception. "We ready for summer?" She bounced over, her fiancé following behind.

"What took you so long?" Ashleigh hugged her old friend. "Hi, Mike," she said over her embrace, waving him in to join the love.

"No fair, I'm all the way back here." Liam pouted.

"Snooze you lose, brother." Mike's voice was deep and playful, and in a second he broke off and gave Liam a hearty handshake. Liam leaned over the bar and kissed Shauna's cheek.

"What can I start you guys off with? Beers, shots, something fruity?"

"You know me," Shauna said. "Tito's and cranberry all the way."

As Mike leaned close to read the draft list and discuss options with Liam, Shauna looked between Ashleigh and Kellan waiting for an introduction. Ashleigh snapped into action.

"Shauna, this is Kellan. She was in the Army with Liam."

"Nice to meet you." Shauna extended her hand, and while still holding it, she turned back to Ashleigh openmouthed, leaving no room to question what she thought of Kellan.

"Behave yourself," Ashleigh ordered.

"Never," Shauna countered.

"You're taken, anyway."

"Don't play." Shauna shook her head and waved one finger. "We both know I'm not talking about me." She gave Kellan another once-over. "Last I checked, you don't have a date for my wedding, and I bet she cleans up real nice."

Ashleigh shot her a look that could kill, but before she could further scold her, a crowd of their colleagues burst through the back door into the courtyard.

"Saved!" Shauna laughed at her timely joke, waving their friends over hurriedly. Liam sprang into action, ready to get everyone served. The group multiplied quickly, and before long, Ashleigh fell into a small circle discussing summer plans. She listened idly, but her attention kept drifting over to a different clique where Kellan seemed to be in deep conversation with Lisa Carmichael, an over-the-top flirt who loved attention. Ashleigh rolled her eyes as she watched Lisa run her fingers over the ink covering Kellan's forearm. Gag.

"You could go over there and insert yourself right into that convo." Shauna's taunt was barely above a whisper, but Ashleigh heard her loud and clear. "Make a play for that sexy soldier. You're a thousand times hotter than Lisa."

"Not interested."

"Yeah, right." Shauna raised her eyebrows in challenge but seemed intent on entertaining her for the moment. "Okay, fine. Give me one good reason why?"

Ashleigh scrunched her nose trying to come up with something plausible. "For one, she's not my type."

"Please, girl." Shauna dismissed her with a wave of her hand. "You dated one person your whole life. And then you married her. You have no idea what your type is."

It was technically true, and it annoyed her that Shauna had a point. But even putting Reagan aside, she had always been drawn to women who leaned toward the feminine end of the spectrum. Not that she wasn't into androgynous people or butches per se—it was more that none had caught her attention. Until tonight. But she wasn't entirely sure intrigue equaled attraction. Either way, she was still staring.

"Imma snap a pic for you. Give you something to look at when you're alone in bed tonight." Shauna lifted her phone, tilting for the right angle. Ashleigh wrenched her arm down.

"Are you out of your mind?"

"Are you?" Shauna stirred the ice in her drink. "Kellan is smoking and you're clearly into it. So why are you still talking to *me*?"

"I'm not into it. I'm not anything. Anyway, she's only here for the summer."

"Does this story get more perfect?"

"What does that even mean?"

"Ashleigh, I'm being your friend here." For a moment Shauna seemed uncharacteristically serious. "You should be dating. And I know you're nervous. I get it—I was single for a long time." She smiled at Mike across the yard. "It can be brutal out there. What better way to ease back into the scene than by testing the waters with a hot visitor, someone whose days here are literally numbered."

For a split second she pondered how the evening might unfold if she listened to Shauna and chucked her straight edge rules out the window. She felt a head rush when an image of Kellan passionately kissing her in the crowded courtyard filled her brain. She blinked it away just as quickly. "I don't do that."

"What? Have fun? You're divorced now. Carte blanche to do whatever and whoever you want. I say you start with that sexy beast over there." She pointed her tumbler right at Kellan. "But what do I know?" Shauna kicked back the rest of her vodka cranberry and sauntered over to Mike.

Alone, Ashleigh found herself considering the option, as she assessed Kellan from afar. She was all confidence and charm as she leaned on the staircase railing, drinking her beer and listening to Lisa and the science staff talk about God knew what. What could she possibly get out of that conversation? Ashleigh lost track of how long she was staring, but Kellan caught her eye and smiled.

Embarrassed, Ashleigh shifted her glance around the courtyard, thankful for the rescue when Liam signaled her over from behind the bar.

"You having fun?" he asked.

"Definitely. Good turnout, right?"

"You're the best, Ash. I owe you."

"No, you don't. Everyone's having a great time. That's good PR for me too."

"Oh my God, I have the best idea." He was talking fast, like he always did when he was excited about something. "It just came to me. I can't believe I didn't think of it before. Kellan!" he called out, before she could press him for specifics. "Kellan, get over here."

His urgency must have counted for something, because Kellan was there in a second.

"What's up, buddy?"

"I'm a genius." Liam worked away, straightening up the bar as he spoke. "The thing is, I know you're here for the summer. And I want you to have a great time. God knows, if I was out in Colorado you'd show me around for sure. But the timing…it's just that I've invested a lot in this place, and I sort of need to be here—"

"No worries, bro. I can take care of myself. Honest."

"That's just it. You don't have to."

Ashleigh felt her heart rate speed up, knowing where Liam was headed. As if reading her mind, he nodded right at her. "Just the other day, Ashleigh told me how she's got this whole summer plan to see the city. Right, Ash?" There was no chance to answer as Liam launched into a hard sell. "You know how it is when you grow up someplace, and you take all the cool stuff for granted? Ashleigh pointed out that we have this amazing city right at our fingertips and we haven't done squat."

She let Liam talk, barely listening as she racked her brain for a way out. It wasn't that she didn't want company. She'd loved the idea of Liam coming along. But Kellan unsettled her in a way she couldn't quite understand, and even though she knew it would be the hospitable thing to do, she longed for an excuse to bail.

Kellan must have read the distress on her face. "That's all right." She smiled, but it didn't have the same spirit as before. Ashleigh couldn't help being affected.

"You should come," she said, surprising herself at the offer. "If you want."

"I don't want to horn in on your plan. It's fine."

She seemed so earnest that it tugged at Ashleigh's sensitivity. "Well, you don't have to. But it might be nice to have company." She cast a glance at Liam and then back to Kellan. "Any friend of Liam's is good people in my book."

"If you mean that, I might take you up on it. Only when you're in the mood for company, though. I don't want to hijack your entire summer." Gone was the cocky charmer who'd walked into the bar full of swagger. That person had been seemingly replaced by this well-mannered, chivalrous twin. Just as captivating, perhaps more dangerous.

"How about this." Ashleigh took out her phone and handed it to Kellan. "Put your number in and I'll send you my itinerary. You can take a look and tell me what interests you."

Kellan smiled as she keyed in her number. "Honestly, what interests me is that there's an itinerary."

Ashleigh felt like she had to defend herself. "I like to have a plan."

"And I am not knocking that. At all," Kellan added as she handed the cell back.

Liam finished shaking up a fruity red concoction and filled three shot glasses.

"What's this?" Ashleigh asked.

"Just a little something I whipped up to commemorate the occasion. To old friends," he said, acknowledging Ashleigh and Kellan with a raised glass.

"And new ones," Kellan responded, smiling big at Ashleigh.

Ashleigh couldn't help but join in. "To summer," she said, clinking their glasses in unison. "Let the adventure begin."

CHAPTER FOUR

How do you want to do this?
     Should I come to you?
Did you want to swing by my place?
Meet somewhere in the middle?
The string of texts came in succession, the chime of the first one dulled by the others that followed. Ashleigh had been up for an hour, lying in bed in a daze of half sleep, too tired and hungover to move yet.

The enthusiasm in Kellan's messages implied she was not as similarly affected.

How do you have so much energy? Ashleigh typed back.

A split second passed before Kellan's response appeared. *I'm so sorry. Did I wake you up?*

No. Technically, it was the truth. She'd even gotten out of bed at seven to take some Motrin, which were finally doing their job of keeping her headache at bay. *I'm just slow moving today.* She threw back the covers and slipped into a sweatshirt and slippers as she headed downstairs.

"Morning, Gran." Ashleigh deposited her phone on the kitchen table next to her grandmother. "Where is everybody?"

"Billy is golfing with your uncle Jack." It was cute that she referred to her dad as Billy, as though he was a still a little boy, not a grown man in his sixties. "Your mom went to the farmers' market."

"Everyone's off to an early start today." Ashleigh checked the coffeepot for signs of life, but it was empty.

"It's beautiful outside. The water's still hot if you want tea."

"Thanks," she said as she reached for a mug, reigniting the burner under the kettle. Tea wasn't what she wanted, but she didn't want her grandmother to feel bad, and she was too lazy to brew coffee.

"How was your night at Liam's?" Granny closed *The Daily News*, clearly ready for gossip.

"Fine. Nice." Ashleigh poured the boiling water over a tea bag of Barry's Gold Blend as she took the spot kitty-corner from Granny at the kitchen table. She pulled her legs up onto the seat of the chair, then twisted the handle of her mug, encouraging her tea to steep. "Liam's place looks great. He redid the back courtyard. It was a lot of fun. I have pictures—do you want to see?"

"Oh yes, that'd be lovely."

Ashleigh scrolled through the pictures on her phone, but they were mostly group shots of her colleagues, making it hard to see the remodeled look of Connolly's Public House.

"Hang on, I have an idea." She opened Instagram and went right to the bar's account. She scrolled through promo photos and was surprised to find that Liam had already posted a ton of pics from last night. She backed up a little so her grandmother could get a feel for the change.

"It looks wonderful." Granny enlarged a picture to get a closer look. "That's a pretty dress you're wearing. Tell me, who are all these people?"

Ashleigh leaned forward. "Mostly friends from work." She pointed closely. "There's Shauna. The tall guy behind her is her fiancé, Mike."

"I love weddings." Granny beamed.

Ashleigh had too, once upon a time. The fact that she had to help her best friend prepare for her mid-August nuptials was dulling her enthusiasm over the institution. Not because she wasn't happy for Shauna and Mike, but all the preparation was a constant reminder of how she had failed at her own so miserably.

She blocked it out for the moment, focusing instead on the picture from last night. Immediately her eyes went to Kellan standing next to Lisa at the end of the group. Even in the grainy cell phone shot, Kellan's green eyes popped. She tilted the phone to get a better look, mildly irked to see how close Kellan and Lisa were standing to each other.

"What about you?" her grandmother asked.

"What about me?" she responded, even though her grandmother's tone told her exactly what she was angling at.

Granny peered over the rim of her proper teacup. "Any new suitors?"

It was sweet that she asked, but Ashleigh hated feeling the pressure of letting her down with the truth. Still, she couldn't lie.

"Sorry to disappoint you." She stood from the table to get the milk and sugar. She touched her grandmother's shoulder and gave it a gentle squeeze as she passed. Granny patted her hand in return.

"There's plenty of time, dear. You're so young still."

"Thanks, Gran."

Ashleigh sat down and squeezed out her tea bag, hoping for every last drop of caffeine, before she placed it next to Granny's on the saucer in the center of the table. Her phone dinged with two new texts from Kellan.

"Kellan Dwyer," her grandmother said as if making an announcement. She widened her eyes in implication. "That's a name I've not heard before."

"Look at you, trying to get the scoop."

"I'm an old lady. Amuse me. Texting at eight thirty in the morning seems full of potential." Ashleigh loved the way her grandmother delighted at the thought of a little scandal. "But why did you do that whooshy thing with your finger that makes it disappear, instead of reading it?"

She burned her tongue as she laughed into the scalding tea. Her grandmother was still sharp, no worries there. Swallowing a grin, she opened the text from Kellan.

Not trying to be a pest. Just wondering if we're still on for today. A second message followed. *No pressure.*

What had they decided on last night that had Kellan champing at the bit? For the life of her she couldn't remember the specifics of their conversation. All that came to mind was a vague memory of almost leaving before Kellan stopped her by the door. But damn if she didn't have a clue what they talked about. The only thing that was perfectly clear was the spirit in Kellan's eyes, a sprinkle of freckles dotted across the bridge of her nose, the way she wet her lips with her tongue as she spoke. For fuck's sake, she needed to get her shit together. Fully aware the mature thing to do was simply ask, she started a response.

Yes, she typed, feeling the need for control. *Just getting moving over here. I'll come to you.* Somehow admitting she was lost felt embarrassing. At least this stall tactic bought her more time—maybe caffeine and a hot shower would jog her memory. *Text me your address.*

111 Furman Street.

Ok, how's 10:00?

Looking forward to the spontaneity ;)

What was the joke she was missing? Was Kellan being sincere or making fun of her? Either way she didn't like it. She was doing a favor here. She was being put out. The fact was she had zero reservations about exploring the city by herself. She didn't need a companion. There was even a small part of her that had been looking forward to the alone time. Ignoring the text, she stood up, crossed the kitchen to the sink, and dumped her full tea out.

"Well?" Her grandmother was clearly waiting for the lowdown as she nursed her tea. "Who has you so frazzled this early in the day?"

"I'm not frazzled." Annoyed was more like it. She willed some details to surface. Preferably ones that would shed some light on Kellan's last text message. Nothing came.

"Is it one of the girls in the picture?"

"No. I mean yes." Ashleigh fought for composure despite the butterflies she felt zipping around her belly. "Yes, she's in the picture. No, it's not like that."

"Show me."

"Uh-uh." She could get away with baiting Granny for a few minutes. "I'm getting in the shower."

"Oh?" Her grandmother had game too. "Are you going somewhere?"

"I'm going to meet Kellan. She's a friend of Liam's in town for the summer. That's all. I told her I'd show her around a little."

"That sounds promising."

"Keep this up and you'll be walking yourself to the senior center." She bent down and placed a kiss on her grandmother's soft cheek. "Be ready to go in an hour, okay, old lady?"

"Oh good. Plenty of time to put my face on!"

On the walk to the center, Ashleigh indulged Granny with additional details of the previous night, or what she could remember anyway. She played up Liam and the bar, the crowd, her teacher friends. For a thrill, she made her grandmother's morning by pulling up the Insta pics and pointing out Kellan. On this second viewing, Ashleigh found herself far less affected by Kellan's appearance, and that relaxed her. Granny simply nodded and said *very nice*, but Ashleigh wondered what she really thought. Kellan's style couldn't be more opposite her own conventionally feminine appearance, and that of her ex too. Ashleigh was fairly certain she and Reagan made up the sum total of lesbians Granny knew personally. But if she had an opinion, her grandmother kept it to herself, simply squeezing her arm and wishing her a fun day as she headed into the Park Slope Senior Center to spend the day with her peers.

Ashleigh ordered a rideshare to take her the rest of the way to Kellan's place. It wasn't far, only about two miles, but she was still low on caffeine and didn't want to be late. As the driver navigated the way, she pulled up her summer itinerary on her phone.

There it was. Splashed across the top of the spreadsheet she'd created was the title in bold: *Spontaneous Summer of Fun*. It came back like a flash. She'd sent it to Kellan last night after she'd left the bar. She wanted to die and felt herself get infinitely smaller as she sank into the leather of the back seat. Why did she have to be such a total dork?

Her phone vibrated with a text from Kellan. *Hey, I'm at the Brooklyn Beanery. It's a coffee shop right near my building. Do you want anything?*

Coffee, desperately. But she didn't want Kellan to buy it for her, and she wanted to doctor it herself. *I'll meet you there.* She glanced at the navigation app on the dash. *Three minutes.*

Cool.

As she followed the cobblestone walkway to the coffee shop, it occurred to Ashleigh that she hardly frequented this area. There were outdoor movie screenings at night, if she was remembering correctly, and she had a flash memory of reading something about a beach volleyball event. Kellan might be interested in those things. Perhaps she should add it to the schedule.

"Hey."

"Oh, um, hi." Even though they had discussed meeting at this very spot, Kellan's husky voice behind her caught her off guard.

"Do you want coffee?"

"Yes. Yes, I do. Did you get some already?" Kellan's hands were empty. "No, I guess." She laughed anxiously. Oh my God, why was she having nervous giggles? She wasn't a teenager on a first date. In fact this wasn't a date at all. It was simply coffee with a new friend. One who happened to be incredibly attractive in the most unconventional way, but still.

"I waited for you." Kellan opened the door to the coffee shop, and Ashleigh refrained from staring at her toned biceps as she passed through the opening.

"Thank you."

They ordered their coffees individually and Ashleigh was glad for the separation. She needed a tiny bit of space to get her act together. Plus she didn't want any awkwardness over payment. Side by side as they prepped their drinks, Kellan spoke first.

"Should we grab a spot outside?" Kellan gestured with her chin. "Those two look like they're leaving."

"Yes, that'd be perfect."

Ashleigh smoothed her cotton skirt over her thighs as she sat down. Kellan planted herself firmly in the rickety iron chair on the other side of the small table, leaning her tattooed forearms on the table.

"How gorgeous is it out here?" It wasn't a question so much as an observation, but Ashleigh agreed with a nod.

She took a sip of her Ecuadorian roast and almost melted into a puddle right on the spot. "Oh my God, this is good coffee."

"Right? I stopped here yesterday. Plus, the view."

"It is beautiful," she said. She took in the sun reflecting off the skyscrapers and the body of water between the two boroughs, pondering whether it was technically part of the Buttermilk Channel or the East River. "I haven't spent much time over here," she said.

"How come?"

"No reason, really. This area has only been built up in the last ten years or so." It wasn't an explanation so much as a fact. God, she sounded like an idiot. "Anyway, I'm sorry it took me so long to get over here. I hope I didn't mess up your morning."

"Not at all. I'm sorry I texted you at eight." She laughed a little. "It's just...you said you wanted an early start."

"I did?"

"When you were leaving last night. You said you were a morning person and I'd have to keep up if this was going to work. No big deal though. I'm an early riser too."

"I didn't really say that, did I?" This was exactly why she didn't drink. She liked having inhibitions. They made her feel safe. In control.

"Maybe not those exact words. But something to that effect. You don't remember?"

"I don't really drink that often. Last night is kind of fuzzy."

"Well, in that case, you also said all sorts of flattering things about my looks, my buff body, my charming personality."

"I did not." She blew into her coffee, using the action to mask her smile at Kellan's teasing. The drawn out moment gave her time to regain some composure.

"No, you didn't. That was Lisa." Her smile was marginally irresistible, tainted only by the overabundance of self-confidence she possessed. "Seriously, though, you did say that you wanted to get going bright and early. So I got up at six and got my run in. I didn't want to slow you down."

"You already went running today?"

"Just a few miles. Exercise helps me stay focused. Otherwise I tend to have too much energy. I can be a lot to take, I think."

Ashleigh was moved by her forthrightness. It seemed genuine.

"Anyway, I realize that I'm totally tagging along on your thing. And you know…" She made eye contact and Ashleigh burned her tongue for the second time at Kellan's serious expression. "You don't have to do this if you don't want to. Liam kind of backed you into a corner yesterday." She spun her to-go cup in her hands and removed the lid, the steam drifting toward her chiseled jaw.

"No, it's fine. Honest." She reached out and covered Kellan's hand with hers, surprising herself with the familiarity of the gesture. "It'll be fun."

"If you're sure."

"I am," she lied. She was certain of nothing. Not how the summer was going to go, or how she would get along with a virtual stranger day after day, if she'd be able to stop thinking about what it would be like to kiss her.

"Okay, but if you change your mind, you have to promise you'll tell me. I have thick skin, I swear. I get that you have a whole plan figured out. One that did not include company."

She actually found herself endeared by Kellan's honesty at acknowledging the situation for what it was. It reminded her that Liam surrounded himself with good, kind people. Kellan was probably as decent as they came. Without even contemplating it further, she felt her defenses drop. "What did you think of the itinerary?" she asked.

"It was good." Kellan paused before adding, "Detailed."

Ashleigh detected sarcasm, and her face must have showed her resentment at the judgment.

"I'm just teasing," Kellan said, reading her expression. A playful smile lit up her face as she continued. "It's just that, usually, spontaneity involves less planning." She winked.

"Fine. I get it. Make fun of the geek." She took a swig of her coffee. "Have Lisa show you around the city. Be prepared to do a lot of shopping. Hope you're into the outlets." She lobbed a fake smile at Kellan. Two could play at this game.

"Ah, Lisa." Kellan leaned back into her chair, seeming to reminisce. "She was very nice. In fact, all of your friends were. Everyone was very welcoming. Thank you for that."

"For what?"

"Including me in your party yesterday. Not making me feel like an outsider. I appreciate it."

How did she do that? Bounce from snarky to sincere in an instant. It was hard to keep up with.

"You're welcome, I guess."

"You guess?"

"I didn't really do anything."

"I think you did. Your friends associated me with you, and they were nice to me. Accepting."

"I don't want to burst your bubble, but Lisa is that nice with everyone. Just so you know." Ashleigh covered her smile with her coffee cup as she drained the last sip. Her eyes met Kellan's sexy smirk.

"Touché, Ashleigh. Touché." Kellan nodded at her empty cup. "You want another one?"

"No. I'm good. Do you?"

"Nah."

Ashleigh followed Kellan's gaze across the expanse of the water to the skyline of Manhattan, wondering where things went from here. Her itinerary kicked the summer off in two days, on a Monday, naturally.

As if Kellan was reading her mind, she said, "Let's do something."

"Like what?"

"I don't know. I know your schedule has the Statue of Liberty and Ellis Island slated for Monday, and this meet-up was just to see if we're compatible, but I'm kind of itching to get into the city. This is my first time in New York. I was thinking…Central Park."

"Right now?"

"Oh, hey, I didn't mean to imply you have to come with me. If you've got plans, I'm totally fine on my own."

"I don't but—"

"Do not feel like you have to entertain me—I'm a fully functional adult."

"No, it's actually a beautiful day for it." She was oddly excited by the unexpected plan and reached for her phone. "Just give me a second to make sure my mom can pick up my grandmother later." She messaged her mom and was pleased when the response was immediate. "Okay, I'm all set. Let me just see what subway we should take from here. I'm not a hundred percent familiar with the public transportation options over this way."

Kellan tapped out a quick rhythm with her empty paper cup. "Actually, the East River ferry stops just over there." She pointed in the distance. "The next one comes in five minutes. We can make it."

"But where will it leave us?"

"If I'm reading the app correctly, this one is heading back from the city, so Dumbo is the last stop in Brooklyn. It'll drop us over by Wall Street, we can grab a subway there, right?"

"We can." She collected her purse and tossed out their cups, smoothing her skirt as she stood up. "Dumbo. Look at you, already mastering the lingo."

"My doorman explained it to me. What a weird way to name a town."

Ashleigh held back on explaining that while New Yorkers often came up with the name of a neighborhood based on an acronym describing its location—*SoHo* stood for South of Houston street, *Dumbo* simplified Down Under the Manhattan Bridge Overpass, and *Tribeca* was a shortened version of Triangle Between Canal—they absolutely never referred to those neighborhoods as towns. Instead, she smiled and held out her arm, indicating Kellan should lead the way.

"I have to follow you. I honestly don't know where I'm going," she explained with a laugh.

"All right then, let's do this."

CHAPTER FIVE

"Did you grow up with Liam?"

Kellan looked out over the Great Lawn littered with picnic blankets and people frolicking as they walked the paved path that looped around Central Park.

"Right next door. Our grandparents were friends in Ireland. Mine came over first. Well, my granddad did. My grandmother is from America. Liam's grandparents and my grandfather were all from the same place."

"Where's that?"

"County Laois. Do you know it?"

Kellan shook her head, unable to stop asking questions. "I was just wondering how long you've known each other. You seem very close."

"We are. It's nice. I was devastated when he joined the Army."

"Were you two, like, a couple?"

Ashleigh's look of shock told her that was a ridiculous question, and she started speaking before Kellan had a chance to qualify it.

"He's gay. You know that, right? I am too."

"No, I know. I mean about Liam anyway." She was making a mess of this. She took a slow breath hoping to channel her inner suave. "I just…I wasn't sure. I don't know. People change. Like I said the other night, Liam talked about you in the Army, but I didn't know the entire history. I didn't want to assume anything."

What she wanted were facts. She was dying to know Ashleigh's status. Gay, straight, bi, single, coupled, dating. At present all she had was old intel from Liam, dating back to when they were overseas together. While she thought she remembered that Ashleigh was married, she wore no ring and hadn't mentioned a partner at all. When she'd tried to probe last night, Lisa steered the conversation back to herself every time. Even though she thought she detected an energy between them, she might be wrong. It had been a while since she'd dated anyone, so perhaps she was misreading the vibe. It didn't matter. Attracted to Ashleigh or not, she knew better than to try for a summer fling with the best friend of her buddy. There were plenty of women in Brooklyn. She'd have to find someone else to fulfill those desires.

"Liam is the best," she said, hoping to get her mind back to a safe place.

"He's like a brother to me."

"Cool. Do you have any? Brothers or sisters?"

"I have two sisters. Stella and Siobhan. They're twins."

"Older or younger?"

"Younger. By seven years. In a way it was like I was an only child." Ashleigh tapped her arm. "Up this way is Strawberry Fields. Are you a Beatles fan?"

"Not really. Be cool to see it anyway." It was cute that Ashleigh asked for her input, but she was enjoying the conversation as much as the walk. It was nice to be outside on a gorgeous, mild, windless day. "You're not close with your sisters?"

"I am now. But growing up, I was a lot older, and they had each other, you know? The twin thing. I was closer to Liam in a lot of ways. Plus, we were both gay. Not that it's the same, but we could relate to each other. We're both from working class immigrant families. Irish, Catholic."

"I'm sure. How is your family? Are they accepting of you?"

Ashleigh waved her hands, shaking her head repeatedly, and Kellan watched her blond waves bounce around her shoulders. "I'm sorry, I should be clear. My family is great. Honestly, they have always been super supportive. I didn't mean to suggest otherwise. Liam just understood me in a way they didn't. We clicked."

"I totally get that. I connected with him that way in the Army. Probably for some of the same reasons."

"I always worried about him being gay in the military. The rules seem to change all the time. I suppose it wasn't easy for you, either."

The way her voice lilted up made it seem as if she was asking a question, and when Kellan looked at her, she saw genuine concern in her lovely blue eyes, and she longed to put her at ease.

"It wasn't as bad as you might think. The policy was a wreck sometimes. But the people were amazing. Including Liam. That's what matters." They had stopped walking and she wondered if it was so Ashleigh could search her face for battle scars. With only a few feet between them, Kellan couldn't help but focus on Ashleigh's soft full lips, parted ever so slightly as she listened to her talk. "Anyway, there it is, right?" The "Imagine" mosaic appeared in the nick of time. She needed a distraction, and quick.

"There it is." Ashleigh walked closer, taking out her cell to snap a pic.

"Take one with me?" Kellan asked, before she could overthink it. "For the scrapbook I'm sure you've got planned already."

"Jerk." Ashleigh nudged her with an elbow to the ribs, all but admitting Kellan was on the money. "Who are you kidding anyway?" Ashleigh asked, as she smiled into the camera. "My photo books rock. You'll be begging me for a copy."

"Begging, huh?" Kellan used her thumb to snap a series of pics of them together in front of the memorial and the flowers around it. "That's a bold statement."

Ashleigh's shrug was full of spirit. "What can I say—I'm good at some things."

"I don't doubt it."

It was almost flirting and she knew it, but Ashleigh had started it, right? Either way, it was harmless. Even though it was a terrible idea, she found herself strongly attracted to Ashleigh. After passing the boathouse and the lake, and debating the zoo—Ashleigh found them sad, but was willing to go if she wanted—Kellan wondered if they'd call it a day. She didn't want their time together to end, which she knew was absolutely ridiculous, because they literally had the rest of the summer together, so long as Ashleigh was willing to let her tag along. She was enjoying listening to Ashleigh teach her the facts of the park and the city around it. She liked the light pitch in her tone, how excited she seemed to share the history, the way she tucked her hair behind her ear, how soft her skin was when their forearms brushed against each other.

"Do you want to pop into the Museum of Natural History?"

"What?" Kellan was completely thrown by the question.

"It's just a few blocks away. We're already here. I know it's on the agenda for later in the summer, but it's enormous. If you're into it, we could always come back again."

"Are you sure we're allowed to manipulate the schedule like that?"

"Don't push it."

"I'm just teasing you." She bumped Ashleigh's shoulder with hers. "Can I grab a hot dog first, though? I'm starving."

"You're not going to eat a dirty water dog. We can do better than that."

"Wait, is that really what they call them?"

"Unfortunately, yes."

"Now I definitely want one. Part of the New York experience." She turned around and walked backward so she could get the full view of Ashleigh's disapproval. "Come on, you know you want one."

"I definitely don't."

Kellan jogged the last few yards up to the vendor, then purchased a hot dog with mustard and sauerkraut and two waters.

"Here." She handed Ashleigh a bottle of water and slipped the other into her pocket as they exited the park onto Central Park West. She spotted the museum directly across the street. "Holy smokes. It's right here."

Ashleigh's smile was confident and beautiful and Kellan felt her pulse race. "I told you." Kellan felt the touch of her hand at her elbow. "Come on, let's cross while we have the light. We can sit on the steps while you eat."

They sat in companionable silence against the constant rush of the city around them, people watching the hordes as they entered and exited the park and the museum, fiddled with strollers, hailed cabs, jogged, rollerbladed. It blew Kellan's mind that there wasn't a collision every second.

"What brings you to the city again?" Ashleigh broke her train of thought. "Something having to do with your aunt?"

"Yes. Aunt Holly is away for the summer for work. She has a new cat and didn't have the time to find a pet sitter. Or maybe she didn't want one. I'm not really sure. My mom asked me if I'd do it."

"That was nice of you."

She'd been elated at the opportunity, mostly because she thought proximity might open a window to her past, but she opted to keep her response simple. "It wasn't a big deal, honestly."

"And you were able to get off from work with no problem?"

"I work for my parents, so yes."

"Oh, right. At a resort. What do you do there?"

"Whatever they tell me." She laughed at her own joke, even though it was kind of true. She didn't have an official title or job description just yet. Her niche at the resort would develop organically, and until then she was happy helping out any way she could. "Odds and ends right now. My parents are halfway retired, so they're transitioning the business over to me and my brother." She finished the last of her hot dog and wiped her mouth with a paper napkin. "He's been home longer than I have, so he's basically leading the charge right now."

"Is that frustrating? Being here while he's learning the business?"

"Not at all. Turk's been home three years. He was in the Army too. That's how I met Liam. They were in the same unit. Anyway, he knows Mom asked me to help Aunt Holly. Family first. He gets that." She took a sip of water. "I think he was just happy he's got a wife and three kids of his own. He was off the hook." She finished with a laugh.

"I know you Army folk are used to it, picking up and leaving at a moment's notice, but it still can't be easy to move to a place where you barely know a soul."

"Well, I knew Liam was here. Or at least I hoped he was. I didn't know for sure until the other night." But she knew Dara was here. It was a truth that both excited and scared her. Being geographically close provided an opportunity to mend their friendship face-to-face. Her gut told her that in each other's presence the distance would melt away instantly. How could it not? Their connection was deeper than with almost anyone she knew. Of that she was certain. After all, it wasn't every day a person underwent actual surgery for their bestie. But she'd done it without hesitation. To this day, she had no regrets. Just confusion over how a decision that should have bonded them forever had somehow contributed to their undoing. The clarity of a decade gone by made the answer to that question starkly obvious, to her, at least. The only question now was whether she'd find the courage to contact Dara and figure a way to get things back on track.

Decisions for another day. "Shall we?" Kellan asked, pushing it out of her mind as she stood to brush off her shorts. She offered a hand to help Ashleigh stand.

"We shall." Ashleigh accepted the assistance but let go of her hand the second she had her footing. "You ready to be completely overwhelmed?"

Kellan didn't have a clue what Ashleigh meant, but by the time they worked their way through the Neanderthal section, she realized it was about the crowds, not the displays.

"Is it always like this?" She had to stay close so Ashleigh could hear her over the noise.

Ashleigh closed her eyes and seemed to sigh. "I probably shouldn't have brought you here on the weekend. It's always crowded, but a Saturday during summer…" She covered half her face with one hand. "Not my best decision."

"Well, you did make a schedule, and this was not part of it," Kellan said.

Ashleigh's expression hinted that she thought Kellan was teasing her, but nothing could be further from the truth, and she wanted her to know it. "No, I mean it. I'm taking the hit for this."

"You just said the Park. I suggested the museum."

"So we're both to blame." She shrugged, hoping Ashleigh knew she didn't mind at all. "We're here now. You gonna show me some dinosaurs or what?"

Ashleigh's face lit up. "Follow me—I know a shortcut."

"Of course you do."

Three hours later, they had viewed all the big attractions, but Ashleigh had led them through some lesser known exhibits as well—a marble courtyard replicating the architecture found in ancient Greece, old artifacts used for teaching arithmetic that Ashleigh photographed extensively, explaining that she'd use them in lessons with her students next year.

Kellan finally felt herself relax as they descended the stairs to the sidewalk.

"That was intense." But so unbelievably enjoyable. Being in Ashleigh's presence, even surrounded by hundreds of people, felt intimate. What was happening here? She checked the time on her phone, hoping their day wasn't over.

"Sorry. I know it was a lot for your first day."

"It was perfect. Thank you for coming with me." They were walking south, and Kellan wondered if they were headed home. "What now?"

"I'm kind of hungry. I know you just ate—"

"Just ate!" Kellan interrupted. "That was hours ago. I honestly don't know how you're surviving. I haven't seen you eat a thing."

"I didn't feel great this morning."

"You were that hungover, huh?"

"I really don't drink much. I'm a lightweight."

"I just wish I had known. I wouldn't have dragged you all over the city."

"It's okay. I had a nice day." Ashleigh looked at her watch. "How do you feel about heading back to Brooklyn and going over to Liam's place for dinner? I bet he'd love to see us."

She couldn't think of a more perfect idea.

"Well, if it isn't my two favorite people in all of Brooklyn." Liam's enthusiasm met them the second they came through the door.

"Your favorites are starving," Ashleigh said dramatically. "Feed us."

"You want to sit inside or out?"

Kellan registered Ashleigh checking to see if she had an opinion, and it touched her that she cared. As for where they parked themselves, it didn't matter one bit. She was having a great time. The fact that the afternoon had stretched into dinner was an absolute bonus.

"Wherever," Ashleigh answered, reading her perfectly.

"I'm working in here tonight," he said. "Why don't you grab that corner table so I can come visit you. Or you could eat at the bar, if you want. Then I could really talk to you."

"That's cool," Kellan said, hoping it was okay with Ashleigh.

"Excellent."

He reached under the bar to grab some menus, and Kellan took the opportunity to guide them to the corner of the bar. She pulled out a stool for Ashleigh. "This okay? He seemed excited for the company."

Ashleigh's sweet smile told her it was perfectly fine, the look in her eyes echoing the sentiment. "It's perfect."

Liam hooked them up with drinks—seltzers with lime for both of them—before taking their food orders. While he was busy serving other customers, they perused the day in pictures on their phones, leaning over to share and inspect the moments they'd captured. Even with the congestion of the museum and a packed subway, this was the closest she'd been to Ashleigh. She could smell the light aromas of shampoo and perfume and the heat of the day combining together like a summer elixir drawing her in.

"What are you guys looking at so intently?"

"Pictures from our outing together," Ashleigh answered.

"No shit. That happened already? Am I a genius or am I a genius?" He laughed at his own joke. "I knew you two would hit it off."

Without another word, he was off mixing a series of drinks for some new customers but was back almost as quickly.

"So, what did you see today?"

Kellan looked at Ashleigh to give her the opportunity to explain, but Ashleigh conceded the explanation with a smile. Her heart skipped a little at the ease with which they were able to wordlessly communicate. Kellan could feel herself starting to overthink it, so she stopped on the spot, instead taking the nonverbal cue and walking Liam through the day, starting at the coffee shop.

"Nice." He seemed impressed when she finished. "Sounds like a long day, though. You sure I can't interest you in a beer, Kell?"

"I'm still paying for last night, bro."

"It was a good time, though, right?" He leaned over and touched Ashleigh's nose. "You get all the credit for that." He nodded thanks at the waiter who brought their burgers over. "Speaking of…" He reached under the bar once more for a tiny bottle of ketchup. "Did you go home with that girl you were talking to all night? What's her name?"

"Lisa?" Ashleigh's voice held genuine shock and something else. Was it jealousy?

"Lisa. Is that it?" Liam looked at her for confirmation.

With a mouth full of food, Kellan couldn't say anything. She felt their eyes on her as she choked it down. "Lisa, yes." She coughed at the burger stuck in her throat. "I did not go home with her," she clarified.

"I'm surprised," he added. "When I saw you leave together, I thought for sure it was on."

"You left with her?" Ashleigh asked.

"She ordered a rideshare. I just made sure she got in okay. Then I headed back to my aunt's. I was pretty tanked."

Kellan saw something in Ashleigh's expression change. It seemed like she was relieved, which was...interesting.

"So what's on the agenda tomorrow, people?"

Kellan looked over at Ashleigh. "What's the itinerary say, boss?"

"I love that there's an itinerary." Liam flashed his million-dollar smile at Kellan. "How cute is she?"

Kellan focused on her plate, playing bashful for the moment. "She's cute," she said, not bothering to filter. It was bold and maybe too much, but Liam tossed her a softball, and damned if she wasn't gonna crush it.

"Sorry to disappoint everyone," Ashleigh piped up. "Tomorrow I have to help Shauna with wedding stuff."

"You met Shauna, right?" Liam obviously wanted to make sure she was in the loop.

It was nice that her friend was looking out for her. "I did," Kellan responded. "Very nice. Her boyfriend too."

"Mike. Yup. Good guy." He poured some pints for four dudes who'd just arrived. "Kellan, if you're bored tomorrow, you're welcome to hang out here. There's a bunch of soccer matches I'll have on the big screen if you're into that. Baseball too. If you don't feel like being alone."

"Or you could call Lisa." Ashleigh smirked. "I'm sure she'd make herself available."

"Soccer sounds cool," she said with a hearty laugh. "Plus I already have a tour guide. Don't I?" She raised her eyebrows, praying it came off hopeful instead of pathetic.

"If you're okay with nerdy me and my schedule instead of Lisa and her low-cut tops."

"When you put it that way..."

Ashleigh whacked her arm, but it was all in good fun, she could tell.

She rubbed the spot on her biceps for sport. "That kind of hurt."

"Good." Ashleigh's eyes danced under the low lights of the bar, and Kellan couldn't help but be completely turned on by this devilish, impish side of her new friend. Whether she was more enticing than the sweet, regimented schoolteacher she'd spent the day with remained to be seen. She smiled to herself, sure of one thing. Where those were the choices, there was no wrong answer.

CHAPTER SIX

Phone, keys, wallet. Check.

"Okay, Blue, I'm out." Kellan took a quick glance at his water bowl just to make sure it was full. A last-minute scan of the weather verified today was going to be a scorcher, so she dropped the thermostat an extra two degrees just to be on the safe side. "Be good. I'll see you later." He jumped up on the kitchen island for a proper good-bye, and Kellan indulged him with some love. "I do wonder if you're allowed up here." She lowered her face to meet his and winked at him. "Our secret, okay?"

Her phone buzzed in her back pocket, and she pulled it out, expecting it to be Ashleigh saying she was en route, but to her surprise, she saw her mother's face illuminating the screen. Vail was two hours behind New York, making it seven forty in the morning out west. She swiped right, answering the video call.

"Hi, Mom. Everything okay?"

"Hi, honey. We missed your face. Dad's here too."

"Hey, Kell." Her dad popped his head into the frame.

"Pop. Nice beard," she said.

He rubbed his cheeks and smiled. "Just trying to stay current."

"But doesn't he look so handsome?" Her mother turned to gaze at her father. It was cute, if a little gagworthy, her parents' genuine affection for one another, forty-plus years into their relationship. She often wondered if she'd experience anything even close to what they seemed to share daily.

"What's up, guys? You're freaking me out with the early morning call. Everything okay?"

"Fine, honey. We just wanted to check in. See how things are going. We can't thank you enough for doing this."

"It's no sweat, Mom."

Blue nudged his way into the camera view, greedy for more petting. "This is Blue," she said.

"Isn't he precious?" Her mom was an animal lover through and through. "I'm so glad Aunt Holly has him to keep her company. And what about you?" Subtlety was not her mother's strong suit. "Did you meet up with your friend?"

"I tracked down my buddy Liam. He owns a bar-restaurant not too far from Aunt Holly's. He hooked me up with one of his friends."

"Oh?"

She heard hope in her mother's voice and knew she should quash it immediately. Her mom had the tendency to jump to conclusions. "Not that kind of hookup, Mom."

"That's too bad."

It was, wasn't it? She nodded, momentarily forgetting that her mother could see her. "Anyway, Ashleigh, that's her name, she's showing me around New York."

"That sounds nice."

"Yeah, it is. I should probably go, I'm meeting her in a few minutes."

"Okay, but what about your other friend? The one you told me you were going to look up once you got there. Darla."

"Dara."

"Yes, Dara."

Ugh. Hearing her mother say the word out loud made her bristle. She hadn't spoken to Dara in twelve years, so perhaps even calling her a *friend* was a stretch. It was all so complicated and confusing and she didn't have the time or the energy to process right now.

"I'll get to it."

"Well, don't wait too long. The summer will fly by. You don't want to miss your moment. You never know—"

"Loud and clear, Mom." She knew exactly how that sentence ended. She'd been privy to Willow Dwyer's theories on fate, love, and the power of the cosmos since she was in diapers. And truth be told, she didn't disagree. If she was being honest, she knew she'd accepted this assignment so readily, in large part for those very reasons. It might be hokey, but inside, she believed the opportunity to summer in Brooklyn was the universe's way of saying it was time to fix things with Dara. To make amends, bridge the gap of a decade lost, and satisfy the curiosity she'd felt simmering below the surface in those years. But every time she let herself truly acknowledge it, she started to sweat. Right now was no exception.

"I should go, Mom. My friend will be waiting. I love you."

"I love you too, Kellan. Call us more."

She couldn't help but smile. "Okay, Mom."

"And find your friend." Her mother loved getting the last word, even if she had to sneak it in.

"Good-bye, Mom." She laughed. "Tell Dad I love him."

"Bye, Kellan." Her father's gruff voice came through in the distance. "Love you, pal."

She ended the call and saw that Ashleigh had left her four texts in succession.

I'm here. The time stamp told her the first message was sent at 9:55, five minutes before their scheduled meetup at Brooklyn Beanery. The next few messages followed in sequence.

I'm going to start walking toward your building. Hope that's okay.

I think I'm in your lobby.

Is your aunt a bazillionaire?

Kellan laughed out loud at the last text. She was way late, so she grabbed her stuff in a hurry and headed straight for the elevator. In the lobby, Ashleigh had her back to the front desk as she stared out the building's glass facade. Kellan waved hello to the doorman as she approached.

"I'm so sorry." Kellan touched Ashleigh's shoulder gently. "My parents called me and I couldn't respond to your texts. I actually didn't even see them until right now."

"It's okay. Your place is, like, right here. I started walking because I figured I'd bump into you on the way over. But I guess I didn't realize how close it was until I was in the lobby. Then I thought you were probably in the shower or something."

"You could have come up. I'm in 4D."

"I didn't know. And I didn't want to intrude."

"Sanjay would've hooked you up." She turned to the doorman situated behind a high marble counter. "Sanjay, this is my friend Ashleigh."

"Lovely to meet you, Miss Ashleigh."

Ashleigh gave a small wave before turning to Kellan and leaning in as she whispered, "You're friends with your doorman?"

"We chatted a little. He's from Sri Lanka. Nice guy."

Sanjay bowed his head, obviously aware that he was the topic of conversation. Kellan acknowledged him with a smile. "Ashleigh is taking me to see the Statue of Liberty and Ellis Island. Cool, right?"

"Spectacular, yes." Sanjay nodded again. "You have the perfect weather today."

"You think? It's going to get hot as anything."

"I enjoy the heat. It reminds me of home." He smiled happily.

Kellan looked at Ashleigh. "You ready to go? I'm dying for coffee." When Ashleigh nodded, Kellan reached over and extended her arm to hold the door open. Glancing over her shoulder she called out, "See you later, Sanjay."

"Have a wonderful day, Mr. Kellan."

Kellan couldn't help but notice the stutter in Ashleigh's step as she looked at Kellan and back to Sanjay in the lobby. "Did he just—"

"Call me Mr. Kellan?" She finished Ashleigh's sentence. "He did."

"Is that...I mean, does he think you're..."

"A dude?" Kellan shrugged, trying to set the tone. This conversation could be a game changer, but in her heart she didn't believe it should be a big deal. "I don't think so." She fell in step beside Ashleigh. "I don't know, though. Maybe."

"Does that bother you?"

Gender identity was a topic that made people so touchy these days. Kellan wanted to make sure she answered with care, but also honesty. "No," she began. "Not with Sanjay, it doesn't."

"Because you don't know him? Or you don't care? Or because you'd rather be identified that way?"

They were at the door of the coffee house and, man, could she use some serious java. For a day that started with her mom via FaceTime telling her to go find Dara and now was headed into breaking down pronouns and binary issues with a virtual stranger, who was also her tour guide, her new friend, and the person she'd most recently masturbated to, there had not been nearly enough caffeine. She needed coffee, stat.

She opened the door for Ashleigh. "Let's get some coffee. My treat, since I made you wait. Then we talk. Is that okay?"

Ashleigh touched her forearm, seeming to thank her for her manners. "Of course it's okay. We don't even have to talk about anything." Her smile was warm and lovely, and the kindness in her expression told Kellan whatever she said would be okay. It put her at ease in a way she couldn't quite explain. "And I'll let you buy me coffee today, but only if I buy next time. Deal?"

"Deal."

Two large house blends later, they walked over to the ferry station to wait, even though they had almost a half hour to kill.

"So the thing with Sanjay…" Kellan started. She sipped her coffee. "It's like this. We haven't had a conversation about it or anything. But I think he knows I'm not a guy. The first time he said it, he stuttered a little like he was uncertain." She leaned against the railing at the water's edge, turning to make eye contact. "I get it. I know what I look like. I'm almost six feet tall. I have short hair, styled, well, like this." She pointed a finger at her ultra-short pomaded coif. "The rest of this"—she fanned over her clothes—"it's a choice. I choose to dress like this. But it's not to make a statement." She tapped the base of her coffee on the metal railing. "It's just how I feel comfortable. This feels like me."

"I understand."

"So when Sanjay refers to me as mister, even though it's not accurate, the correction is to tell him to call me *miss*, and that feels not right either. Does that make sense?"

Ashleigh nodded, but Kellan could see concern creasing her brow. "What is it? It's better if you just ask."

"Do I ever make you feel uncomfortable? I have referred to you as *she*—I'm sure of it."

Kellan wanted to touch her, to thank her for caring, assure her she'd done nothing offensive, but in the moment, she questioned her own motives for wanting contact. "It's not like that." She met Ashleigh's eyes, even more beautiful in the bright sunlight. "That's what I was trying to say about Sanjay. He's not purposely misgendering me. He took a chance, and I didn't correct him. He's sticking with it. Do I think he knows the truth? I do. I've seen him check out my body. My chest is small, but it is there." She washed down another sip of delicious coffee. "It's almost like we have an unspoken agreement. One we're both okay with."

"Sounds perfect." Ashleigh picked at the plastic tab of her coffee lid. "I bet it's not always that simple."

"I wish." Kellan forced a smile. "The women who accost me in public restrooms could take a lesson from Sanjay, that's for sure."

"Jesus, Kellan. Does that happen?"

She knew her shrug wasn't an answer, but she really didn't know what to say. It happened. More than she wanted to admit. "It sucks. What can you do? This country is weirdly obsessed with who uses which bathroom."

"So stupid. So true." Kellan stiffened at the feel of Ashleigh's hand on her back. She wanted it to mean desire, but it was likely basic support, perhaps even an apology on behalf of the ignorant. "Promise me something?" Ashleigh asked.

"Sure."

"Tell me if you want me to do anything different. If you want me to use the pronoun *they* or anything like that. Would you do that?"

"Honestly, Ash, I'm fine with she or they. I answer to both, and I rarely talk about myself in the third person." She added a laugh, hoping to keep the mood light. "You've not done anything that's made me feel anything other than me. Even this conversation"—she paused to finish her drink—"your answers and your questions, they've been perfect. Truly." She was about to throw out her empty cup, but stopped, wanting Ashleigh to know the depth of sincerity she felt at how natural this conversation flowed. "Thank you."

Ashleigh shook her head. "Thank you. For sharing with me. It means a lot."

"You made it easy."

"I'm glad." Ashleigh ticked her head at the ferry pulling up. "Now, let's go meet Lady Liberty, what do you say?"

"After you," Kellan said, holding her arm out inviting Ashleigh to lead the way.

CHAPTER SEVEN

Ashleigh was mildly embarrassed that, for all her planning, she had never considered the East River Ferry as a viable mode of transportation. This was only her second time, but the more she took it, the more she liked it. The service ran in both directions, making a horseshoe from Manhattan's East Side and stopping in four locations along the Brooklyn waterfront before crossing over to Wall Street. It was convenient and affordable, and it fit nicely with a lot of her summer agenda. While it wasn't super convenient to her parents' place in Park Slope, it was perfect for meeting up with Kellan. The fact that it was a stone's throw from Brooklyn Beanery—her new fave coffee spot— didn't hurt either.

She'd purchased the tickets to the Statue of Liberty and Ellis Island tour months earlier, feeling certain she'd be able to scrounge up a partner for such an iconic visit. When Kellan realized, she immediately offered to reimburse her for the expense. But Ashleigh didn't want her money. In the moment, she was too busy enjoying her company. It was surprising how seamlessly they gelled. Kellan put her at ease in a way that was new to her. Where she was usually worried about being too bossy or too boring, she didn't think about either of those things when they were together. She allowed herself to live in each moment. For the first time in ages, she wasn't worried about pleasing anyone. The reward was a freedom she'd never even contemplated. Damn if she wasn't having a good time.

Kellan seemed completely fine with following her pre-arranged plan with a few minor adjustments, like her aversion to climbing to the crown of the Statue. When she revealed a fear of heights, Ashleigh was taken aback. It was silly to assume that someone brave enough to fight for their country wouldn't be afraid of anything. But what surprised her more was what she learned about herself in that moment. Kellan was content to wait at the pedestal, but Ashleigh didn't want to go without her. She preferred to stay on the grounds of Liberty Island, walking and talking with Kellan. She even weighed in on the souvenirs Kellan purchased to bring home to her brother's kids, ultimately offering to hold them in her oversized purse for safekeeping as they disembarked from the boat at Ellis Island.

"Are there things you might like to do that aren't on the schedule?" Ashleigh asked.

"What do you mean?" Kellan said.

"You know, go to a ball game or something."

"And buck the system you've put in place?" Kellan faked horror. "I wouldn't dare."

She poked Kellan playfully with three fingers to the side of her arm. "I'm trying to be nice and you tease me. I take it back. I'm in charge of everything."

"You love it." Kellan poked her back and Ashleigh found herself resisting the urge to touch her again. "I'm just kidding. I like the schedule. As for a ball game, I don't know." She stuffed her hands in her pockets. "I could take it or leave it, I guess. I'm not a huge sports fan. I like them okay. Watching live sports can be fun."

"Did you play anything growing up?"

"I skied, of course. Vail, and everything." Kellan looked out at the water and Ashleigh wondered if she was reminiscing. "I was on my high school team. But I was only so-so. My brother was an all-star. He almost qualified for the Olympics."

"That's exciting."

"But then when he didn't, he got super depressed. I think he joined the Army just to get away from it all."

"Sad."

"It seemed so at first. But he loved the military. I loved the way he talked about it. Constant travel, always something new. It sounded awesome. I was sold by the time I was a junior in high school."

"And?"

"And what?" Kellan asked.

"And was it what you thought it would be?"

Kellan's smile said there was a story there and Ashleigh longed to hear it. "No, I guess it wasn't. It was awful in ways I hadn't imagined. War is crazy." Her eyes filled with emotion and Ashleigh longed to comfort her, if only she knew how. "It was also wonderful in ways I didn't expect," Kellan said. "The people I met there, served with…there aren't really words to convey how I feel about them." She wiggled her eyebrows, breaking the moment and somehow undercutting the depth of her statement. "Come on, let's go find your ancestors on the Wall of Honor."

No doubt about it, the topic was closed for now, but Ashleigh hoped they'd revisit it at some point. She found herself wanting to know details about Kellan and her life, and that caught her off guard. It was just that she'd never known anyone quite like her, she rationalized. And yes, she was attractive. Almost objectively. Already today, she'd counted five women completely checking her out. None of them were subtle. It shouldn't matter. They weren't a couple. She had no grounds to be irked by the attention Kellan received, and yet she was somehow irrationally jealous.

"Do you know which section of the Wall your grandparents are on?" Kellan asked as they walked through the rows of the monument.

"I looked it up last night. My mother's parents are on panels fifty-seven and two hundred fifty. My dad's father is on panel one twenty-three."

"Okay. Let's start at fifty-seven and work up. Sound good?"

"Sorry if this is boring."

The look Kellan dropped on her said she needn't worry. "Are you kidding? I think this is cool. I'm the boring one here." There was kind of a line forming, and Kellan directed Ashleigh in front of her. "This way, I think." Ashleigh could feel her hand barely touching her hip as she guided her, half a step behind. "Here." She stopped them and stood behind Ashleigh to make space for the other visitors. "What name am I looking for?"

All she could concentrate on was Kellan's breath, warm against her ear, her voice soft and husky at the same time. She felt the heat between them filling the small space between her bare shoulders and the cotton T-shirt covering Kellan's chest. She almost forgot which grandparent she was looking for. "McAllister. John McAllister."

"I see it." Kellan pointed high. "All the way on the left. Third from the top. Do you see?" She took a step to the left, bringing Ashleigh with her. "Here, is that better?"

Ashleigh nodded. It was all she could do. She could feel herself getting hot, and she knew it wasn't a result of the day's temperatures. It wasn't really Kellan either, she told herself. It was simply that it had been ages since she'd had any kind of closeness with another human being. She took a deep breath to gain her composure and was careful to slowly release the air, hoping Kellan didn't notice.

"Are you okay?" Kellan asked.

No such luck. And now Kellan's hand was on her shoulder.

"It's emotional, I'm sure," Kellan said.

Emotional. Not really what she was feeling, but she took the out. "Thanks." She needed to get a hold of herself and quick. Reaching in her purse, she took out her phone to snap a pic. Her grandmother would appreciate it later. "Sorry about that," she said.

"No apologies necessary." Kellan's smile was genuine and Ashleigh found that looking into her eyes grounded her in the most unusual way. She was even able to completely focus on the next two panels as she found Catherine Leonard and Martin Buckley with ease. Dutifully she took photographs of her ancestors' names to document the occasion.

"My mom will be excited to see her parents' names on the wall, I think."

They walked through the museum, examining the history of America and the great many folks who'd left their families in search of a better life. Ashleigh stopped by a small exhibit dedicated to emigrants from Ireland.

"Have you ever been?" Kellan asked.

"To Ireland? Yes," she answered.

"Did you love it?"

Ashleigh took a second to think about the question, knowing the answer was so much more complex than she wanted to admit. "I did." Kellan seemed to search her face, which surely revealed the conflict in her heart.

"I met my wife there," she said. "My ex-wife, I should say."

"Oh. Wow." Kellan nodded. "That explains the look."

"Yeah, well." Ashleigh looked down to avoid eye contact. She didn't want to discuss her relationship with Reagan today. Or any day, for that matter. Kellan was only here for the summer. She could certainly make it through a few weeks without looking like a pathetic failure. "Anyway…" She walked toward the building's exit.

"Hey, don't do that."

Ashleigh turned around, continuing to shuffle backward toward the door. "Do what?"

"I don't know. Walk away when you seem sad. Let me help you."

"You're sweet, but I'm okay."

"Are you?"

She was, mostly. "I've been divorced for almost a year. According to Liam, and most certainly according to Reagan, my marriage was over long before that."

"What if I don't care about what Liam and Reagan think? What if I want to check in with you?"

"Why are you being nice to me?"

"What kind of question is that?" Kellan ushered her into a seat on a deserted bench overlooking the harbor. "You seem, I don't know… sad, angry, annoyed. All of the above, maybe. I'm an outsider. Talk to me. It might make you feel better. It probably won't make you feel worse."

"I don't even know where to start."

"I could ask questions." Ashleigh couldn't help but notice Kellan's eyes widen as she kicked the soles of her Vans together. "I have about a million."

She smiled. "You do?"

"Uh, yeah." Kellan picked up a pebble and moved it between her fingers. "Gorgeous blond divorcee, living with her parents, no dating prospects—that she speaks of, anyway. You bet I have questions."

Ashleigh was flattered and touched that Kellan was trying to cheer her up. She ignored the flutter she felt at Kellan's compliment and didn't even allow herself to think the words were anything more than supportive. Still, it made her smile as she let her defenses slip away. She put a hand on Kellan's shorts and gave her thigh a small squeeze. "Ask away," she said.

"Really?"

Ashleigh couldn't imagine what anyone would find interesting about her humdrum life, but she was enjoying the attention. "Why not?"

"Okay." Kellan seemed to dig deep for her first question. "Here's one. Did your ex move back to Ireland after you split up?"

"Ha! No." She was laughing even though Kellan wasn't in on the joke. "She lives around the block from me. In our old apartment. With her boyfriend."

"Ouch." Kellan covered her heart with both hands. "Didn't see that coming."

Ashleigh ticked her head to the side. "Me either, honestly."

"Well, what can we do to encourage her to move back to her homeland?"

"Sadly, nothing." She scrunched her nose up. "Reagan's American. We met in Ireland during college. We both were in a study abroad program. Even though we were from different schools, everyone in the program hung out together. We had some classes in common. She was studying education too. We fell in love. After the semester was over, she transferred to Columbia to be with me. It was romantic."

"Where was she in school before that?"

"Notre Dame."

"And she can't go back to Indiana now?"

"Well, now she's in love with Josh. So it's unlikely."

"I'm sure there's space for both of them."

Ashleigh touched the fabric of her skirt, considering the sweetness in Kellan's support. "It's actually fine. I don't hate Reagan. Or Josh." She toyed with the hem to feel the stitching against her fingertip. "I just wish I didn't bump into them all the time. It's…awkward." Although, even as she said it, she wondered if they felt uncomfortable at all.

"I can imagine."

"Not because there's feelings, though. I mean there are feelings, but not *those* kind of feelings. It's true that things were over for a very long time before they officially ended."

"How long were you two together. Total?"

"Seventeen years. Married for twelve."

"That is a long time."

"Yes. And now I just feel, I don't know, like a fool, I guess." It was the first time she admitted it out loud. And to someone she hardly knew. Perhaps that detail made it easier. With Kellan she had nothing to prove. No guard to keep up to prevent everyone from seeing the particulars of her divorce hurt her ego as well as her heart.

"Why?"

She rolled her neck in three circles, wondering the best way to phrase what she felt inside before going with pure honesty. "She seems so happy now."

"That doesn't mean she wasn't happy with you."

Didn't it, though? Ashleigh crinkled her eyebrows, openly challenging Kellan's statement with the look. Kellan obviously understood the unspoken comment.

"What I'm saying is I can't believe, over the course of so many years, you two didn't have a lot of wonderful times together."

"I guess we did."

"Of course you did." Kellan touched her knee with the back of her index finger. Logically, she knew it was just a small gesture of encouragement, but it made her heart pound anyway. She closed her eyes and forced herself to focus as Kellan continued. "Sometimes things run a course. Other times we just don't know what we want until we find it, if that makes sense." Ashleigh felt Kellan lean in close, pressing their shoulders together. "The bigger question is, why aren't you dating anyone now?"

Ashleigh tipped her head all the way back and held it there, her gaze fixed on the clear sky above. "Oh my God. You sound like my grandmother."

"Not at all what I was going for."

"Also Liam. And Shauna. And my parents."

"See, there's truth in numbers. We can't all be wrong."

"Come on, let's walk." Ashleigh stood up simply because she was having trouble convincing her starved libido that Kellan's small touches were nothing more than friendly reassurance. Walking side by side helped quell her ridiculous desire, but it seemed her body had a mind of its own, and a few paces in she hooked her arm through Kellan's. Something about their interaction throughout the day felt deeply personal and emotional, and on the spot she gave herself permission to need the physical contact. "I wouldn't even know where to begin with dating."

"Who does?" Kellan shooed an overzealous pigeon from their path. "You just put yourself out there with the rest of us. It's not easy for anyone, I don't think."

"Oh, please." Ashleigh didn't even try to cover her doubt. "Women have been scoping you all day. You know, I should be offended at their brazenness. I could be your girlfriend. Do they care? Nope. All day with the goo-goo eyes."

Kellan bent her head in laughter. She'd obviously seen the looks. "See, you even know it."

"How do you know these women weren't looking at you?"

"Because they were looking at you. I saw them. I have eyes."

"I know. Gorgeous blue ones."

Wait a second. She wasn't crazy—this was friendly support. It couldn't be flirting, right? She was truly at a loss and had no idea how to respond. "Very suave," she finally said, hoping the chill words masked the excitement racing through her body.

Kellan tucked her hands in the pockets of her shorts, and with their arms still intertwined, the action pulled her just a bit closer. "I'm just stating a fact. You don't have to believe me."

They stopped at the end of the line for the ferry that would take them back to lower Manhattan. "That's actually an opinion," Ashleigh said.

Kellan turned and faced her, shaking her head. "Nah, it isn't."

Ashleigh could feel herself blush, and even if this was simply Kellan trying to help her out of a funk or restore her confidence, she appreciated it. "Are you hungry?" she asked.

"Thank God." Kellan pretended to go weak in the knees. "Yes. Of course, I'm hungry. You never let me eat."

"You should say something." Ashleigh slapped her arm, almost scolding her for her politeness. "You like Italian?"

"Yes."

"Great. Little Italy, it is."

They ate outdoors, and as the sun set, the heat broke. Over red wine and pasta, they philosophized about life and love, family, the summer ahead. Ashleigh inquired about the small scar on Kellan's temple and learned it was the result of a grade school ski pole duel with her brother. Kellan asked what it was like to teach high school math and whether she found it fulfilling. And while the conversation never got as personal as it had earlier in the day, the foundation of those talks made Ashleigh feel comfortable in a way that was deep and fresh and utterly unexpected.

Perhaps because they had both allowed themselves to be vulnerable, the playing field was balanced. Or maybe it was simply that it felt good to talk freely and not stress over anticipated judgment or expectation. Maybe it was just that when Kellan looked at her, she seemed to really listen. And God, it didn't hurt that she had the most unbelievable green eyes Ashleigh had ever seen.

When the check came, they split it down the middle, each tossing a card into the billfold. As the server left to run the credit through, Ashleigh opened the ferry app.

"There's a boat in twenty minutes. We could probably make it," she said checking the schedule against the time.

"That ferry can't be convenient for where you live." Kellan slid her card into her wallet. "I appreciate you coming to me, but I know it must be a pain for you to get there."

"I usually grab an Uber or a Lyft."

"I could do the same and come up by you. We could take the subway from Park Slope. I'm sure that was the original plan." She led the way out of the trattoria courtyard, holding the door as they passed through the main dining room and out onto the narrow street. "It shouldn't always have to be you coming to me."

"It's sweet of you to offer," Ashleigh said. "And I might take you up on it sometimes, depending on where we're headed. But most days, I drop Granny off at the senior center on my way out, so this works. Plus"—she paused for dramatic emphasis in the middle of the sidewalk at the ferry stop—"the Beanery coffee. It's only been a few days, and I'm hooked. I may never be the same again."

"It is good. I'll give you that."

"How do you like your aunt's apartment? The building itself is gorgeous. The lobby was something else. Does the apartment live up to the grandeur?"

Kellan nodded. "It's very nice. Small, though. It's only a studio. But the view is amazing. You should come up and see it."

Ashleigh wasn't sure if the invite was generic or specifically intended for tonight. She was afraid to ask, but more than that, she was afraid of the answer. With a full glass of wine coursing through her, she didn't trust herself alone in private with Kellan, especially after Kellan had been so sweet to her today. And maybe they had flirted. But what if she had misread those signals entirely? She was rusty when it came to romance, and she couldn't take being shot down and then having to see Kellan for the next two months. Better to play it safe.

"One of these days I will," she responded. "I want to meet Blue."

"I'm going to hold you to that," Kellan said. As they disembarked from their final passage of the day she added, "You should see if there's a car nearby."

"Okay, I'm going to put in your address and see what comes up."

"Good thinking." They walked along the path, which was peopled with a few late evening joggers and folks walking their dogs. The shops and restaurants were catering to sparse crowds. Even Brooklyn Beanery was almost empty. On this quiet Monday evening in late June, the atmosphere was vibrant and chill and Ashleigh wondered if that was always the case. Something about the lovely evening and easy company gave her peace beyond words. She could happily end every night just like this. Except right now, she didn't want it to end.

In front of Kellan's apartment, a black Toyota matching the plate in her app was waiting for her. She ignored the sadness over having to leave as she walked to the car and turned around for a last look, absorbing it all before she spoke.

"This whole neighborhood is really beautiful. I'd like to spend some time here. Would you be okay with that? If I penciled it in to the schedule?"

Kellan opened the rear passenger door for her to get in. "You don't even have to put it on the chart. Surprise me."

Ashleigh paused by the door before she slid onto the seat, only half kidding when she replied, "You know I can't do that."

"We're going to work on your definition of spontaneity. By the end of the summer, I bet you're doing all sorts of things you never envisioned." Kellan's eyes sparkled and she winked as she closed the door, tapping twice on the roof as a signal for the driver to go.

Ashleigh let her body go limp, virtually melting into the leather interior as she thanked baby Jesus himself for the ultra-dark window tint that covered the desire that was surely written all over her face.

CHAPTER EIGHT

"How's things going with GI Jane?"

Shauna stood on a small pedestal in the dress shop as a seamstress marked a slight modification to her wedding gown. Breaking her pose, she asked, "Are you, ahem, showing her around?" She dropped air quotes around the phrase just in case Ashleigh missed her overt implication.

"It's funny—I never think of Kellan as a soldier," she answered, ignoring the comment.

"Too busy thinking about her rocking your world?"

"You're obsessed." Ashleigh scanned the headlines on her phone to avoid eye contact with Shauna. "I'm just being a good friend."

"Mm-hmm."

"Why does there have to be more to it than that? Can't one kind individual assist another in navigating a foreign city that happens to be her hometown?"

Shauna gave a loud fake snore that made both Ashleigh and the busy dressmaker laugh. "I'm sorry, what did you say? That sentence was so boring I fell asleep halfway through it."

"Sorry to disappoint you, Shauna. I know you have this fantasy that Kellan is going to be the source of my sexual awakening or something, but it's not like that."

"Slow down, honey. I didn't say any of that." Ashleigh watched her friend give her a thorough once-over as she added, "But the fact that you did…color me intrigued."

Ashleigh swallowed as she tried hard to keep her composure, surprised by her own disclosure. Shauna was just making simple conversation to kill time during her fitting. But the truth was she thought about Kellan. A lot. Their two outings had been nothing but friendly, and maybe some harmless flirting. Or was that wishful thinking? Either way, when Ashleigh looked through her photos of their days together, she found herself focusing on Kellan. Those amazing green eyes, that fantastic smile. The sleeve of tattoos. Were there more? More than once she pictured her body and that had slipped right into wondering what it would be like to be with Kellan. Would her kiss be hard and passionate, or soft but leading? Would Kellan explore her body immediately? Would she stop her?

Kellan's hands were sturdy but soft at the same time. She could almost feel her fingertips caressing her face, her breasts, her belly, and beyond. Two evenings ago, this particular fantasy had taken over and segued right into an image of Kellan using a strap-on to take her over the edge. It wasn't anything she even thought she wanted, and yet, she'd been drenched at the mere thought. The orgasm she gave herself was proof that she was way into it, at least in theory. Of course, make-believe had a way of being astoundingly better than real life, and afterward she'd reminded herself that the few times she and Reagan had delved into using toys had been a complete bust. Still, something told her with Kellan it would be different.

"Um, hello. Ashleigh?" Shauna snapped her fingers. "What do you think? Do I look all right?"

Ashleigh focused on her friend as she shook free from the daydream she'd allowed herself to get caught up in, again. "Oh my God. You look amazing." It was true. She watched Shauna smile in the mirror and reveled in excited anticipation right alongside her. "Mike is gonna die at the altar when he sees you."

"For real?" Shauna tilted a little to get a view of the detail in the back.

"Definitely."

"I hope so. You know, not die, obviously. But I hope he loves it."

"He will."

With the help of the attendant, Shauna stepped out of the strapless gown, and Ashleigh handed over her clothes.

"Hey, when did you get abs of steel?" she asked, trying not to stare at Shauna's six-pack.

Shauna pulled on her shorts and tank. "About that," she started. "I was trying to stay in shape, you know for the big day—"

"As if you haven't been in shape your whole life."

"Hey, I was a super-chunk baby. But cute as all get-out."

"I take it back. Your whole adult life."

She followed Shauna to the counter and watched her sign the sales slip indicating consent to her modifications. "Mike has some hikes mapped out on our honeymoon. Maui has an inactive volcano. They do tours, I guess. It sounds fun and supposedly it's beautiful. He promised me beach time—I promised him hiking."

"Sounds like fun," Ashleigh said.

"But I wanted to make sure I could keep up." Ashleigh picked up on her hesitation and wondered where this was going. "So I joined CrossFit." Boom, there it was.

"Home of the happy couple." Ashleigh hooked her purse over her shoulder as they exited the boutique dress shop onto Seventh Avenue. "How are Reagan and Josh at the gym? Do they make out while they train?" She was only half kidding, and she knew Shauna wouldn't judge her snark.

"I'm sorry, Ash. I should've told you before. Now I feel like a cheat. But it's kind of why I needed the adjustments on my dress. That shit is no joke."

"It's paying off. You look fantastic. I mean it." She loved Shauna, and once upon a time she'd loved Reagan. And deep down she knew Shauna did too. The three of them had been inseparable during the years they taught together at John Jay High School, before Ashleigh and Shauna left for faculty positions at Brooklyn Tech's elite STEM program. "Do you all work out together?" she asked.

"During the school year we were at a lot of the same sessions. Mostly because we were on the same schedule."

"Makes sense."

"Are you mad?"

"Of course not." She forced a smile, not wanting her to feel bad. Truthfully, it wasn't anger she was feeling anyway. "I know you guys are friends. Honestly, Reagan and I get along fine. We're both pleasant when we see each other. I promise not to cause any drama at your wedding."

"Please, that's not what I was getting at." Shauna stopped in the middle of the sidewalk. "You didn't think that, did you?"

"I just don't want you to worry on your special day."

"*Pshh*. You and Reagan, furthest thing from my mind." Shauna waved her off and continued walking. "How my mother's relatives from DR are going to get along with my dad's family from Grenada... that's a different story."

Shauna's long-storied family feud had been a source of low-grade aggravation for years, and Ashleigh scrambled to distract her.

"I was actually thinking about inviting Kellan as my plus-one." Ashleigh surprised herself with the spontaneous utterance. Also, it was a fabrication. Asking Kellan to accompany her to Shauna and Mike's wedding was not at all something she'd considered, not even for a second, but it was out before she could stop it. Whether it was the thought of being the lone spinster at the wedding or the idea of sitting across from Reagan and Josh all night that sent her off the deep end, she wasn't sure. But now it was out there, and she needed to do damage control before Shauna jumped to conclusions.

"Well, well, well." Shauna's face was full I-told-you-so smug. "I guess things *are* sparking off. I fucking knew it."

"Stop. It's not like that. I just figured"—she played with the zipper on her purse as they strolled through Park Slope—"it's a month and a half away. I probably won't be seeing anyone by then. Certainly not anyone I'd bring to your wedding. And the vineyards out in Long Island are supposed to be beautiful. I figured we could make it a part of our summer tour." She hoped her nonchalant explanation passed the test. "I mean, would that be okay? If I invited her? For all I know, she'll be gone by then."

"I thought she was here for the summer."

"She could have plans, though."

"Only one way to find out."

"Settle down. It was just a thought."

"Well, I think it's perfect." If Shauna saw through her, she was at least playing along for the moment. "So, tell me, how is the *touring* going?" Air quotes again.

Ashleigh tilted her head and gave her friend an obvious eye roll, so there was no mistaking what she thought of the innuendo. "It's going fine. I was busy earlier this week with family stuff, so we've only spent a few days together, but I like her. She's easy to talk to."

"Do tell." Shauna hooked her arm through Ashleigh's, clearly expecting something juicy.

"There's hardly anything to tell. Like I said, we've only hung out a couple of times."

"And yet you want to invite her to my wedding." Shauna drummed one finger on her chin. "I detect some strong undercurrents here."

"Undercurrents of what? We go to museums together. Are you picking up on our shared love of history?"

"Nuh-uh-uh." Shauna wagged her finger. "I know you. This *I'm just going to put my uptight persona on the shelf and check out New York with a hot butch stranger?* This is not typical Ashleigh. Don't get me wrong. I'm Team Kellan all the way. But do not pretend this is all part of some tour guide nonsense. I am not some damn fool."

Ashleigh couldn't help but laugh at her friend's honesty. "There is no Team Kellan."

"And why not? Explain it to me. You could use a distraction. She's here for the summer. You're both single and attractive. You spend every day together—"

"Not every day. I just told you that."

"Where are we headed right now?" Shauna asked, even though they both knew the answer.

"To Liam's."

"To meet Kellan," Shauna added. "To go where again?"

"The Cloisters. But only because you have plans."

"Ooh, if you're going to be in the Heights, you should go to my Uncle Mervin's place to eat. I'll text you the address." Shauna walked into Liam's pub, not bothering to lower her voice. "And anyway, even if I didn't have shit to do right now, I'd make something up, because I am rooting for this." Her gesture between Ashleigh and Kellan was overt. "Hey, studs," she said, shifting gears to address Liam and Kellan at the bar.

"Ladies." Liam leaned across the bar and gave them each a kiss on the cheek. "Can I get you something to drink?"

"I can't stay." Shauna pouted effectively. "I just wanted to say hi. Nice to see you again, Kellan."

"You too." Kellan raised a pint. "How was the dress fitting?"

"Very nice, thank you for asking." She looked right at Ashleigh, widening her eyes in obvious approval of Kellan's manners. "Kellan, before I forget, do you have any plans on August fourteenth?"

"Uh, no." Kellan's slight laugh sounded uncertain. "What's happening on the fourteenth?"

Shauna backed through the restaurant to the door. "I gotta run. Ash will fill you in. See ya soon."

"What was that about?" Kellan asked.

"Nothing. Shauna's just...being Shauna." She hoped her frustrated act played to her favor and kept Kellan from pressing for details. "Are you ready to go, or did you want to finish your beer?"

"Nope. I'm good. I was just killing time with Liam while I waited for you."

"Let's go, then."

They said good-bye to Liam and headed straight for the subway that would take them through the first leg of their journey to Washington Heights. It wasn't a long trip, just over an hour total, but since they were getting a late start, Ashleigh used the city planner app to ensure they traveled via the most expeditious route. Since the Cloisters were technically an extension of the Metropolitan Museum of Art, they had a strict closing time of 4:45 p.m., and Ashleigh wanted to make sure they had ample time to view the treasures.

After a solid hour and a half perusing Medieval architecture, sculpture, and decorative arts, Ashleigh and Kellan were among the last visitors to leave the monastery-inspired building as they exited into the grounds of Fort Tryon Park.

Kellan turned around to get a look at the building's facade up close, snapping a pic on her phone.

"One for the scrapbook?" she asked, waving Ashleigh toward her in front of the building.

"Okay, but"—Ashleigh ticked her head in the opposite direction— "there's a better background this way."

Kellan looked over and Ashleigh registered awe in her expression. She wasn't surprised—she still remembered the first time she'd seen this view as a kid. But watching Kellan take in the scene she knew so well did something to her. Gave her a thrill of excitement. Or maybe it was just Kellan's strong jawline and muscled physique against the beautiful backdrop that gave her a chill.

She blinked the thought away. "Pretty amazing, right?" she asked, finding her voice.

"Holy smokes, Ash. How did I not notice this when we got here?" Ashleigh laughed, fully aware of the reason for the oversight. "Because I rushed you. It's just that I knew the museum closed kind of early and we'd have a chance to take a walk around here after. But I have to say, it was worth it to see your expression right now."

"That's the George Washington Bridge?" Kellan asked.

"It is. And the Hudson River below it. Just over there is New Jersey." Ashleigh walked closer to the edge of the park's ridge, situated a few stories above the highway. "Come, look." She leaned on a brick wall overlooking the expanse. "I'm sure this is nothing compared to the mountains in Colorado. But I thought you'd appreciate it anyway."

"It's beautiful," she said, resting her arms over the divide. "Colorado is spectacular too, of course. I guess it's just that I didn't expect to be hit with so many trees and so much open space here. My vision of New York was all buildings and subways. Does that sound small-minded?"

"Not at all. It's what everyone thinks about New York City. And it's mostly true." The sun was beginning to set, and the late day light shone on Kellan's face, highlighting the light freckles on the bridge of her nose and various hues of green in her eyes. They were so deep and rich and enticing that Ashleigh thought she might melt on the spot. "Should we walk a bit?" she asked, if only to keep from staring.

"Yes. But first, you promised me a picture."

"I almost forgot." Ashleigh nodded and bit her cheek to control her reaction as Kellan pressed against her, positioning them as she angled the lens to capture the bridge, the river, and the cliffs of New Jersey behind them.

"Tell me about Vail," Ashleigh asked as they made their way along the paved path in the park.

Kellan picked up a leaf and inspected it before letting it fall to the ground. "Sure. What do you want to know?"

"I don't know. Everything, I guess. I know virtually nothing about it."

"That's not true. Everybody knows something."

"Fair enough. I know that there's skiing. And other winter sports. I image it's all picturesque mountains."

"That's actually true." Kellan looked off into the distance. "The streets are heated—did you know that?"

"What?"

"In the winter. They heat the streets to keep them from icing over. Helps with tourism."

"Also genius."

"I guess. It's nice to always be able to get around."

"Did you miss it? I mean do you miss it, now?" She had a million questions, but realized she was coming off kind of intense. "I'm sorry. That's two different questions. I was wondering if you missed home when you were in the Army and also if you were sad to be away now, since you've only gotten out and now you're stuck in New York."

"No worries. I'll answer both." Kellan's smile was so easy Ashleigh couldn't look away. "I'll go in order, if that's okay."

"Very soldierly of you."

"Yes, ma'am." Her voice was smooth, her smile wolfish and intoxicating. It made Ashleigh swoon on the spot. Why did Kellan have such a visceral effect on her? She didn't do flings or hookups or one-night stands. And despite her late-night fantasies and Shauna's ridiculous suggestion of a summer tryst, she knew it was a terrible idea. There was nothing about this that could end well.

"I did miss home when I was away," Kellan said, interrupting her train of thought. "Especially when I was in the desert. I think being someplace so opposite Vail made me think of my family. I'm pretty close with my parents and Turk."

"Did you see him at least, when you were overseas?"

"Our paths crossed a few times over the years. It was nice."

"I didn't even ask—what did you do in the military? Were you on the ground fighting? I'm sorry, I should have asked you sooner."

"It's fine. I was in an intelligence unit."

"What does that mean exactly? Wait, can you not tell me? It's okay if you can't."

"I can."

"I'm sorry—I just realized we talked a lot about me the other day, and I barely asked about you at all. I don't want you to think I don't

care. I do. Care. About you, I mean. You know, your service. Your life."
Oh my God, why was she such a dork?

"You're cute when you're nervous. Do you know that?"

Ashleigh covered her face with both hands, mortified at how she was butchering her attempt at sincerity. She felt Kellan's hands on her shoulders before she could say anything else.

"Breathe." Kellan massaged her for a second. "It's all good."
Ashleigh felt Kellan's hand slide down her back and away as she spoke. "I was an E-5 Specialist—that was my rank. Technically, my job was to analyze intelligence. That means"—she seemed to search the air for the right wording to explain—"like, we would get some intel from headquarters, or troops in the field, assets, a whole bunch of resources, and then my job was to vet the information. Scrub it, drill down as far as possible to see if the information was legit."

"That sounds interesting." It actually sounded dangerous, but then everything about the military required bravery, in her opinion. In the moment, she was thankful she didn't know Kellan during her active service. She would have been worried sick the whole time. "Did you do that from a base or were you in the field? I don't even know if I'm using the right terminology." She hoped she didn't sound like a moron.

"You're fine," Kellan answered, as if she understood her unspoken concerns. "Both, to be honest. I was lucky. Early on I met a colonel who took a liking to me."

Ashleigh stopped in her tracks and she suspected her face revealed exactly what she was thinking, a combination of surprised and scandalized.

"Not like that. Get your mind out of the gutter," Kellan teased. "About three years in, I was stationed in the Middle East. We were out on a field mission. Two teams of us. I was there as the analyst for one team, but we were all kind of working together. In the middle of the op our main radio malfunctioned and we lost communication. It was pretty dicey because we were in, let's just say, not friendly territory. There was a communications guy there with us, but he was useless. I ended up just tinkering around with the radio and got us back online. I'm actually pretty good at stuff like that."

"Impressive."

"I think Colonel Smith was scared he was never going to see his family again. After that, he was taking no chances. I was assigned to his team permanently. He was the commander of a military outreach unit. We went to a lot of interesting places in Europe, Asia, and Africa, also—obviously—the Middle East. He was a decent guy to work for. Honest, fair."

"Sounds like you enjoyed it."

"I did, most of the time."

"Was being gay ever an issue for you?"

"In the Army or in life?"

"Both, I guess. Although I was asking about the military."

"I had my fair share of run-ins while I was in the Army. There are jerks everywhere, as I'm sure you know. But the colonel protected me. He once told me that I reminded him of his daughter. I don't know if that means she's a lesbian or butch or non-gender-conforming or what."

"You didn't ask?"

Kellan shook her head. "It wasn't that kind of interaction. He mentioned it once in passing. Beyond that, he was always kind, respectful. By the same token, I was a hard worker. A good analyst. I can fix almost anything. I was a valuable member of the team."

Ashleigh had plenty of questions she still wanted to ask, but she didn't want to pry and put Kellan off. They still had the whole summer ahead of them.

Kellan leaned in close to her. "By the way, getting back to the original question, I don't feel stuck here. Yes, coming to New York wasn't part of my original plan, but I'm enjoying myself. Thanks to you." There was a genuineness in her tone and her expression that transcended flirting. It rang of absolute sincerity, and it touched Ashleigh in a way she didn't quite expect.

"Are you hungry?" she asked, changing the subject entirely.

"You know the answer to that." Kellan's smirk was dangerous and charming as hell.

"Great." Ashleigh pulled her phone from her purse. "Shauna texted me the address of her uncle's restaurant not far from here. Apparently, it can get crowded, but she called ahead and her aunt is holding a table for us. Her mom's family is from the Dominican Republic, so it's authentic Dominican food. Is that okay?"

"Sounds amazing. So nice of Shauna to set it up for us."

It was nice. A touch manipulative, but it came from a good place. Shauna was clearly going to do her part to make Team Kellan happen.

Ashleigh smiled to herself as they exited the park and walked along the streets of Washington Heights.

"Hey, what was Shauna talking about before? That stuff about August?"

Ashleigh felt her heart pound. How was she supposed to explain this without sounding crazy or pathetic or both?

"Oh, that," she said with a wave of her hand like it was no big deal. "Shauna's getting married in the middle of August out at the end of Long Island, by the wineries. She thought if you were still around, you might like to come. You know, just to experience that side of New York. She was pushing me to bring you as my plus-one." It was a harmless stretch of the truth.

"Wow. It's so nice of her to include me."

"I told her you were probably busy."

"You tell me. You're in control of my schedule." Kellan laughed out loud. "But I imagine you might want to bring a real date."

"Well, there's no one on the horizon, so you might get lucky," she said, as they squeezed into Uncle Mervin's. She regretted her word choice the second it was out of her mouth and hoped Kellan didn't pick up on it, but when she glanced up, the twinkle in Kellan's eyes told the story.

"A vineyard wedding *and* I might get lucky? I'm in."

Ashleigh shook her head and rolled her eyes, feigning disinterest, because she was ridiculously and completely turned on at Kellan's playful suggestion, and she was sure she was blushing. She sent all her prayers to the sky, hoping if there was a God above, Kellan wouldn't see right through her.

CHAPTER NINE

I don't know how you could possibly have room for anything else."
"I can do it." Kellan felt confident inside, but she heard doubt
in her tone that contradicted the words.

She and Ashleigh were two hours into Smorgasburg, Brooklyn's
open-air food festival located in the Williamsburg section. So far they'd
indulged in Korean barbecue tacos, a Wowfull—some genius's sweet
and savory play on waffles—and a small order of truly stellar Buffalo
wings. And even though they'd split everything between them to avoid
this very problem, Kellan was stuffed. But there were still tons of
vendors whose offerings piqued her interest. She patted her abdomen
for support and inspiration as she considered hitting up one more stand
just to get the most out of her experience. "I'm no quitter."

"Don't feel pressured." Ashleigh scooted next to her to make room
on the picnic bench for another customer. "We can come back anytime.
Smorgasburg is here every weekend. Plus, we still have all afternoon.
We can even walk around Williamsburg and come back in a bit, if you
want." Ashleigh arched her back, stretching deep as she tilted her face
toward the sky.

It was ridiculous, but Kellan could be perfectly content just
watching Ashleigh bask in the sun for the rest of the day. Eyes closed,
her smooth skin was slightly flushed from the temperature and open
exposure to the UV rays, the sun highlighting her dirty-blond hair as
she tossed it slowly back and forth across her shoulders. The movement
itself was innocent, but it sent Kellan's mind to all sorts of non-PG
places. She forced herself to turn away and focus on a row of tents
lining the perimeter. She dug deep to find her voice.

"I still can't believe you surprised me."

"I knew you'd get a kick out of it. You're always teasing that I never let you eat." Ashleigh scrunched up her nose and her smile was positively irresistible. "Plus, I figured Brooklyn Flea wasn't high on your must-see list."

Kellan hung her head and laughed. Ashleigh already had her number. "True, vintage clothes shopping isn't high on my list, I'll admit, but I wouldn't have minded," she said, the second half of her statement just as true as the first. "I like hanging with you." She shrugged, hoping it made her comment come off breezy.

They'd only spent a handful of days together, but Kellan was having a fantastic time. It wasn't just the sightseeing, although that was proving fun. But instead of whittling down her list of tourist attractions to catch, or figuring the right way to reconnect with Dara, she spent her free time thinking solely about Ashleigh. Counting down the hours to their next adventure, wondering what they would talk about, what Ashleigh might wear. It was harmless. Fun little daydreams she indulged in, knowing the real thing couldn't happen.

"What do you say, champ?" Ashleigh patted her thigh. "You have another meal in you, or what?"

"Champ?"

"You wrecked those wings like a champion, so, yeah."

"Were they not fantastic, though? Hot, tangy, crispy."

"My mouth is still on fire a little bit."

"Ooh, let's have a beer." Kellan nodded in the direction of the beer garden.

Ashleigh squinted, a quizzical look taking over her expression. "I thought that just makes it worse."

"Eh, only the first few sips." Kellan stood up and offered her hand, pleased when Ashleigh took it. "Come on, let me buy you a drink. It's the least I can do, since you spoiled me rotten with this event."

At the bar, Kellan ordered them each a local brew and was mildly taken aback when the bartender asked for ID. She reached into her back pocket and took out her thin wallet, retrieving her Colorado driver's license and handing it over. The guy gave it a glance, accompanying his inspection with a nod that almost seemed like an apology.

Ashleigh pulled her attention away from her phone. "Did you just get carded?" she asked, her voice full of surprise.

"I did."

"Wow. I haven't been proofed in years. That's got to feel amazing." Kellan scrunched her face in response, knowing she needed to let Ashleigh in on what really happened. "Don't get all excited. It's not what you think." She tapped her credit card on the bar as she waited for their drinks. "It's less about me looking like a twenty-one-year-old woman." Kellan leaned in close and lowered her voice, mostly because she didn't want the bartender to feel bad hearing her explain it to Ashleigh. "More that I look like a nineteen-year-old dude." She shrugged. No biggie.

"Oh." Ashleigh nodded, seeming to analyze the explanation. "Really?"

Kellan nodded, knowing it was the absolute truth. This wasn't the first time her physical presentation had caused this type of confusion. She was used to it. And she didn't mind. Especially when things proceeded as smoothly as they had in this interaction. She checked Ashleigh's expression to see if she was freaked out.

"You okay?" she asked.

"Me?" Ashleigh touched her chest. "I'm fine. I do have one concern, though."

Kellan felt her blood pressure rise a little. "What's up?"

"I need to see your wallet."

"Uh, why?"

"Because if I'm not mistaken, when you were putting your license away, I caught a glimpse of your military ID. And I'm going to need to see that picture of you in uniform."

"You wish." Kellan couldn't contain her grin or the speed of her pulse at Ashleigh's perfect response.

They had a good spot at the corner of the bar, and Kellan was enjoying people watching the crowd behind Ashleigh. The bartender returned with their order and Kellan's credit card, and when she reached for her wallet, Ashleigh made a play to snag it away.

"Nice try."

"Come on. Please?" Ashleigh batted her lashes for effect.

"Nope." Kellan didn't really care about the picture, but she was too heavily invested in the back-and-forth to give in so quickly. She raised her eyebrows and held the slim billfold just beyond Ashleigh's reach. "What's in it for me?"

Ashleigh dropped a look that indicated she couldn't believe Kellan had gone there. "Hardball, huh?"

Kellan responded with a playful arch of an eyebrow, so Ashleigh would know it was all in good fun.

"I guess we're going to do this the hard way." Ashleigh's tone was so measured Kellan didn't expect her to lunge for the wallet so quickly. Still, she was so much stronger that Ashleigh wasn't able to loosen it from her hand. Their bodies were pressed close together, and they were both laughing from the silly struggle. Kellan knew she was enjoying the contact too much as she held the wallet behind her back and felt Ashleigh's breasts graze her torso.

"All right, you win," Kellan said, ready to give in.

"Ash?" A spirited voice caught them both off guard, and Ashleigh froze as she stopped playing and turned around. "I thought that was you."

Kellan slipped the wallet away and looked between Ashleigh and the mystery brunette closing the distance between them.

"Hi. Reagan…hi."

Reagan. Of course. Leave it to the ex to interrupt their most flirtatious moment ever. Without even seeing Ashleigh's face, Kellan could sense that she was unnerved by Reagan's presence. Immediately, she was annoyed in solidarity.

"Hi, Josh." Ashleigh looked right at her ex-wife's significant other. Her voice was even, almost friendly, but Kellan felt Ashleigh's body stiffen and knew it was all stress. "I'm sorry." She pivoted and touched Kellan's midsection ever so slightly. "This is Kellan. Kellan, this is Reagan. My ex-wife," she added. Did Ashleigh really think she didn't know who Reagan was? Her usual easy cadence was replaced by sheer unrest. "And her boyfriend, Josh."

"Nice to meet you both." Kellan extended her hand and gave them each a tepid greeting, unsure what her role was.

She could feel Reagan analyzing her from head to toe. Did she think they were together? More importantly, was Ashleigh trying to play that off? She was standing closer than usual, but the bar area was packed, and they'd just come off their frisky moment. It was hard to split the difference.

"I'm actually surprised to see you here," Reagan said. "You hate stuff like this."

"Yeah, well." Ashleigh moved closer and pressed into the front of Kellan's body to make room for a patron in a rush to get to the bar. "Sorry, Kell," she said, shortening her name for the first time ever.

"No worries." She wanted to slip her hand around Ashleigh's waist possessively just to let her know how okay it was. If the situation had been at all different, she might have gone for it. But the timing was wrong for such a bold move, and it might never be right. Instead she subtly touched two fingers to the small of her back, hoping Ashleigh felt her support over this less than ideal situation.

Ashleigh's eyes held gratitude, and Kellan felt her heart pound unexpectedly. "Kellan's a foodie," she said, answering Reagan's comment. "She's here for the summer. This was sort of a no-brainer." Her words were calm, but her smile stressed. Kellan hated that if she noticed, surely Reagan did too.

"Nice." Reagan nodded, clearly still trying to assess their dynamic before she made full eye contact. "Where's home?" she asked.

"Colorado."

"Cool." Josh turned from the bar. "You guys need drinks?"

"No thanks," Ashleigh said.

"I'm good," Kellan echoed.

Reagan reached out and took a plastic cup of ice water from Josh, downing half of it immediately. "I was dying of thirst. So hot today," she said to no one in particular as she dabbed at her brow before giving her attention to Ashleigh. "How was your class this year? Shauna said you had some troublemakers second semester."

"Shauna exaggerates. You know that."

Reagan took another swallow of her water, then laughed softly in silent agreement.

"How's things at John Jay?" Ashleigh asked.

"Great," she said. Kellan caught Reagan looking at Josh. Was she really checking for approval before answering? "Our math team almost made it to regionals. I thought of you. You would have gotten them there."

"They did great. I saw them compete during the city finals."

"Of course." Her nod was a touch wistful, a smidge complimentary. It annoyed the fuck out of her. "What do you do, Kellan?"

"I just retired from the Army."

"Wow." She and Josh looked at each other again. "That's amazing. And now you're in Brooklyn?"

"Like Ash said, just for the summer." *Ash.* It oversold their connection, but only slightly, and she still didn't know how they were playing this. She didn't want to assume anything, but she didn't want to blow it up, either. She hoped Ashleigh would give her a sign.

"We should actually get going." Ashleigh picked up the momentum. "Are you ready?" She found Kellan's hand and laced their fingers together.

Kellan squeezed her hand in response. "Whenever you are."

"Good seeing you, Reagan." Kellan saw a practiced smile emerge across her beautiful face. "You too, Josh."

She let Ashleigh lead her through the packed bar area and kept hold of her hand as they walked to the street and along the sidewalk. They reached the corner and she was bummed when Ashleigh dropped her hand.

"I'm sorry, I don't know why I did that."

"Are you okay?"

Ashleigh nodded, but her eyes were closed and her lips pursed, and Kellan felt genuine concern course through her veins at the sight of her obvious angst. It killed her to see Ashleigh hurting. "Are you sure?" She bent down to make eye contact. "It's okay not to be. You know that, right?"

"It's ridiculous not to be." She tucked her hair behind her ears and crossed her arms over her chest, seeming to steel herself, even though the hard part was over. She let out a long breath and Kellan thought she might say more, but their Uber pulled up to the curb. "Did you get us a car?"

"I got the feeling you might want to get out of here."

"When, though?"

"Just now, when we were walking out. We lucked out. It was a minute away."

They slid into the back seat, and Ashleigh relaxed her head against the headrest and looked out the window. "Where are we headed?"

"I just put in my address because it was easiest. But we can go anywhere. Liam's, if you want. Or I can drop you off at home. Whatever you say."

"Let's go down by you, if that's okay. It's pretty there. I don't really feel like going home."

Fifteen minutes later the driver deposited them outside Kellan's apartment building. Kellan wasn't really sure what the plan was from here. She loitered by the front door. "Do you want to go upstairs or walk for a bit? Grab a coffee, maybe?"

"A walk sounds nice. Would I be able to wash my hands first?"

"Of course." Kellan led the way through the lobby and waved to Sanjay. "I'm up on the fourth floor," she explained to Ashleigh as they stepped into the elevator. "Blue will be so excited to meet you."

"Is he friendly with new people?"

Kellan laughed, realizing she didn't know the answer. "No clue." She opened the apartment door, ready to find out. "Blue? *Blu-ue?*" she called out, shutting the door behind them. "The bathroom is just over there," she said to Ashleigh.

"Thanks. I'll just be a minute."

"Take your time."

While Ashleigh freshened up, Kellan grabbed the cat treats. "Come on, Blueberry," she said, using her special nickname for him. "Don't embarrass me."

"Found him." Ashleigh walked slowly into the studio space holding the petite gray cat. "He was in the shower," she said. "I only had a tiny heart attack when he poked his head out." She pressed her face against his head.

"Look at you two. I think I've been replaced."

"He's a sweetie." Ashleigh turned around to take in the space. "And if the apartment comes with him, I'm sold." She placed Blue on the ground. "Kellan, this place is sick. Look at that view."

"I'm enjoying waking up to it every day. The apartment is not at all what I expected. Small, but really lovely."

"I don't even think it's that small, really."

Kellan had almost forgotten that Ashleigh shared a living space with her parents and her grandmother. An empty studio with a sole feline roommate and a view of the Manhattan skyline probably seemed like winning the lottery. For a split second she wondered what Ashleigh's old apartment was like. Was it sleek and modern like the space they shared right now? Did the aroma of her light perfume and shampoo linger like she hoped it would tonight?

"What do you think so far? Of New York?" Ashleigh interrupted her thought with the question as she turned away from the window.

"I love it." Her answer was a reflex, but it was honest. What she didn't elaborate on was that her pleasure had as much to do with Ashleigh as it did with the city itself.

"For real?"

Kellan drew her finger in a square across the surface of the kitchen island, not ready to hold eye contact. "What's not to love? I live in a great apartment. Rent free, I might add. I have a cool roomie." She tossed a toy and watched Blue pounce on it. "I'm seeing all the key spots, thanks to my fabulous tour guide. Who even rearranges her airtight schedule to surprise me." She looked up. "Thank you for that, by the way."

"You're welcome." Ashleigh walked over and reached up to kiss her cheek. "Thank you for being sweet. Let's go for a walk."

She didn't want to overthink it. Truly, she didn't want to. But was a kiss really necessary? Even as a thank you? There was definite energy between them. No doubt about it. Ashleigh had to feel it too. Their conversation often veered into that gray area that was beyond friendly but not quite flirtatious. And today with the wallet—that interaction felt like a scene right out of one of those rom-coms she hated watching. But fucking Reagan had shown up just in time to destroy their mojo before anything more could happen. Somehow the aura she cast over the day seemed to linger, even still.

She looked at Ashleigh waiting by the door, her expression one of peace and gratitude, but beneath it there seemed to be something else. Maybe heartache, she wasn't sure. Whatever the cause, she longed to put a smile back on Ashleigh's face. She pushed away her selfish concerns. If there was a vibe she was picking up between them, it would keep. Right now Ashleigh needed a friend. She grabbed her keys and slipped them into her pocket, then killed the lights behind her.

"Let's roll."

❖

Brooklyn Bridge Park was alive with walkers, joggers, and outdoor diners. It seemed they weren't the only people jonesing to be outside. It made perfect sense. As the day progressed, the heat had dissipated some, giving way to a cloudless, warm evening. The ideal summer night. As they passed a crowd gathered outside a restaurant, Ashleigh turned to her.

"Did you want to eat?"

It was a considerate question, and Kellan was touched, but she was still full from the afternoon. "I'm okay. Do you?"

"No. I know sometimes I forget to ask. That's all."

"I ate way more than you did at the festival. I might snack on something later, but I'm good for now."

"I knew you'd love Smorgasburg," Ashleigh said. "I'm glad you got to experience it." Her voice faded as she looked out over the water. Kellan wondered where her head was. She hugged herself, and it made Kellan long for the contact of her touch from earlier, even if it had been just a guise to escape an awkward situation.

"I am sorry about everything with Reagan," Ashleigh said, seeming to somehow channel into her thoughts. "You know, cutting the day short. Also acting like we were together. It was stupid."

"It wasn't." Kellan hoped her sincerity came through. "I would have done the same thing."

"I doubt it."

"Why do you say that?"

"Come on." Ashleigh shot her a wry smile, in obvious disbelief. "Like you've ever had to pretend to have a girlfriend? Please, I see the way women look at you. Even that woman who passed by with the black schnauzer two minutes ago. She practically broke her neck craning to gawk."

It was true. She got a fair amount of attention. But she hadn't had as many significant relationships as Ashleigh seemed to think. "That woman was not looking for a relationship."

Ashleigh faced her and Kellan saw her jaw drop a little. Right away she realized how it had come out. "What I mean is, a lot of those women, they're not interested in me. I'm a fun experiment for them. Someone they can live out a fantasy with and move on."

"What do you mean?"

Kellan struggled for the best way to explain what she meant. She wasn't being vain. In fact, the opposite was true. "Take Lisa, for example."

"Wait. My Lisa. From school?"

"Yes."

"You slept with her?"

It was the second time Ashleigh seemed irritated at that particular possibility, and while that intrigued her, it derailed the message she was trying to convey. "I did not have sex with Lisa. Once and for all."

"But you just said—"

"I was trying to make a point."

"That you could have slept with her?"

"No. Yes." She shook her head taking another stab. "No. What I'm saying is the Lisas of the world see me as their shot at a guilt-free one-night stand. I'm not a guy, which somehow makes it less real, if that makes sense. Also, I'm not a jerk. I enjoy spending time with them. And they get to have their *fantasy*, their experience." She emphasized the word to make her point clear. "But then the novelty wears off. They go back to their boyfriends, their husbands. It rarely turns into anything real."

"Rarely? Does that mean sometimes it does end up being something longer?"

"There have been a few serious relationships."

"Will you tell me about them?"

Kellan wanted to tell Ashleigh everything. But the truth was tricky. Yes, she'd had girlfriends in the Army. She'd even had a steady hookup in Vail when she visited home over the last decade. But if she was being honest, none of those relationships felt as effortless and exciting as the connection she felt whenever she was with Ashleigh. That knowledge made her head spin, forget about what it did to other parts of her body.

"You don't have to tell me," Ashleigh said, misreading her extended silence. "You've done so much for me today already. I didn't mean to pry. I just thought…I don't know. If I could return the favor, somehow."

"There's no favor to return. I had a great day."

"Even when I forced you to be my pretend girlfriend with no warning?"

"Who said that wasn't my favorite part?" It might have been the truth, but she was playing it for laughs, and it made her feel good when Ashleigh giggled.

"God." Ashleigh let out a loud sigh through her laughter. "I do not know how I let her get to me so much. I don't even want to be with her. I swear."

"I believe you."

"I'm honestly fine. But then I see them together, and I don't know. It gets under my skin."

"The boyfriend. Josh." Kellan didn't want to push, but she had questions. "Is he the reason why you split up?"

Ashleigh took a minute and Kellan worried she'd overstepped. "Ultimately, yes, I guess he was the reason we finally got divorced. But our marriage was over way before he was in the picture."

"What happened?"

They were walking slowly near the water's edge, the sun was just starting to set, and Kellan almost couldn't get over how beautiful the sky was. Without discussing it, they both stopped to lean against the railing under the shadow of the Brooklyn Bridge. Ashleigh folded her pale, slender fingers together and leaned her arms over the railing. She bent her head all the way forward against the bend of her elbows.

Kellan touched her back gently. "I'm sorry. I didn't mean to upset you."

"I'm not upset." Ashleigh turned her face toward Kellan. "I just have no idea where to start that story."

"Well, I know you met in college in Ireland. So you can skip the beginning." Kellan winked as she joined Ashleigh in leaning over the railing.

"We were so young." Her smile was nostalgic, the worry lines softening in the late day breeze. "Sometimes it seems like forever ago. Other times, like it was yesterday."

"I get that."

"We were crazy about each other. We did everything together. Attended the same graduate program, applied for jobs at the same school. Took great vacations."

"Did you get married right away?"

Ashleigh tapped her light pink fingernails against the thick railing, stopping to inspect them as she spoke. "Not right away. We moved in together straight out of college, though. We got married a few years later. We were twenty-five. Actually, I was twenty-four. I turned twenty-five on my honeymoon."

"Wow. That's…very young," she said. But then, she'd already been in the Army six years by then. And made arguably the biggest decision of her life, but they weren't talking about her. "But you two were happy for a long time, I assume. Your divorce is recent, right?"

"We were happy, yes. Actually, I wouldn't say we were ever unhappy. It's not like we fought all the time or anything. But I think because we were young when we got together, when we grew up, or changed—which is natural—we simply evolved in ways that made us not as compatible as we once were. There was no hero, no villain."

"Eh, I'm going to label Reagan the villain if that's okay with you." As far as she could tell, Reagan was at fault for making Ashleigh feel responsible for the way everything had unraveled. It clearly still caused her stress, and where Ashleigh might be willing to give her a pass, she wasn't so forgiving.

Ashleigh rested her hand on Kellan's forearm. "That's truly not fair. If anyone is the villain, it's me."

"I don't believe that."

"You should. Reagan acknowledged the truth about what was going on in our relationship long before I was willing to."

"What do you mean?"

"We were living separate lives under the same roof. She addressed it. She wanted to break up. Like, a full five years before we did." Ashleigh shook her head almost dismissively. "I insisted we go to therapy."

"Did it help?"

"Yes and no. It felt like we were trying. I considered that progress. But the problem wasn't fixable. We loved each other. We just weren't *in love* anymore. But I fought to stay together. And Reagan, to her credit, she stayed. For a very long time. In a strained, sexless marriage. But then she fell in love with someone else."

"Josh." Kellan's heart broke to see Ashleigh assume all the blame for things. "I should have known he'd be the bad guy."

"That's just it, though. I don't think he was." She touched the corner of her eye and Kellan wondered if she was crying. "I don't think he was anything but a friend to her initially. Reagan and I were together for such a long time, and we had the same circle. I think he was someone she could talk to, really talk to, who wasn't in our group." She leaned all the way back, gripping the railing as she shook her head toward the evening sky. "I honestly don't even think she cheated on me. She said she didn't, at least. I'm inclined to believe her. She was so miserable at the end. I don't imagine she was being fulfilled in any respect. I feel guilty about that."

"You shouldn't."

"I should. I do. Logically, anyway." Ashleigh rubbed her forearms and seemed to steel herself with the small action. "What I mean is, when they're not right in my face, I can see things clearly. For what they were. What they are now. And I'm fine. I care about Reagan. She was a huge part of my life and I'm happy she's happy. I want that for her. But, I don't know…" She made a noise that almost sounded primal. "Ugh. It just irritates me when I see them together."

"Why do you think that is?"

"I'm embarrassed. It all feels like a failure."

"Come on, you don't really feel that way. More than fifty percent of marriages end in divorce. It's a statistical fact."

"It's like…" She closed her eyes and Kellan wondered if it was a type of self-protection as she spoke. "I feel like Reagan being with Josh now, somehow it invalidates our relationship."

"It doesn't." Kellan was trying to be supportive, even though she understood where Ashleigh was coming from. She might feel the same way in similar circumstances. But Ashleigh was special. Over so many years with her, Reagan had to have experienced what Kellan had seen in such a short time. "You don't really believe that."

"I don't know. Maybe she never loved me."

"Ash…" She looked at Ashleigh, but her eyes held so much sadness, all she wanted to do was pull her into her arms and hold her. Fold her in her embrace and kiss her and make her feel loved and valued and complete. She was so overwhelmed with the thought that whatever she'd planned to say fell right out of her mind.

"What?" Ashleigh asked.

"She loved you," Kellan said, fighting to keep her own desires in check. "You know she did. And hey, she was even jealous today. You heard her make that little dig about how you hate stuff like we did today. Which, by the way"—she leaned in to press her shoulder against Ashleigh's—"really meant a lot to me. I enjoyed being your fake girlfriend today." She leaned closer. "You're the real deal, Ashleigh McAllister. Never doubt that."

Ashleigh looked right at her, and Kellan watched her eyes go to her mouth for the briefest moment. But then she looked away, diverting her glance back to the water. "Thanks, Kellan." Ashleigh leaned her head against Kellan's shoulder as the last of the daylight turned to darkness. "You're not so bad yourself."

CHAPTER TEN

You ready, Gran?"

"You look lovely today, Ashleigh. Is that a new dress? And you're doing something different with your hair." Her grandmother studied her for a moment. "I can't put my finger on it. But something's different." Granny hooked her arm through hers as they left the family brownstone and walked in the direction of the senior center. "I don't suppose your new friend has anything to do with this? The one you spend all your time with. No, no. That would be ridiculous." She brushed the thought away with a swipe of her hand, just to be dramatic.

It was nice to see Granny still had wit to match her energy, even if she was fishing.

"Look at you, trying to get the skinny."

"Heaven forbid." Granny fake gasped. "I'm just taking an interest in your life." Her grandmother patted her arm. "There does seem to be a spring in your step these days. I suppose I'm just curious if Kellan doesn't have something to do with it."

Granny wasn't wrong. The days she spent with Kellan were nothing short of divine. They went sightseeing, they talked. And not just about the mundane. Sure, some of their conversations were small talk, but they also chatted about their lives. Just the other day she had opened up to Kellan in a way she hadn't with anyone else either before or after her divorce. To her credit, Kellan had been wonderful and kind. And yeah, sexy as hell, but that wasn't the point.

"I don't know, Granny." She held on to her grandmother's arm as they crossed Sixth Avenue. "I'm having a nice summer with Kellan— it's true. But it's not like you think."

"And why not? It's a long time since I've seen you smile that way you do when you tell me about your adventures together. Why not… kick it up a notch? Is that the terminology you kids use these days?"

"Granny!"

"Oh, please. If I were your age and single…" Granny waved her off again. "What's holding you back, dear?"

"For starters, Kellan's only here for the summer." Was she really testing these waters with Granny?

"And then she returns to Colorado, correct?"

"Yes."

"Do they not teach math in the Southwest?" Her grandmother's response was loaded with sarcasm.

"Now you want me to leave Brooklyn?" Ashleigh decided to play along. "I think you're just after my room."

"But you forget." Her grandmother raised a crooked finger. "It's technically my room. I'm not dead yet. The house may be in your father's name, but if I ask for your room, who's going to say no? I'm a feeble old woman, after all."

"Ha! Far from it." As witnessed by this conversation, she wanted to add. But Granny was yapping away.

"All I meant to say was that every relationship starts somewhere. If you and Kellan hit it off, geography shouldn't stop you."

"You are way ahead of yourself. We're just friends. Honest."

"Friends do not get all dolled up like this. With the dewy cheeks and perfect mascara."

"We're going to see a Broadway show. I wanted to look nice. And you should talk. It took you a half hour to get ready today."

"I like to look nice too. I'm not getting any younger either."

"Granny, you look amazing. And you have more energy than half my friends. I would never guess that you're in your eighties."

"Which is why you should listen to me. I know a thing or two, so I'll let you in on a little secret." She held her arms in front of her and lifted her face into the warm breeze, basking in the beauty of the weather. "Summers are for love. If you and Kellan get along and it blossoms into something—wonderful. If not, a little fling might be just what the doctor ordered."

Her grandmother was advising her to consider casual sex. This was a twist she did not see coming.

They arrived at the center, but Granny paused outside to continue talking. "Happiness is found in all sorts of different ways. In books, in music, the great outdoors." She reached up and booped Ashleigh right on the nose. "Sometimes life surprises you. You know, Frank's Henry goes by Genevieve now. And she's happy as can be." Ashleigh's confusion must have been obvious because Granny explained, "Frank's granddaughter. She's beautiful and we love her. We accept her."

"That's great." Ashleigh tried to get a handle on the unexpected turns in the conversation. "Who's Frank?"

Ashleigh followed Granny's gaze to the center's entrance, and sure enough an elderly gentleman was standing behind the tempered glass.

"He's *my* friend," Granny said, clearly taking a page out of Ashleigh's book as she sent a flirtatious wave in his direction. "We looked at the pictures on Instagram from the party you had at Liam's restaurant. We both think Kellan is very attractive. A touch of masculine and feminine mixed together, if you will. Very captivating, if I do say so myself." Granny poked her chest with a bony index finger and a devilish grin. "I think you should go for it. Frank does too."

"You go on Instagram?"

"Frank has a smartphone. We don't just sit around and play cribbage all day like some old bats. We like to stay current." She delivered the statement with an air of determination and won Ashleigh over in a second.

"Granny, my head is spinning." She laughed a little, hoping her grandmother understood that while she was appreciative, she was also mildly blown away. "But you are really sweet. So thank you. As for me and Kellan, I don't honestly know what's happening between us."

Her grandmother's eyes lit up.

"Let me clarify," Ashleigh said, feeling her cheeks get hot. She needed to get the conversation back on track "There's nothing happening. Not yet, anyway. Sometimes I feel like there's an energy between us, but then I wonder if I'm just lonely and I'm misinterpreting the signs."

"Oh, Ashleigh." Granny leaned forward to caress her exposed arms. "Your generation. Always analyzing and processing." She clenched her hands and brought them together under her chin. "Stop overthinking everything. Listen to your heart. Or at least your hormones."

"Granny!"

"You are only young once." Her grandmother waved in warning. "Have no regrets."

Ashleigh gave her a nudge. "Get out of here, old lady. Tell your boyfriend I say hi."

"Said the pot to the kettle," her grandmother teased.

Ashleigh shook her head in an attempt at being dismissive, but try as she might, she could not shake the smile off her face.

❖

Leaning back against the wrought iron chair, Ashleigh studied the illuminated marquee visible from the rooftop bistro they'd decided on for dinner. It wasn't completely exposed, but it had an open air feel and a glass ceiling that allowed a full view of the city skyline.

"I think I forgot it would still be light out." She took in the ornate gothic buttress of a building in the distance before turning to Kellan. "What did you think of the show?"

"I liked it," Kellan said. "I wasn't really sure if I would. But it was fun. The music was awesome."

At Ashleigh's insistence, they'd waited in line at the Times Square TKTS booth for discounted tickets to a matinee. Because the options changed daily, the experience was somewhat of a gamble, but the risk paid off when they ended up with twofer tickets to one of Broadway's hottest musicals.

"It's kind of crazy to me that people live here." Kellan touched the base of her wineglass as she scoped the restaurant's clientele.

"In New York City?"

"I mostly was referring to this area. It seems kind of intense. Crowded. Loud. Busy. But I saw people walking into their apartments with groceries on our way here. It's wild to me that this is a neighborhood. With all this going on around it."

"This neighborhood is Hell's Kitchen." She paused to consider the accuracy of her statement. "Actually, it's also referred to as Clinton," she corrected. "But I think most people still go with the former. Don't quote me on that, though."

"How does anyone come up with a name like that?"

Ashleigh pulled a crusty end of bread from the basket in the center of their small table. "Before the turn of the century this whole area was an immigrant ghetto. Irish, mostly. And really tough, like, dangerous. Constant riots. Gangs. Murders. The saying went that it was a hotbed of criminal activity, more perilous than if the devil himself lived here." She broke the bread in half and popped a tiny piece in her mouth. "Later it became home to the Westies—that's the Irish Mafia."

"I love that you always know the history."

"I do not." She pointed with her crust. "For all you know, I'm making it all up."

"You're not, though."

"Maybe I am." Ashleigh raised her glass in the slightest challenge. "You don't know."

"I guess I'm going to do some fact-checking then." Lifting her phone off the tabletop, Kellan leaned in close. "I bet I'm right."

"What are we wagering?" she asked, purposely loading her tone with innuendo.

"You tell me." Kellan met her stare. Her slight grin was wolfish and enticing, her green eyes full of temptation.

The intensity of the moment rattled Ashleigh, and despite her initial courage, she was out of clever responses. Rather than say what she really wanted—there wasn't enough alcohol in her system for that kind of bravado—Ashleigh laughed the moment off, angling Kellan's forearm toward her under the guise of getting a better view of the phone's screen, but it was just a ruse to touch her, and she wondered if Kellan knew. Keeping her fingers in place she felt the muscles move beneath Kellan's smooth inked skin as she thumbed in the search terms. Sitting so close, she was intoxicated by Kellan's scent, a mix of musk and sage, and she felt her own heart rate climb ridiculously in response, so much so that she was having a hard time focusing on the Wikipedia information as it appeared.

As Kellan scrolled the page, a text popped up, but she dismissed it immediately.

"Olivia 4C. Hmm," Ashleigh mused playfully. "Should I be jealous?"

Ashleigh had no idea what the hell she was doing, but she channeled Granny and tried not to overthink it.

"That depends," Kellan countered with a mischievously arched eyebrow. "Are you?"

She was spared figuring out a comeback when their server arrived with the entrées, placing the plates down and topping off their wine. Kellan cut into her steak as she spoke. "Olivia lives in the apartment across the hall." She stopped to take a sip of wine. "She checks in on me once in a while."

"I bet she does."

Kellan laughed, but her eyes were dead serious and it seemed like she was looking right through her, trying to figure out if this was for real. Ashleigh wasn't sure if her uncharacteristic behavior was the result of Granny's advice, the wine going to her head, or the simple math that it had been ages since she'd spent this much one-on-one time with anyone. Let alone a person who flirted and doted and was possibly interested, even if only for the summer. Not a good idea, she repeated in her head. She'd do well to get a handle on herself before she lost her inhibitions completely.

"Do you like the beach?" she asked, changing the course of the conversation drastically.

Kellan's expression showed confusion for a half a second before she caught up to the shift. "I do." Kellan speared a green bean with her fork.

"Would you be up for going on a day trip?"

"Isn't that what this entire summer is about?" Her smile was charming and sweet, and Ashleigh felt just the teensiest bit foolish.

"You're right. I just meant…there's beaches around here, obviously. But I was thinking about going out to Fire Island. It's a bit of a hike, but it's really quaint and super gay and has a sunset that's truly unbelievable."

"You don't need to convince me. I'm down. When should we go?"

"Tomorrow?" Ashleigh asked.

Kellan cringed and Ashleigh felt her heart drop with disappointment. "There is a tiny problem." As if to illustrate how tiny, Kellan held her fingers *thisclose* and crinkled her forehead. "It's not on the schedule. Are you sure you're going to be okay with the change?"

"Jerk." Ashleigh poked her. "I actually got nervous."

"Over what?" Kellan laughed. "Did you think I wasn't going to go with you?"

She didn't know how to respond because the truth was, in the fraction of that small second, she worried that Kellan had other plans.

Possibly with someone else. And what she felt…well, jealousy didn't even cover it.

"I don't know your entire schedule. Maybe you had other plans. We actually had nothing on the itinerary tomorrow."

"Why is that?" Kellan sliced a piece of her filet. "I've been meaning to ask you. I noticed in the amended version you sent you've adjusted so there's more free days. Are you sick of me already?"

"Not at all." The truth couldn't be further from Kellan's suggestion. Ashleigh wanted more time with Kellan, not less, and it scared her more than she was willing to admit. "I figured there might be some things you wanted to do. Either with or without me. I didn't want to monopolize your time."

"I like spending my days with you."

It was such a nice thing to say, yet it sent a rush of panic through her body. Did that mean Kellan spent her nights with someone else? So far, most afternoons had blended into evenings together. And they flirted. Or at least she thought they did. Maybe that was just Kellan's way of communicating with everyone. Or worse, what if she had been fluffing Kellan during their outings only to send her to the waiting arms of Olivia in 4C every time they parted ways?

"Hey, Ash, you okay?" Kellan brushed her leg under the table. "You disappeared on me there for a second."

"Sorry." Ashleigh snapped into action. "I was just thinking about the logistics. For tomorrow," she lied. "I should remember to text my sisters. I had lunch plans with them tomorrow."

"Do you want to postpone the beach? We could go a different day."

"Not at all." She smiled, registering what looked like relief in Kellan's eyes over the confirmation of their on-the-spot decision. "The weather is supposed to be nice. If we put it off, who knows? Siobhan and Stella work right around here. I can see them anytime."

"Are you sure?"

"I am."

They spent the remainder of their meal talking about the show, the city, the mountains of Colorado, their families. Ashleigh told Kellan how her sisters' twin bond carried into related careers in the fashion industry. She listened to Kellan talk about home, loving the way her slight accent came through when she talked about her parents and Turk.

They polished off their bottle of wine, but she was far from ready to call it a night.

"Feel like going to Liam's for a drink?" she asked.

"Definitely."

Ashleigh hooked her hand through Kellan's elbow as they walked to the corner to grab a cab. Riding the high of good wine and even better conversation, she didn't move when their knees brushed in the back seat of the car. She kept them pressed together as she rested her head on Kellan's shoulder and took in the view of the city while crossing the Brooklyn Bridge. It was bold and gratuitous, but utterly enjoyable, and if Kellan minded, she wouldn't know, because Kellan didn't move a muscle.

❖

"Lookee here." Liam looked up from the martini he was shaking. "If it isn't my two favorites. Give me one second and I'll be right with you."

"Take your time," Ashleigh said over the bustling dinner crowd. "This place is packed, Liam."

Kellan claimed some real estate in the corner of the bar area and made room for her to squeeze in. "Do you want me to get you a stool? I think that one's empty." She indicated a vacant seat with a nod of her chin.

Ashleigh was moved by the offer. "I'm fine," she said. She placed her hand on Kellan's hip, rising on her toes to adjust for the height difference as she spoke over the noise. "I'm going to run to the ladies' room. Would you get me a drink?"

The bar was boisterous and crowded, forcing them into each other's space, making any conversation oddly intimate. Ashleigh was enjoying the continued closeness—she could literally feel its effects everywhere—but she worried her defenses might not hold up.

"Wine?" Kellan asked. Her eyes were a touch glassy, and Ashleigh caught her gaze drifting to her lips, over and over.

"How about a cosmo?" She squeezed Kellan's arm gently. "Please," she added, almost as an afterthought.

"You got it," Kellan said.

When she returned, her drink was waiting next to Kellan's pint of lager. She took a sip, and while it was yummy, it was also strong. She was already nervous her restraint was slipping. As the minutes passed, her reasoning against acting on pure attraction was fading. No doubt the alcohol was acting as a coconspirator. And yet she continued sipping away as she squeezed in next to Kellan in the corner.

On the one hand she relished the tight space they were forced to share, because it meant continual contact. At the same time, though, she missed the lively conversation Liam's thriving business made it impossible to have.

Liam was busy and kept apologizing even though it wasn't necessary. After half an hour competing with the loud music, she suggested leaving, blaming the crowd. She was bummed to call it a night, but suggesting a quieter place was out of the question with so much alcohol already softening her resolve.

Kellan agreed amiably and walked her the few short blocks to her parents' house as they discussed the details of the LIRR train schedule which would take them to the Fire Island ferry. As they crossed Sixth Avenue, an overzealous car turned into the crosswalk, and Ashleigh reached for Kellan's forearm to make sure she was out of the way.

"Thank you," Kellan said. "I owe you one."

"You owe me nothing," she said, letting her hand slide into Kellan's. In response, Kellan laced their fingers together. Ashleigh's palm throbbed from the contact, and she was devastated to realize they were already at her house.

"What time tomorrow?" Kellan asked. "Should I meet you here or…"

"That seems crazy. But going down by you is really not convenient either." They were still holding hands, and she turned to face Kellan as she tried to come up with a logical meeting point halfway between them. She'd lived in Brooklyn her whole life, and picking a spot should be simple. But all she could focus on was their fingertips touching lightly and the way Kellan's gaze went from her mouth to her eyes and back again. She prayed she wasn't imagining it.

"I'm trying to think of a good place that's between us to meet up," she said. "I'm blanking."

"I'll be here at ten." Kellan pulled her in close as she took control of the situation. "I'll bring coffee. Sound good?"

"Okay," she said, not bothering to argue. She was too absorbed in the way Kellan was looking at her. Her gaze was boozy but also intense and filled with desire. Kellan was going to kiss her. She was sure of it.

As if the universe was listening, Kellan leaned forward. The kiss she placed was soft but just to the side of her mouth. If Ashleigh turned one millimeter, their lips would touch. But she didn't. She choked. "Text me when you get home," was all she could manage.

"I will." Kellan held eye contact as she backed away, their hands finally releasing as the distance between them increased. "See you in the morning, Ash. Sweet dreams."

Ashleigh shut the front door behind her and closed her eyes as she leaned her whole body against it. Her dreams were going to be something, that was for sure. Sweet was definitely not among the possibilities.

CHAPTER ELEVEN

*D**id you make it home okay?*

Kellan saw the message from Ashleigh when she was halfway to the fridge. She needed a cold bottle of water or a beer or *something* to take the edge off the day that seemed sizzling with undercurrents from minute one. They always flirted a little, but today was off the charts. But Ashleigh had opted to go home early. It was confusing.

A glance at the clock told her almost an hour had passed since they'd parted, and she'd forgotten to text confirming she'd made it home safe. Kellan shook her head. She was usually more accountable. In the service, it was second nature to check in and report back. But damn, her brain was so scrambled over Ashleigh, it was messing with basic manners.

I did! I'm so sorry I forgot to text you :(

You forgot about me already? Ouch.

Far from it. She twisted the cap off a liter of Poland Spring and downed a third of the bottle. *Who says I forgot about you?*

Did you go back to Liam's?

Nope. Came straight home. For someone who wanted to leave so badly, Ashleigh was chatty. Not that she minded, but it did make her wonder if something was wrong.

How come?

This was…odd. Kellan responded with the shrug emoji before sending a second message. *Is everything okay?*

Wait a second. Watching the bubbles roll as Ashleigh crafted her next message made her anxious. Did Ashleigh feel the energy too?

Was it all one-sided? Did it make her uncomfortable? Was Ashleigh about to tell her to back off? Fuck, she hoped not. She was enjoying their flirtation too much and found herself constantly wanting more, not less. Finally, the message came: *Are you busy with Olivia from 4C?* Before Kellan could respond, there was another text: *I can let you go. Although...seems unfair that you're having all the fun while I'm home alone.*

An enormous smile spread across her face. Ashleigh was being playful. And this was definite flirting. "It's on, Blue. It is on."

I think you're jealous. Kellan grinned as she typed it.

Ashleigh's response was quick. *That's not an answer. I can let you go if you're busy...*

Settle down. Just me and Blue here. He's out cold. Kellan flopped on the king-size bed, and Blue picked his head up at the disturbance. She snapped a picture of him by her feet and dropped it into the thread as proof.

So not the pic I was hoping for.

Be specific and you may be rewarded. Too bold? The heck with it, she hit send.

How about a tat I haven't seen? I'm sure there's more than just your arms.

You first.

Ashleigh answered, *You promised* :(

She hadn't promised anything—she'd only said maybe. But she loved where this was going too much to split hairs over the semantics. Kellan lifted her shirt and flexed, trying for a good angle as she took a picture of the design that covered her left hip and part of her abdomen. She sent it through immediately, but at the same time Ashleigh must have been capturing her own body art because the text that bounced onto the chain first was a picture of a heart with purple flowers and some kind of Celtic artistry surrounding it. More importantly, the tattoo she was looking at was just above Ashleigh's bikini line. She was a little bit speechless. Thank God the bubbles meant Ashleigh was typing.

What are you doing right now?

Kellan decided on pure honesty. *Looking at your tattoo. Thinking about a shower.* She waited a minute to send the next message. *A cold one.*

There was silence for a solid thirty seconds, and Kellan felt her heart race from both the excitement of the exchange and the fear she'd gone too far.

Are you mad we left the bar? Ashleigh's text was decidedly tame, but she went with it.

Not at all. I had fun tonight. Do you wish we'd stayed?

There was only one thing I wished for that didn't happen.

Kellan waited for more of an explanation, but when none came, she knew she had to step up. She was curious what was going on in Ashleigh's head, but she also wanted to say something nice and vague and low pressure. *And that would be...* It seemed to cover all the bases. She pressed send before she could overthink it.

I wanted you to kiss me.

It hung there for only a second, and she wondered if just a few miles away Ashleigh's heart was pounding as hard as hers. She didn't even have to think about her response.

I wanted to kiss you.

Why didn't you?

It was a great question, but one she didn't really have an answer for. *You could come over. I promise to kiss you now.*

If I come over, we won't stop at kissing.

And that would be bad because...

We shouldn't, Ashleigh answered.

Right. Kellan hit send, but she didn't really understand why they were holding back at this point. *Why exactly?*

Instead of answering Ashleigh responded with: *Are you in bed?*

"Here we go, Blue. At least I think..." *Yes,* she typed quickly, her pulse pounding like crazy.

I think about kissing you a lot. I'm imagining it right now.

In these thoughts...do we do anything else? Or just kiss?

We do it all.

Boom. It was all the encouragement Kellan needed. *When you think about us, do you do anything?*

There were bubbles, then none. And then bubbles again. Picking up on Ashleigh's nerves, she mentally ran through a set of responses that might put her at ease. But then the answer appeared before she could say anything.

Sometimes.

What about right now? Kellan asked.

At the moment I'm just thinking about it.

I think about you too, she said, hoping her honesty would relax Ashleigh.

You do?

I do. She went all in. *I imagine you here, with me. On the couch. In the bed. Being inside you. Making you come.* She pictured Ashleigh sliding a hand over her flower tattoo, reaching down and touching herself as she thought about Kellan. It made her hard and desperate for contact. But she would wait. For now, Ashleigh was her sole focus. *Is it okay to say that?* she asked. Even though it seemed Ashleigh was into it, the last thing she wanted to do was make her uncomfortable.

Yes.

Are you sure?

Yes.

Kellan was in the midst of coming up with another message, something to convey how attracted she was, both to Ashleigh's mind and her body, how often she thought about being with her, but her train of thought was interrupted with a new message.

We should probably go to sleep. It'll be a long day tomorrow.

It was a rapid downshift, but Kellan considered it entirely possible Ashleigh wanted both hands free. On the other hand, it was also possible she was freaking out.

We good? she asked.

Uh, very.

Whew. *Ok, then. I'll see you in the morning.* She could have left it there, but there was no fun in that. Plus, she wanted Ashleigh to know the effect she'd had on her. *Good night, Ash. I'll be thinking of you.*

The one-word response was immediate and absolutely perfect: *Same.*

"How come you never talk about the Army?"

Kellan laughed out loud at Ashleigh's random question. The whole day had been this easy. There had never been any weirdness about the fact that they dabbled in some light sexting the night before, and if Ashleigh felt awkward, it didn't show. In fact, they hadn't discussed it at all. Which was fine, except that Kellan couldn't stop thinking about it. And she found herself overanalyzing every last thing. Starting from when Ashleigh thanked her with a kiss on the cheek for picking up her favorite blend from Brooklyn Beanery, right through every little touch as they rode the train and the ferry to Fire Island.

"No reason." Kellan tried to stay focused. She kept her eyes closed as she stretched out on Aunt Holly's beach towel. "What do you want to know?"

"I don't know, really. I was just thinking how you know all this stuff about my life. My marriage, my divorce. My insecurities about both. I don't know very much about yours. It feels, I don't know, selfish." Ashleigh paused for a second and looked over at her. "Do I talk too much?"

"No. I like hearing about your life." She touched her stomach to feel the warmth of the sun against her fingertips. "If it makes you feel better, though, you can ask me anything you want. I'm an open book."

"For real? Anything?"

She heard Ashleigh giggle and turned her head just to sneak a look at her beautiful face, but the sun was so bright she had to use her hand to shield her eyes. "Oh, boy, should I be worried?"

Ashleigh shifted from lying on her back to her belly, and Kellan tried not to stare at her gorgeous body covered only by a small black bikini. Ashleigh rested her chin in her hands, seeming to take in their surroundings, before giving Kellan her attention.

"Did you put sunblock on?" she asked.

Kellan snickered. "That's your big burning question? Wow. I expected more."

Ashleigh flicked her with one finger.

"Ow!"

"Serves you right." Ashleigh did it again. "I'm trying to look out for you."

"Stop flicking me." She made sure to keep the levity in her tone. She didn't really want her to stop. She would take any kind of contact from Ashleigh, and she wondered if Ashleigh knew it. "I'm inclined to get tan instead of burning, if you must know. But for your information, I did put sunscreen on before I left the apartment. Did you?"

"I did. I should probably reapply soon." She said it under her breath, and even though Kellan wanted to offer her assistance, it felt like a cheesy line. "Can I really ask you anything?" Ashleigh said.

"Sure." She settled into the sand and closed her eyes, a little worried that Ashleigh would see right into her heart if she kept them open. "What's on your mind?"

Ashleigh rustled next to her and she wondered if she was repositioning again. "When was the last time you had a girlfriend?"

"A true girlfriend? Or just someone I was casually seeing?"

"I don't know. Both, I guess. Start with real girlfriend, first."

"Hmm. A few years ago. I was stationed on a really large base. It had hospital facilities. I dated a doctor for a while."

"Ooh, a doctor. Fancy."

"Yeah, well. She was crazy. Don't get too excited."

Ashleigh laughed. It was so smooth and sweet. She could listen to it all day.

"I should be nicer," she said. "She wasn't totally crazy. She was just a lot to take."

"In what way?"

"She was super possessive. Like, she didn't ever want me to even have a conversation with anyone else."

"You were probably flirting." Ashleigh lightly kicked her shin with the tip of her toe. First a flick with a finger, and now a nudge with her foot. Ashleigh had to know the kind of effect these little touches had on her. Especially after last night. Sure, it had all been in good fun, but still, she'd admitted being attracted to Ashleigh.

"I wasn't, though." Kellan got defensive and she propped up on her elbows. "That's why it was frustrating. I don't do that." She looked right at Ashleigh, intent on making her point. "I don't cheat or flirt. Not if we're dating. If I'm with you, I'm with you. That's it. But Jessica, geez, she was relentless."

She leaned all the way forward to stretch and was surprised when she felt Ashleigh's hand on her back. It was different than their previous contact. Where the other touches were playful, this was sincere. Soft.

"I'm sorry. I didn't mean to hit a nerve."

She allowed herself to indulge in Ashleigh's smooth fingertips on her bare skin, hoping to commit the feeling to memory before lying back down. She turned on her side so she could see Ashleigh and assure her they were fine. "You didn't. It's all good." She was happy her voice didn't reveal the desire she felt at Ashleigh's small comfort. "We were together for about eight months, me and Jess," she said, falling back into the conversation. "Last I heard, she got married."

"She was the last person you dated? A few years ago." Ashleigh turned too, tucking both arms under her head like a pillow as they lay face to face.

"Jessica was the last person I would consider a real girlfriend, yes."

"Since then, just casual dating?"

"There's a woman in Colorado I had kind of had a steady hookup with. Mary Beth Jensen. But it's seemed to fizzle since I've been home. I don't know why but it's probably for the best, I suppose."

"Why do you say that? That it's for the best."

"I don't know." She dusted some sand off her board shorts. "I've known Mary Beth since high school. But we were just friends back then. She dated men. Still does, I think. She got divorced about ten years ago. After that she started working at one of the restaurants at the resort. I think she didn't date much because she had three little kids when she and her husband split, and I guess she was just trying to get by. You know, working and being a good mom and stuff. Anyway, we were catching up one night when I was home on a furlough. Mostly reminiscing, but then one thing led to another. It was easy. Nice. It became kind of a regular thing when I was in Vail."

"But you didn't consider her your girlfriend?"

"Honestly, I haven't been home that often over the years. There have been times an entire year would pass. I didn't expect her to hold out for me." She ran her hand across the patch of sand between their towels. "The truth is, while we had a nice time together, it was never anything that deep. Hardly a relationship." She couldn't make eye contact. "You think less of me for that?"

Ashleigh's hand covered hers. "Of course not. Why would you say that?"

"I don't know. Hearing it out loud, it sounded a little cavalier."

"It didn't." Ashleigh pulled her hand back and immediately Kellan missed her touch. "But you said it's not happening anymore? You and Mary Beth?"

"The dynamic changed, now that I was home for good. I think

that's why I don't feel bad. See, when I was only in town every so often for these short bursts of time, there was no pressure. For either of us. We had fun together. We like each other. Then I'd be gone again. She would go on with her life. I would go on with mine. But now, being home for good, it's like we both want more, expect more, even, but not from each other. And that made it weird. That balance we had was all askew. The good news is we both felt it, so there were no hard feelings. We still chat when we see each other at work or in town."

"When was the last time you had sex?"

"With Mary Beth?" If the words weren't telling on their own, her tone revealed the truth that Mary Beth had not been her most recent hookup. She wished she could take it back, but the question had caught her completely off guard, and the words were out of her mouth before she could stop them.

Ashleigh broke eye contact, nodding as she focused on the hem of her beach towel, her face revealing an expression Kellan couldn't read. "That was what I meant." She hung her head.

"April," she whispered. "When I got home." With one finger she lifted Ashleigh's chin so their eyes met. "Ash, it matters what you think of me." So much more than it should. "I never set out to date casually. But with the Army, I moved around so much. It was hard to form lasting connections."

"You don't owe me an explanation. I would never judge you or your life. Christ, look at the mess I made of my own."

"Stop. Your life isn't a mess."

"I'm going to be thirty-eight and I live with my parents. Not where I thought I'd be at this point."

"But is it so bad? Your parents sound nice. And hey, if it's any consolation, I live with my parents too."

"You do?"

"I have a suite at the resort. It's basically an apartment, but on their premises. So in a way…"

"That is not the same. And you know it." Ashleigh rolled her eyes and flopped back on the towel, but the spirit had come back into her tone. "So since it obviously wasn't Mary Beth, are you going to tell me about the last person you slept with?"

"I wasn't planning on it," she said, matching Ashleigh's lively voice. Her stomach dropped in spite of her charade. This was the last thing she wanted to be talking with Ashleigh about. Kellan rolled onto her back.

"Boo." She felt Ashleigh's hand on her arm. "How am I supposed to live vicariously through you without the details?"

"Kinda thought we were working on that last night," she said, finally bringing it up. Ashleigh let out a squeal, and when Kellan looked over she was covering her face. "Stop." She reached for her arm to pull it away. "Don't be embarrassed. Last night was hot. And fun."

"A little mortifying." Ashleigh's voice came out muffled though her hands.

"Do you really feel that way?" she asked.

Ashleigh turned to her. "I never did anything like that before."

"I wanted to keep going. Thinking about you...doing that." She wanted to keep it light so Ashleigh wouldn't overthink it all. "Picturing me. It turned me on." Fuck, she was all in now. No mincing words.

"It did?"

"Of course." It was now or never, and without even thinking about it, Kellan knew she was going for it. "I'm attracted to you. I think you know that. I think about you a lot."

"I think about you too. Obviously." She heard nerves in Ashleigh's voice but was unsure how to calm them. It didn't matter—Ashleigh continued talking. "I just think we shouldn't necessarily act on that attraction."

"Can I ask why?" Kellan could hear her heart beat in her chest and hoped she didn't sound too pushy, but she was genuinely curious.

Ashleigh started with a deep breath. "You're leaving at the end of the summer. I'm not sure I can be like you or Mary Beth."

"Ash—"

"I don't mean that as a dig. I swear. I just mean...I don't know. I'm not sure I could handle something so...unstructured. But I'm having such a good time with you. Exploring the city. Days like this." Her eyes scanned the beach. "I don't want that to end or be awkward or anything. I'm enjoying being with you"—she slipped her hand into Kellan's—"and touching you. It makes me happy." She squeezed Kellan's hand a little. "If that's frustrating or not what you want, I understand."

When Ashleigh started to pull her hand away, Kellan stopped her. "Hey, that's fine."

"You're sure?" Ashleigh tucked a long piece of hair behind her ear. "I don't want to hold you back. Honest. Women ogle you all the time. I know I tease you about that, but I don't want to get in your way." "You're not in my way. I like being with you. If this is what you want"—she lifted their joined hands and gestured back and forth between them—"whatever this is, is fine." Her laugh was genuine and came from deep in her belly. "If you want to text me late at night…I'm here for that too." She didn't really know what she was signing up for, but she wasn't ready to let Ashleigh go in any capacity. She would be whatever Ashleigh needed her to be. She channeled everything she was feeling into her smile and pulled Ashleigh up off the towel. "But we have got to eat. Because it's been hours, and you know I'm starving."

For the rest of the afternoon, they ambled through Cherry Grove and the Pines, openly holding hands as they talked and laughed and fawned over the friendliest deer they had ever seen. When they hit the dock near sunset, it was so crowded with folks waiting to watch the sun go down that they had to really work to get a good view.

"I'll just stand behind you," Kellan said, making room for a couple as she ushered Ashleigh in front of her.

Ashleigh pressed against her, tilting her head up to whisper in her ear. "Can you see?" Ashleigh asked, but all she could focus on was Ashleigh's breath hot on her neck. She looked out over the bright orange sky at the ball of fire in the distance. "Kell, you okay?"

"Mm-hmm. Yeah." She smiled at Ashleigh but was distracted by her perfect lips, wet and inviting. She shifted her focus to the horizon where the sun slipped below the ocean and out of sight. The crowd seemed to disperse nearly immediately, but she and Ashleigh stayed right where they were, their bodies still aligned. "It's beautiful here," she whispered.

"It is, right?" Ashleigh turned to face her, and in the semidarkness, Kellan would swear she looked right at her mouth.

"Thank you for sharing it with me."

"I know it's far from Brooklyn. Thanks for coming with me." Ashleigh leaned up and placed a kiss on her lips. It was a peck, but it hovered a touch too long to be truly platonic.

"You're welcome," she responded, bringing their lips together a second time to return the favor. Kellan's kiss lingered softly, purposely matching the ambiguous tone set by Ashleigh's, as she was conscious to respect the confusing boundaries. But Ashleigh kissed her back. It was subtle at first, but Kellan read her with ease. Their bodies were close and Ashleigh's hands touched her abdomen, urging her closer. Kellan responded instinctively. She kissed Ashleigh soft and slow, channeling the desire she had felt all day, all summer, if she was being honest. She caressed Ashleigh's face as their lips and tongues found each other, over and over. Her heart was beating so fast she could feel her pulse everywhere. The moment was perfect and sweet and unbelievably sexy. Kellan would have stayed there all night—she didn't care one bit about the ferry docking a few feet away.

"We should get on that boat," Ashleigh said, breaking them apart but finding her hand again.

"I'm sorry, Ash. I feel like that went against everything you said on the beach."

"Why are you sorry?" Ashleigh slid into a seat on the lower deck. "I started it. I should apologize. I don't mean to be a tease. I just…I wanted to kiss you. The moment seemed—"

"Perfect." She slid her arm along the back of the bench seat and kissed Ashleigh's temple. "It was perfect."

They spent a lot of the ninety-minute commute back to the city in comfortable silence as they rode the ferry and the railroad, marginally cuddled together, their boundaries blurring by the second. There was no more kissing, and while it was probably the most rational decision, Kellan was disappointed when Ashleigh suggested separate Ubers to their respective abodes when they reached Atlantic Terminal in Brooklyn. All things considered, though, the events of the day left her too happy to be sad, so she gave Ashleigh a sweet kiss on the cheek as she opened her car door.

"Good night, Kell." Ashleigh hugged her tight. "Thank you for a great day."

"Same." She gave Ash's hand a small squeeze. "I'll be up later if you feel like talking or texting or anything."

Ashleigh paused and her lips parted slightly. For the briefest moment, Kellan thought she was going to abandon her car and change the course of their summer on the spot. But then it was as though she came to her senses. "Maybe," she said.

On the surface, the word selection and its tone seemed cool and collected, but the flash of color in Ashleigh's cheeks told a different story.

CHAPTER TWELVE

Ashleigh stood under the steady stream of hot water, trying to make sense of the entire day. The beach had been amazing and lovely. The lunch place rustic and charming. The conversation delightful as ever. That purple and orange sunset, beyond words. But all of it, every last second, was eclipsed by that kiss. That perfect, decadent, soft, sultry kiss she could still feel in every part of her body.

But then she'd said good night at the train station, when she obviously could've gone back to Kellan's. She imagined Kellan kissing her, touching her, taking her. Doing all the things she dreamed about. Even now, she could hear Shauna's voice and Granny's too, telling her to go for it. There was part of her that wanted to, even though she knew it was foolish. She didn't do well with hasty decisions. Particularly ones made out of pure lust.

That kiss, though.

Just thinking about it made her heart pound. Kellan's lips were gentle but firm, her tongue strong but delicate. She gushed, wanting more. She needed it. Right fucking now. She shut the water off with force, knowing exactly where she was headed. Sure, she could go to her bedroom, live out the fantasy at her own touch. And yes, it was the logical, wise thing to do. But tonight, she wanted the real thing.

She toweled off and pulled her wet hair in a loose messy bun, then tossed a few essentials in an overnight bag. Yoga pants and a loose but flattering tee later, she zipped by the living room where her family was glued to *The First 48*.

"Going to meet my friends for drinks. I'll probably just stay at

Shauna's," she said, purposely avoiding eye contact with Granny as she raced to the car that was waiting by the curb.

Her Uber cut through the empty Brooklyn streets in record time, giving Ashleigh little opportunity to come to her senses. Whether that was a good thing or not, she wasn't sure. Likewise, Sanjay the doorman seemed to remember her right away, as he smiled and picked up the desk phone to announce her presence the minute she entered the lobby. For the briefest second she worried Kellan might not be home, or worse, she might have company, but with a small nod and an even smaller smile, he replaced the receiver.

"You can go ahead up, Miss Ashleigh," he said.

"Thank you," she said over the sound of her heart pounding in her chest. It seemed to get louder and more distinct with each step to the elevator. Her stress completely took over as the doors opened on the fourth floor and she second-guessed every decision she'd made up to this point. What if Kellan didn't want to see her? What if she'd had enough of her games and sent her away on sight? She felt herself shaking but then she looked up and Kellan was standing in the open doorway of her apartment, a slight question in her eyes but a welcoming smile on her face.

"Hey, you," Kellan said, reaching for her arm and pulling her inside. She wrapped her in a sweet embrace. "You okay?"

She felt the heat of Kellan's body through the thin cotton of her V-neck tee, the fresh smell of soap wafting off her skin. Keeping her arms around Kellan's shoulders, she looked up and registered concern in her magnificent green eyes. "I should have called. I'm sorry."

"You never have to call." Kellan caressed her arms and led her to the stools by the kitchen island. "Is everything okay?"

"Yes. I just…" She had no idea what to say.

Kellan read her face. "Did you miss me?" Her tone was the perfect balance of playful and suggestive, and if Ashleigh had any game, she would have leaned forward and kissed her in that moment, but she waited a second too long, and Blue leaped onto the counter, stealing the attention. "Or did you just want to pay this guy a visit?" Kellan held out her hand and the cat brushed into it.

"Hi, Blue," Ashleigh said. "Are you allowed to be up here?" She reached forward to pet him.

"We have an understanding."

"Oh yeah? What's that?"

Kellan smiled and stood, reaching for the cat treats from the cupboard. "He does what he wants, and I don't tell on him."

"He's got you wrapped around his finger, I see."

"He's not the only one." Kellan tossed a treat across the room, and Blue scampered after it.

"I don't know what I'm doing," Ashleigh admitted as she leaned her elbow on the countertop and dropped her face into her hand.

"You don't have to know what you're doing." She felt the gentle brush of Kellan's fingers against hers. Kellan turned the stool around slowly and touched her face. "I'm glad you're here. I didn't want to leave you tonight."

"Me either."

"Good." Kellan touched their foreheads together. "I know the facts of what this is…" Her voice was husky as it trailed off, and she kept her eyes trained on the floor as she continued. "Look, it's all really fast and I'm only here for a short time. I know that makes you nervous." Ashleigh felt her hands move to her hips, and she opened her legs just to bring them closer. "Being around you, it feels right to me—I can't explain it. And if you don't want to do anything but be near each other, that's one hundred percent fine. We can go over to the couch right now, put on a movie. Snuggle if you want—"

She held Kellan's face in her hands, her voice barely above a whisper. "If you don't kiss me right now, I might die."

Their mouths crashed together in absolute synchronicity, the buildup of so much shared tension exploding in one single, perfect, epic kiss. In the moment Ashleigh was aware of every detail, the way their lips parted together, the urgency of their tongues moving desperately to make up for all the opportunities they'd let pass. Gone was the sweetness of the moment they shared on the dock hours earlier. In its place, nothing but passion. Pure and unfettered, and sexy as fuck. For a brief second she panicked it was a dream, but like magic she felt Kellan's hands on her, bringing her back into reality as she caressed her bottom and pulled her flush against her body. Kellan's touch ran the length of her body all the way up her back until she felt hands in her hair, at the base of her head, along the front of her neck as Kellan kissed her deeper and harder than she thought possible.

She was tingling everywhere, her skin on fire. She didn't know if it was because it had been so long since she'd experienced any kind of intimacy at all or if it was because the last few years with Reagan had been so utterly tepid. All she knew was the way Kellan was kissing and touching her right now made her feel wanted and needed and desired in a way that was entirely new. It was freeing and fresh and wholly erotic. She wanted to rip her clothes off and never leave this apartment for the rest of the summer.

Somehow she managed to move off the stool, still finding Kellan's lips as they backed toward the bed. In the dim light, she registered a look in Kellan's eyes that almost seemed to be checking in, making sure it was all right to continue. It was in such stark contrast to their actions, she almost didn't know what to make of it. Still, it moved her to know that even if she pulled back now, it would be okay.

She stood on tiptoe to kiss her. "I want this," she whispered in response to Kellan's unspoken concern. It wasn't racy but it was more than Ashleigh had ever said aloud, and hearing the rasp in her own voice surprised her. She slipped her hands under Kellan's shirt, her fingertips grazing over smooth muscular abs.

Kellan pulled her shirt over her head, and even though her state of nakedness was scant more than Ashleigh saw on the beach hours earlier, the exposure seemed entirely different. She traced the outline of the tattoo that covered Kellan's waist and her rib cage, not brave enough yet to follow it up along the side of her small breast. Kellan leaned forward and pulled her close, kissing her fully, and Ashleigh was relieved and so fucking ready when she took the lead. She felt herself gush when Kellan slipped her hands underneath her shirt and unhooked her bra, her nipples hardening first in Kellan's palm, then against her tongue.

In seconds they were on the bed, Kellan's warm mouth all over her body. She sucked and kissed her everywhere, making gentle circles with her tongue and then escalating to just shy of leaving a mark. It seemed as though she would get almost caught up in the moment and then pull back just in time. Ashleigh couldn't care less if there would be evidence in the morning. Her head swirled in euphoria at Kellan's distinct touch, beautifully hard and soft at the same time.

As they kissed, Kellan was moving between her legs, and she couldn't help but notice the friction caused Kellan's sweats to inch down little by little. Ashleigh spread her legs wider, her breath catching at the heat she felt through Kellan's boxers.

"Do you want me to stop?" Kellan's voice was heavy but measured as she kissed along Ashleigh's neck and jawline, obviously trying for chivalry.

Ashleigh answered with a searing kiss she hoped made her answer crystal clear, but just in case, she held Kellan's face in her hands and looked her dead in the eye. "If you stop now, I'm going to kill you."

A crooked smile emerged, and Ashleigh's heart pounded.

"Let's get under the covers then." With one hand, Kellan pulled back the duvet and smoothly ushered them onto the soft sheet underneath. She didn't ask for any more assurances as she removed what remained of Ashleigh's clothes and tossed them to the floor. She discarded her own boxer briefs at the same time and Ashleigh shuddered at the feel of their naked bodies together. Kellan kissed the spot below her ear, her face, her lips. "Tell me what you like," she said.

Ashleigh wasn't a talker, but if she knew the answer, she would have said it in a heartbeat. Kellan seemed so open that she didn't think anything would be off-limits. But the problem was she honestly didn't know. "I like *you*," she said, hoping it sufficed.

Kellan kissed her hard in response, and Ashleigh heard herself moan at the feel of their bodies touching everywhere. She could feel herself dripping with desire, and Kellan had to feel it too. Still, she took her time as she kissed down her body. Kellan hovered for a second, her breath hot against her throbbing center. Kellan kissed her softly there, holding back from giving real satisfaction as her tongue teased in a delicate, divine kind of torture.

"Oh my God." It was a breath more than a statement, and Ashleigh wasn't entirely sure she vocalized it at all, but she felt Kellan smile against her skin, the thickness of her tongue making real contact a millisecond later. The moan that escaped her was completely beyond her control, but Kellan responded with the perfect amount of pressure in exactly the right spot. Her hips bucked wildly, but Kellan stayed with her as the orgasm rushed through her entire body.

She knew it was fast, but in her defense it had been forever since she'd had sex—not that Kellan knew that. Or maybe she did. She was so out of practice that she had no idea what even passed as normal.

Kellan seemed undeterred, still kissing her thighs and caressing them gently with her soft fingertips.

"I'm a little embarrassed at how quick that was." Ashleigh let out a laugh, hoping it might balance the awkwardness of her admission. She reached down and ran her hands through Kellan's hair, feeling the short ends bristle against her palm.

Kellan turned her head and kissed Ashleigh's hand. "Oh, I'm not done with you yet." She smiled devilishly, her mouth grazing along Ashleigh's wrist and forearm as she baby kissed her way over her shoulder and along her collarbone. When she reached her mouth, her kiss was thorough and passionate, her tongue gentle and strong and leading. Ashleigh was wet and pulsing and so ready when Kellan slipped inside her. She cringed a little and heard herself whimper at the fullness of Kellan's fingers.

It only took her body a fraction of a second to adjust and find the right rhythm as they moved together. She gasped and moaned and gripped Kellan's shoulders, as her legs opened wide. Before long, Kellan's breathing got heavy, and she could feel her starting to sweat as she pumped faster. It was raw and hard and it felt amazing. Her nipples got hard against Kellan's chest as she started to come. But instead of subsiding, a second orgasm followed in sequence, and then another, and another, the sensation cascading through her body like a domino of nerves crashing into each other until there was absolutely nothing left.

Ashleigh could form no words, and her body went completely limp as she basked in an afterglow like no other.

Chapter Thirteen

I cannot believe I fell asleep." Ashleigh covered half her face as she curled into Kellan's side. She'd woken up with competing thoughts vying for space in her mind. Her conscience was trying to convince her she should feel bad for sleeping with someone she wasn't dating, but everything in her being said she'd made the right choice. There was zero guilt present. Honestly, what she felt was alive. And comfortable. And relaxed. She brushed a hand on Kellan's worn tee. "I'm not a pillow princess, I swear." She placed a kiss on Kellan's shoulder, snuggling in.

Kellan draped one arm around her, pulling her close, and Ashleigh felt her pulse regulate. "I'm not worried." She kissed the top of her head. "Plus, I'd be lying if I didn't admit to taking complete pride in totally knocking you out." Kellan grinned, and it was sexy even if it was unabashedly arrogant.

"Maybe I was just tired." She let her hand drift to Kellan's soft belly under her shirt. "You don't know," she added, employing full sass. "Long day at the beach. Full exposure to the sun."

"Mind-blowing sex," Kellan finished. "It is a lethal combination. I get it."

"This is what I have to put up with now?" she teased. "So cocky."

Kellan answered with a killer smile. "Good morning, Ash." She dropped a soft kiss on her lips. "Coffee?"

"Oh my God, yes." She watched Kellan crawl out of bed in a fresh shirt and boxers and Ashleigh scooted up, pulling the covers around her naked body. "When did you put clothes on?"

"After you passed out. I can't sleep naked." Kellan spoke matter-of-factly as she slipped into sweats. Ashleigh idly wondered what other tidbits she might learn if they continued down this path. She leaned back against the headboard as she watched Kellan walk to the kitchen. Blue followed, weaving around Kellan's legs until she scooped him up and kissed his head. She wished him a good morning as she rubbed between his ears and got his breakfast. Sexy and sweet. Could this honestly be for real? She was leaving at the end of summer, she reminded herself. She blinked slowly as she consciously kept her budding feelings in check. When she opened her eyes, Kellan was looking at her, holding a bag of freshly ground coffee from Brooklyn Beanery.

"Colombian roast okay?"

"You have coffee from the Beanery. You are my hero."

Kellan's smile seemed genuine as she prepped the coffee, and it touched her in spite of the internal warning she'd given herself not two minutes ago. She scanned the room for last night's discarded clothes until she spotted them in a heap on the floor. She stretched for her shirt, and Kellan took a few steps forward, picking it up and handing it to her.

"Here." Kellan sat on the edge of the bed. "Do not misunderstand this kind gesture. I'm only helping because I saw you struggling to reach. I'm not endorsing you putting on clothes at all."

Ashleigh felt her heart pound ridiculously. She swept her hand down the side of Kellan's chiseled face, bronzed after a day in the sun, as she put on her shirt and stood up. "A true gentleman," she said with a snicker as she tugged lightly on Kellan's bedhead before padding down the hall.

In the bathroom, she brushed her teeth, washed her face, attempted to do something with her hair. But there was no saving the mess, wild from the combination of vigorous sex and falling asleep while it was still damp from the shower. She gave up and pulled it off her face.

"You know we have nothing on the agenda today," she said, as she walked back into the main space.

Kellan was at the kitchen island pouring their coffees. "I saw that on the schedule." She reached for the cream and sugar, offering it to Ashleigh first. "Do you have anything going on with your family, your friends?"

"Not a thing." She stirred her coffee and took the first delightful sip. "You?"

"Just this." Kellan smiled. She nodded to the clouds out the window. "Sort of the perfect weather for holing up and doing nothing really."

"Cheers to that." She raised her drink to Kellan's and felt a major rush when their eyes locked. A whole day together with no plans—she shuddered at the possibilities. But the morning unfolded slowly. They nursed their coffees. Kellan made spinach and tomato omelets. They ate together side by side at the island, talking about the basics. Families and work and friends. It was easy and chill and she felt herself slipping deeper into the comfort zone they'd come upon so naturally since their first real outing together. There was zero awkwardness at having slept with each other. If anything, their interactions were smoother than before, and when Kellan flopped on the bed to relax, Ashleigh followed suit, resting her head against her chest.

Kellan stroked her hair. "Are you tired?" she asked.

Ashleigh was wide awake. She just wanted closeness. And well, to be honest, nakedness. She'd passed out so quickly last night. She was dying for more. Even still, she had no idea how to make the first move.

She shook her head and tilted it slightly to make eye contact.

Kellan was there. "Good," she whispered, finding her lips. The kiss that followed was deep and soft and full of promise. In a second, her shirt was off, Kellan's too. Kellan was assertive and sure and confident, seeming to know exactly where and how to touch her. Everything about it turned her on.

This time, after she came, she didn't pass out immediately. She channeled all her endorphins, feeding off their energy to overcome the slight trepidation she had over the fact that it had been eons since she'd done this. Ignoring her mild neuroses, she kissed her way down Kellan's fantastic body.

She started at her neck but quickly moved to her strong shoulders, her muscular chest. She was distracted by Kellan's tattoos, some colorful, others designed in various shades of gray. She kissed them all religiously, running her lips and tongue over the delicate lines, a ridiculous attempt at tasting their significance.

Without notice her anxiety faded, replaced by the encouragement of Kellan's gentle touches guiding her the whole time. There was something about the way Kellan was able to maintain control but still allow her to feel in charge that was intoxicating. The dynamic moved things to a level she hadn't known existed. She was dying to taste Kellan, and when she finally did...Oh my God—it was amazing. She could have stayed in place for hours, her tongue buried deep inside. But after a solid few minutes, she felt Kellan's hand press firmly against the back of her head, and she registered the change in the cadence of Kellan's breathing, her hips bucking slightly forward.

Ashleigh rested her face on Kellan's stomach, tracing the outline of her hip with one finger.

"Come up here," Kellan said, pulling her into a lingering kiss. "You didn't have to do that." Kellan touched her cheek. "You know that, right?"

"I wanted to." Ashleigh's blood pressure started to rise. "Was it okay? I mean, did you not want me to?" She squeezed her eyes closed and touched her forehead to Kellan's bare chest, embarrassed that she might have crossed a line and been so caught up she didn't even notice.

"Stop." Kellan lifted her chin with one finger. "It was perfect. And hello, clearly I enjoyed it."

"You did, right? I wasn't sure. It's just been a while and—"

Kellan silenced her with one finger to her lips. "Ash, relax. It's just me. Quit stressing." Their faces were close, and she felt Kellan's hand fall into a familiar spot at the small of her back. "You don't have to worry about me. I promise to tell you if there are things I'm not into." She kissed each of her eyelids, the gesture sweet and oddly sincere. "I hope you'll do the same for me. That's the reason I said something. I don't ever want you to feel pressured into doing anything. Or, you know, feel too shy to tell me if there *is* something you want."

"Okay." It felt like a weak response, but it was all she could come up with. This three-minute conversation was more than she and Reagan had talked about sex in twelve years of marriage. She sighed inwardly, realizing that was perhaps part of the problem. "Thank you," she said, genuinely appreciative of Kellan's willingness to talk and effortless way of making it all seem like no big deal. As for actually verbalizing things she thought she might be interested in trying, she wondered if she'd ever have the courage to say those words aloud. But Kellan's willingness at least made it a possibility.

Ashleigh touched a cluster of stars dotted near Kellan's shoulder and collarbone. "What now?"

"That's a big question," Kellan said. "Do you mean, like"—she wagged her finger between them—"here?"

"Uh-oh. Who's nervous now?" Ashleigh caught Kellan's finger and brought it to her lips. She gave the tip a small playful nibble. "I meant today. It's still overcast, but there's no rain." She ran her hand through Kellan's thick dark hair and placed a kiss on her forehead. "How about a walk? I hear an iced coffee beckoning to me."

Twenty minutes later, Ashleigh treated them to large cold brew coffees, because even though it was cloudy, the temp was still mid-eighties. On the walking path that wound through Brooklyn Bridge Park, they sipped their beverages, talking about the city and the days ahead as the afternoon slipped into evening. When they reached the end of the park, Kellan took her hand and held it, and Ashleigh couldn't help but smile at how natural it felt to walk the streets of her neighborhood together. She led the way through Cobble Hill and Carroll Gardens, pointing out the senior center when they reached the border of Gowanus and Park Slope.

"Did I tell you that my grandmother has a boyfriend?"

"No way. That's fantastic."

Ashleigh rolled her eyes but felt a smile emerge just the same. "Apparently, they play on the phone together."

"Wait." Kellan stopped in her tracks. "You mean like we did the other night?"

Ashleigh squealed. "Argh. No." She covered her face in spite of her laughter. "I can't believe you even suggested that. They go on social media sites together." Her shiver was half embarrassment at her own recent foray and half aversion at the thought of Granny doing anything even remotely similar. "I may never get past that image."

"Well, I didn't know what you meant." Kellan laughed with her, and Ashleigh enjoyed hearing the sound of her deep, throaty chuckle. "You always talk about how she has a ton of energy and is young at heart." She was smiling big and her eyes danced in the evening light. "I'm sorry." Kellan pulled her close and touched her cheek with the pad of her thumb. Ashleigh felt her body purr in response to the simple gesture. "Forgive me?"

"We'll see," she teased.

Kellan leaned forward and placed a soft leading kiss on her lips. "If I beg?"

"Maybe." She tilted her head back, and Kellan seemed to accept it as the offer it was, finding her neck and kissing it over and over. The feel of Kellan's body, the way she touched her, kissed her...she wanted more. But they were in the middle of the sidewalk on busy Fifth Avenue, a scant few blocks from her parents' house. "Come," she said, forcing herself to unwind from Kellan's embrace. "Nothing good will come of this." Ashleigh tugged Kellan along down the street.

"I wholeheartedly disagree," Kellan said, even though she followed dutifully behind. "Where are we going?" she asked.

Ashleigh sighed, tipping her head toward the sky. "I should probably go home," she said. "I've been gone for a while." She saw Kellan pout and it made her smile. "You probably wouldn't mind some time to yourself."

"I have plenty of alone time. Come back with me."

"I would. I want to," she said, adjusting her statement with the truth. "But if I don't show my face soon, there'll be drama."

"I'm not following." Kellan kept them from crossing on the red signal, and against the dark sky the color in her eyes was as vivid and bright as the Connemara hills. It almost broke her resolve.

"The thing is...living with my parents is fine, for the most part. Not that I plan on staying here forever. But when Reagan and I separated nearly two years ago, at the time I thought the break might bring us back together somehow. It sounds ridiculous now."

"It doesn't."

"I didn't want to get a place, commit to a lease. This just seemed like a better plan. When it became clear things weren't going to work out and we started the divorce process, it was nice being here. Not being alone. My parents are wonderful. My grandmother is a trip. It's actually been a way easier transition than I ever expected. That said, I can't just disappear for two days. They will worry."

"Wait a second. Don't they know where you are?"

"Well...not exactly."

The expression on Kellan's face said she was confused, not angry. Still, Ashleigh owed her an explanation. "It was late when I left last night. I just said I was meeting Shauna for a drink and was going to crash there. Even at my age, there is something inherently awkward about explaining to your parents that you are going out and hoping to… you know." She felt her cheeks getting hot and was thankful they were walking so Kellan couldn't see her blush.

"Hoping, huh?"

"Shut up, jerk."

They stepped up onto the curb, and Kellan gripped her hand to stop them for a second. She leaned in and pressed a sweet kiss on her lips. "I was hoping too. I'm glad you came over. Even if they think I'm Shauna," she joked. They strolled on and Kellan laced their fingers together. "Is that what you always tell your family? Do you and Shauna have some kind of code in place?"

"What do you mean?"

"You know, for situations like this. When you stay out?"

Mortifying. That's what this was. Ashleigh wasn't sure how they'd veered into the very topic she was planning on avoiding altogether. It wasn't required information. They weren't girlfriends by any stretch of the imagination. Kellan didn't need to know she hadn't slept with anyone since her divorce or that she had only ever been with Reagan, for that matter. For all Kellan knew, this could be something she did every summer, every school break. Heck—every weekend, if she wanted. But in the absence of a response, her silence answered for her.

"Hold up." Kellan stopped walking and faced her. "Ash, have you not…I mean since Reagan, am I…" Her voice faded, but the words were already out there. She knew.

"I've only been divorced since September," she said as though her decision needed justification. But the reality was Reagan and Josh had started dating the moment they'd separated. There was absolutely no reason she couldn't have done the same. She placed both hands over her face solely so she didn't have to look Kellan in the eye.

Kellan's touch was soft as she slid her fingertips along her forearms and eased her hands down. "Uh-uh. Nope," she said, tilting her face so their eyes met. "Don't do that. Please?"

"It's embarrassing."

"It's not. It shouldn't be." Kellan touched her face. "You loved your wife. You wanted things to work."

"Meh."

"Don't blow that off. It's true and it's honorable. And it makes you who you are. Don't belittle it."

It was only part of the reason, and she hated giving Reagan all the credit. "It's more that all this is foreign to me. I met Reagan when we were kids. I never did the dating scene. Not really."

"You didn't date before Reagan?"

"A few boys here and there in high school. Nothing serious. Even then I knew I was attracted to women. I didn't have a clue how to make that happen. Not entirely unlike now." She hoped her self-deprecation played as cute instead of pathetic.

"You're doing just fine now." Kellan's smile was enough to make her melt on the spot. "Although for the summer, I'm hoping to get all your attention. There's still a lot of New York to see, and I like having a personal tour guide."

"So you're in it for the historical anecdotes?"

"There might be a few other perks too."

Ashleigh squeezed their clasped hands and tried for a playful punch to Kellan's biceps. Her strength was way outmatched, but Kellan let her land the shot anyway, faking a wince that was both over the top and still adorable. They held hands for the remaining few blocks to her parents' house on Garfield Place, and standing outside the family brownstone, Ashleigh went for a real kiss, not even caring that they might have an audience.

CHAPTER FOURTEEN

"How are things going with Ashleigh?" Behind the bar, Liam washed glasses and prepped drinks for a respectable dinner crowd, but he turned as he did his chores, clearly expecting a response.

"Awesome. She's great people." Kellan opted for a safe answer, but only because she didn't know how much to reveal. Since their adventure to Fire Island four days earlier, she and Ashleigh had slept together two more times. The sex was beyond good, and each time she felt Ashleigh come out of her shell a little more. The first encounter followed an afternoon at the Guggenheim Museum where they could barely keep their hands off each other as they perused the exhibits. Kellan had wondered a little bit if they were even going to make it back to her place as they eye-fucked each other the entire subway ride back.

Likewise, when the sky opened out of nowhere and cut short a leisurely stroll along the Coney Island boardwalk, they'd raced to the shelter of her swank Dumbo crib. Stripping out of their sopping wet clothes, she'd turned Ashleigh around, bending her over against the kitchen island to take her from behind. Ashleigh didn't stop her. On the contrary, she begged for more when two fingers weren't enough to satisfy her. In the corner mirror she'd glimpsed Ashleigh writhing and reaching back to grasp for her. Ashleigh had pulled her forward by her hair, demanding a kiss that was both hard and possessive. The action had taken her by surprise. Something about the assertive way Ashleigh begged to be overpowered was a complete turn-on. Combine that with the X-rated image in the mirror...she'd nearly come on the spot.

Liam reached for her empty pint, bringing her back to the present. "You two are hitting it off then?"

"Yep. For sure."

That was putting it mildly, but in addition to not knowing where Ashleigh stood with making anything public, she was floored at the insane connection they'd made in such a short period of time. She blamed it on summer—vacation and the heat toying with reality. Because if it was anything else, well, that scared her even more. "How's business?" she asked, looking around the semifilled space.

"Decent." He coupled his answer with a definitive nod. "It's still early and I've got asses in chairs, to borrow a phrase from Lieutenant Ambrose. Remember him?"

"Hard to forget a personality that strong." She took a sip of her fresh beer. "You have to let me pay for my drinks. I'm on to that trick where you take my card and don't put any charges on it."

"I can do what I want." He met her eye roll with an arched eyebrow. "I'm actually the boss here. How do you like that beer?"

"Nice. Hoppy."

"Too bitter?"

"No. It's good."

He lifted a case of bottles from atop the ice cooler and started to restock the bar fridge with some local craft brew. "Do you keep in touch with anyone? From your platoon? Your battalion?" His question, more specifically the way he asked it, sounded calculated, like he was leading up to something, but she was probably just being paranoid.

"I check in on Thad Dussaint here and there. Do you know him?"

"Big guy? Football player?"

She nodded. "His time is up in eighteen months. He's counting the days. I keep tabs on some of the others on Facebook. It's nice to see everyone getting by in the real world."

"You ever talk to Dara Torres?"

There it was. She was sure her expression revealed some emotion, but she tried like hell to keep stoic. "Nah."

"And you're just fine with that? Never talking to her again?"

It was so much more complicated than he was making it sound, but Liam didn't know that. "I don't know, bro. It's been a minute."

The bottles clanked as he stacked them on top of one another. "Look, it's none of my business and I'm not trying to pry, I swear." He shut the fridge door and made quick work of the thick cardboard box. "But I also know when I met you a million years ago, in Germany, I think it was"—he paused, seeming to assess whether or not the location was correct—"you two were inseparable."

"It was Germany. Baumholder." She took a long sip of her drink, unable to keep the memory at bay.

"That's right. The Rock," he said, invoking the base's nickname. "God, that was a good assignment." He seemed nostalgic for a moment. "Anyway, a few years later when we met up in Iraq, y'all were still tight. Cut to three years later…you and me together again in the Middle East, Afghanistan this time. Dara had left the military and you were a hot mess. When I asked, you said you two had a falling-out. You tried to play it off like it was no big deal, but you were pretty busted up. And look, from my limited exposure, there was no debate, you two were absolute besties. You had that kind of friendship that comes around once in a lifetime. If you're lucky. So seeing you in that state, I knew what went down had to have been major."

"Dude, you make it sound like I was barely functional." Defensiveness seeped into her tone and she forced a smile, hoping he didn't notice.

"That's not what I mean at all." Liam looked right at her, and his soft blue eyes held only kindness. "I'm just saying it was clear you missed her. Whatever your disagreement was, you were hurting." He wiped the bar top clean and stood upright, seeming to survey his small domain. "Even though you barely talked about it. My guess is that it had something to do with her husband." Liam tidied his bar stock as he spoke, straightening the napkins, coasters, and straws. "I'm not asking for confirmation, but every time I had any interaction with Ronnie Torres, he was a total prick."

"That is an understatement." She turned her pint in her hand and examined the logo on the front. "It's funny actually. Initially I avoided Dara on base because I knew she was married to that jack-off. I figured anyone with taste like that…no thanks."

"Crazy, though. Dara was a gem. Sweet, funny. Fucking brave too. A medic gig is no-nonsense."

Kellan hated that she felt a tug in her heart. But it was true. Dara was the real deal. Kind and hilarious, she couldn't have been more opposite than her husband. They'd clicked from their first introduction and their friendship blossomed immediately. Before long, they were spending all their downtime together talking about home, their dreams beyond the Army, philosophizing about life and love, lifting one another up when they were homesick or tired or just plain sad.

"I know you're a smart person." Liam checked his citrus supply. "Army intel and all that. So I'm going to assume you've done your research. And I'm not aiming to get in the way. Honest to God." He looked up at the ceiling, paying homage to a deity she wasn't sure existed. "Dara lives in Brooklyn. And she's divorced. I can't imagine that didn't affect your decision to spend the summer here. What are you waiting for? Go find her and make things right already."

"Just for the record—me and Dara, it wasn't romantic. There were never any kind of feelings. On either side. You do know that, right?" She knew she'd told Liam that much, but she also knew about the rumors. It seemed no one could resist a juicy story, even when there wasn't one.

His look told her she was crazy for even giving voice to a notion so ridiculous. "What, you're too good to have friends now?"

"No, I just know people talk. And, I don't know. Ronnie wasn't a fan of mine. I didn't know what he might have said that made its way back to you."

"First off, if you were hitting that, I'd know. Like I knew when you broke rank and hooked up with Captain Regina Espinoza. You"— he snapped his bar rag in her direction—"have a terrible game face."

She laughed into her drink at the truthfulness of his statement. Her emotions, whether they were good, bad, or completely indifferent, might as well be embroidered on her sleeve.

"I know all about your bizarre connection with Dara." She froze for a second at the possibility he knew the whole story. A wave of both fear and relief shot through her, but it was for naught. "Remember, I spent a fair amount of time with you both. I watched you two connect on, like, an organic level. You finished each other's sentences. It was like you shared a brain."

The wheels in her head turned, and she swallowed a smile in spite of the fact that she hadn't made a decision yet. "She's divorced, huh?" She ran her hand along the edge of the bar considering that detail.

"She is. She's working as an ER nurse in the city."

"How do you know so much about her?" She was trying to be cool, but in all honesty, other than a few basic internet searches, she had kept her word and stayed out of Dara's life. She hadn't even known about the divorce.

Liam started to fill an order from one of the servers. "I talk to Joe Salvo once in a while. He's like the social director. Stays in touch with a lot of the guys. He lives out in Queens. Apparently, he and his wife used to get together with Ronnie and Dara, here in New York, when their kids were little. I guess they were the same age. Roughly anyway. You knew Dara had a kid, right?"

"Yep." It was a detail she could never forget.

"Anyway, whatever the fallout between you guys was, it's none of my business." He lined the drinks up on a bar tray, then wiped away the excess moisture rings. "You two had a bond unlike anything I've seen. True, genuine affection. Beyond kinship, in a way. Now you're here. In Brooklyn." He held his arms out wide. "Track her down and talk it out."

"It's not that simple."

"I'm sure it isn't. But you knew she was here. So you've at least considered contacting her."

"I haven't spoken to her in over ten years."

"Do yourself a favor and don't make it twenty."

Liam went back to doting over his spotless bar, perhaps to give her time to let his suggestion sink in. Thankfully, he didn't seem to expect a more detailed explanation than she'd offered. Because she had no idea how to even begin to explain the depth of what she and Dara had shared and how it had all come apart.

She studied the diminishing layer of froth halfway down her glass. She wondered what would happen if she told him everything. It was weird, but the person she wanted to tell was Ashleigh. She'd almost come close the day at the beach when they'd discussed serious relationships. Ashleigh had point blank asked about her life, and she'd opted not to share. She was only partially sure why. Without a doubt, her friendship with Dara surpassed anything romantic she'd experienced. A decade might have gone by, but Dara Torres was still the most significant person in her life. But how to convey that without telling the whole story, she had no idea.

"Whoa! McAllisters. The whole clan!" Liam's voice boomed in excitement, and she looked up to see him scooting under the bar to greet Ashleigh and her family with full hugs and kisses. "What a treat."

Indeed. Ashleigh had been tied up with commitments for two days and Kellan hated herself for missing her so hard. She couldn't even dial back the smile that broke out the second they made eye contact. She didn't hope for more but her heart pounded when Ashleigh sent her a look and blew a subtle kiss in her direction as Liam got them settled at a corner table. She let her eyes stay on Ashleigh's lips for only another second as Ashleigh's family chatted away, before she took out her phone for a distraction.

"Hey." Ashleigh was suddenly next to her, rubbing her back and gently dropping a discreet kiss on her shoulder. "I didn't know you'd be here."

"How was shopping?" she asked, casting a look over at Ashleigh's parents and grandmother talking to Liam.

"Ugh. Shopping." Ashleigh made a tortured face before seeming to shift gears. Kellan felt her soft fingertips brush the bare skin of her biceps. "Is there any chance you'd join us for dinner?" Ashleigh ticked her head toward her family, and her voice had an adorable lilt to it, like she might be nervous to ask.

"For real?"

"I'm sure it's not on your list of fun summer activities, but you're awake, so I know you're hungry."

"We know that's true." She let out a slight laugh at how well Ashleigh already knew her. "I feel bad crashing into your family time."

"I live with them. Every day is family time. Plus..." Ashleigh scrunched her nose and her eyes sparkled. "Be nice to see you."

"Yeah, okay. If you're sure."

"I am." Ashleigh let her hand linger the whole way down her arm and she felt her body buzz in response before her touch was gone.

She followed Ashleigh to the table and almost made it free and clear until she saw Liam assessing them as he walked back to the bar. With a wave of his hand, he signaled his waitstaff to bring over another place setting for her. The smile he laid on her was loaded with inference, and as they crossed paths, he grabbed her arm and leaned in.

"Dude, never play poker," he whispered. "Seriously, I mean that," he continued at full volume. To the average person his words might have been confusing, but his tone was all support, and the hefty thump he landed on her shoulder clearly signaled she had his vote.

God bless the US Army and the fellowship it fostered.

❖

"So, Kellan, Ashleigh tells us you're retired from the service." Bill McAllister sipped on a beer several shades paler than hers.

"Yes, sir." She glanced at the bar where Liam was working away. "That's where I met Liam."

"And you're here apartment-sitting for your aunt?" Peg chimed in. "Whereabouts is that?"

"On Furman Street. Down near the water. Her building is right next to Brooklyn Bridge Park."

"Ooh, very nice. I've only driven by the redevelopment there. My father was a longshoreman on those piers when I was growing up. So interesting to see how that neighborhood has changed."

"Where's home?" Bill asked as he split his attention between the conversation and Liam's updated menu.

"Colorado, sir. Vail, to be exact."

"Skiing sounds so exciting," Granny mused. "Ashleigh, do you ski?"

"Gran." Ashleigh shot her grandmother a set of daggers from both eyes, but in the moment, Kellan realized she wanted to know the answer.

She turned to Ashleigh. "Do you?"

"I haven't ever. When I was in high school, they did a ski trip to the Poconos every year, but it was always over winter break, and it coincided with practice for the Math Team." Ashleigh's shrug was positively adorable. "It was important to come out strong in the second semester."

"So no skiing."

"Sorry."

"Well, don't be sorry, dear." Granny straightened her silverware. "It seems like the perfect time to learn. Now you have someone to teach you."

"Except it's July in New York."

"Don't be obstinate, Ashleigh. Of course I meant when you visit Kellan in Colorado."

She saw Ashleigh roll her eyes at her grandmother, but she was down with the old lady's spunk. It was cute that she was trying to play matchmaker, and Ashleigh looked adorably flustered to be on the spot. "We usually have snow as early as October. I bet there's a school break you could sneak away for." She smiled big, knowing that even though it was offered in sport, her invitation was a hundred percent real.

"Stop it, you." Ashleigh's tone was all spirit. "Do not encourage her." Ashleigh nodded toward her grandmother as she gave Kellan's thigh a playful squeeze under the table.

She looked at Ashleigh and tried hard to keep her tone free of flirtation. "You should come visit. Vail is beautiful." She covered Ashleigh's hand and laced their fingers together out of view. "I'll even do the bunny slope with you."

Bill turned the conversation to dinner as he debated trying Liam's trendy take on shepherd's pie, versus soy-glazed baby back ribs, versus a standard burger.

"Oh, don't get a burger," Granny said. "Be adventurous—try something new. Anyway, we're barbecuing on the weekend. As good as I'm sure the chef here is, nothing beats the way Peg seasons her sliders. Which reminds me"—she placed her menu down on her bread plate—"Kellan, will you be joining us for Ashleigh's birthday?"

She almost choked on her beer and had to force it down, making her eyes water.

"Oh, you must," Granny continued. "The weather is supposed to be lovely. Peg's going to cook up a storm. Stella and Siobhan will be coming with their boyfriends. It's going to be a real party."

"Stella broke up with Blake," Ashleigh said, taking a sip of her seltzer.

"She did?" Peg was obviously surprised. "When?"

"She doesn't want to make a big deal of it. I'm sure she's going to tell you the whole story. Let's just say he was being a jerk."

"That guy's always been a jerk in my book," Bill added. "Such a know-it-all. I'm glad she's done with him." He sipped his beer in closure. "Anyway, three o'clock Saturday, Kellan. What kind of beer is that you're drinking? I'll make sure to have some on hand."

"Slow down, everybody." Ashleigh halted the conversation with outstretched arms. "Easy with the strong-arming. For all we know, Kellan is busy." She felt Ashleigh's hand on her thigh giving it a reassuring squeeze before she turned to face her. "But if you're free, I'd love it if you came." Her smile was warm, and it took every ounce of restraint to avoid kissing her right at the table in front of her parents and grandmother, who would no doubt cheer in support anyway.

"I would love that." She gave her attention to the other three. "Thank you so much for the invite. Please tell me what I can bring."

"Nonsense," Granny said. "Just bring yourself."

After they placed their dinner selections, Liam returned with an offer to show them the remodeled back courtyard. Granny and Bill and Peg jumped at the opportunity for the behind-the-scenes tour. She stayed put at the table with Ashleigh.

"I'm sorry about my grandmother," Ashleigh started. "She can be a bit heavy-handed."

"She's fantastic. I do feel bad about your party, though. She kind of left you no choice in that one." Kellan was ecstatic to be included, but she wanted to make sure Ashleigh was cool with it.

Ashleigh's hand was at the base of her neck, touching her buzzed hairline. "I'd like it if you were there. Unless...do you have other plans?"

"I don't. You know this."

"You always say that. But I don't know if you make plans on days that I'm busy with my parents or Shauna." Ashleigh's finger dipped below her crewneck, drawing a lazy pattern on her skin. It was intimate and understated, but the effect it was having was not conducive to having to sit through dinner with the fam.

"I don't. I haven't yet." She reached for Ashleigh's hand and took it away from her neck and brought it to her lips, sneaking a quick kiss on her knuckle while her family was still outside. "I love the way that feels, but it's doing all sorts of things to me right now." For the last half hour, she hadn't stopped thinking about how she might be able to convince Ashleigh to go back to her place.

"Is that so?"

Ashleigh looked at her mouth and started to lean in, but the back door opened and her family reentered. Liam steered them to the wall of history—pictures of Ireland and his family, Park Slope in the middle of the century, some early shots of the bar from back in the day. Ashleigh sat all the way back in her chair, the moment gone, but she continued to hold Kellan's hand under the table where they could still touch out of sight.

"Can I see you tonight?" Ashleigh asked.

"Yes. Of course." She breathed a sigh of relief that Ashleigh needed her too.

"Stick around after dinner. I'll walk these guys home, pack a bag, and meet you here." Even if Ashleigh didn't say the words, the spirit in her eyes said she'd missed Kellan in their time apart. Thank God, because she was practically in withdrawal. She didn't even try for chill.

"I can't wait."

Chapter Fifteen

"My parents could not stop talking about you the whole way home." Ashleigh dropped her purse and her overnight bag on a chair in the corner. "My grandmother, forget it."

"Your family is awesome. Although I do feel bad they treated me to dinner."

"You didn't think my dad was going to take money from you, did you?"

"No, not really." Ashleigh watched as Kellan filled Blue's dinner bowl and gave him fresh water. "You will have to tell me what I can bring Saturday, though. I'm not showing up empty-handed."

"You're cute." She kicked off her strappy sandals and sat at the kitchen island just to be close to Kellan. Blue hopped up on the counter clearly expecting some love, and she rewarded him, happily petting his small head with both hands. "Hey, Blue." She brought her nose close to his. "Did you miss me?"

"Don't be a hog, Blueberry." Kellan placed the filtered water back in the fridge. "I missed her too. And I didn't get any kisses yet."

As Kellan spoke, she came around the island, swiveled Ashleigh's chair, and kissed her delicately on the lips. It was lovely and comfortable, but she wanted more. She reached one hand up behind Kellan's neck and pulled her in for a deeper kiss. She spread her legs wide and found the waistband of Kellan's jeans, hooking a finger through the belt loops to inch her closer. The kiss was thorough and perfect, and she felt herself react everywhere.

"You missed me, huh?" she asked as Kellan kissed her face, her neck, her throat. She slid her hands under Kellan's shirt, basking in the feel of her muscular body.

Kellan nodded and dropped a kiss on her lips. "Maybe a smidge."

"Good." She traced the vague outline of Kellan's abs while enjoying the feeling of her mouth as she teased along her neck. Kellan sucked deeper, and she panicked, pulling away immediately. "Don't give me a hickey. Not on my neck."

"So many rules." Kellan teased her but held her face gently, dotting baby kisses everywhere. "I am not going to give you a hickey. I promise." Kellan took her hand and led her to the bed.

"I should tell you something," Ashleigh said. She registered concern in Kellan's lovely eyes, and she backpedaled immediately. "It's not bad. I just..." She tucked her hair behind one ear. "I told Shauna about us. Yesterday—I had lunch with her, and it just came out."

"Okay."

"I only mention it because I know we haven't really talked to each other much about what this is. Or really defined it, what we're doing here."

Kellan sat on the edge of the bed, her expression completely unreadable. "Do you want to talk about it?"

"Not really. No. I think we're just enjoying each other's company. A lot." A nervous giggle escaped, and she started to pace a few feet in a semicircle. She brought her hand to her face. "What I mean is—"

"Ash." Kellan caressed her elbow, and when she relaxed her arm, Kellan found her hand. "I like you. I'm attracted to you. We have fun together. I think you feel the same. Why does it have to be more complicated than that?"

"It doesn't. You're right."

She let Kellan pull her close, and when she reached the edge of the bed, she lifted her knees up onto it so she was full-on straddling Kellan.

"That's better." Kellan caressed her bottom and kissed along her neck, stopping just shy of her mouth. "Anything you want to talk about, I'm here. Okay?"

She nodded, a sense of relief washing over her. Even though they hadn't discussed anything really, Ashleigh felt like the opportunity was there if she wanted to. More importantly, it seemed they were on the same page. A summer romance based on mutual attraction and hot sex. Not what she'd expected, but pretty great so far. She just had to make sure to keep her feelings in check. No big deal. Kellan's mouth was torturing her with open kisses along her jawline and over by the sensitive spot just below her ear.

"For the record, Liam knows too." Kellan slid her hands along Ashleigh's thighs and lifted her light summer dress over her head. "I didn't tell him, but he figured it out. Is that okay?" Kellan kissed along the top of her breasts above her braline.

"That was bound to happen. He knows us both too well to not pick up on the signs. Did he say anything?" She pulled Kellan's hair to see her face but also because she liked the tiny feeling of control it gave her.

"Not really," Kellan said, following her response with a kiss. "Did Shauna?"

Ashleigh rotated her neck, remembering in detail the grilling she'd gotten from her bestie. Kellan took this as an invitation to unhook her bra and kiss her breasts. "Did she ever. Shauna had about a million questions."

Kellan released her nipple immediately. "Wait. For real?"

Ashleigh sighed at the loss. "Yes. I got the third degree."

"What did she say?" Kellan lay back on the bed but didn't stop touching her. In fact, the way she was holding her hips in place as she moved beneath her was teasing her in the most delicious way.

"She just wanted to know things. Details."

"Like?" With one hand Kellan held her in place, still writhing, while the other covered her breast, massaging it with just the right amount of pressure. Her body was sizzling, like there was some kind of hardwired connection between her nipple and her clit.

"Like this." She was breathing heavily, and she couldn't help it.

"Did you tell her it was the best sex of your life?" Kellan was all smug charm. "You don't know how you survived without it so long?"

Ashleigh dug her hips down deep, grinding hard against Kellan. She bit her lower lip, hoping it looked as sexy as it did in the movies. She leaned all the way forward and met Kellan with a searing kiss before pulling back just slightly. In a low voice she said, "I told her it was decent. On a scale of one to ten, a solid three."

She broke into hysterics as Kellan flipped her over, laughing with her. She wasn't about to admit Kellan's skill in bed was off the charts.

"A three? A three!" Hovering over her, Kellan was all smiles as she looked deep into her eyes. "You're killing my ego."

"I'm teasing you." She touched Kellan's gorgeous face. "You know that."

"I guess I have to work harder to impress you." Ashleigh felt Kellan's hand slide smoothly over her stomach, slipping into her panties. Kellan's groan was guttural and Ashleigh knew she was turned on.

"You're so wet. I love it."

"Of course I am. You tend to have that effect on me." Kellan kissed her neck, her fingers still teasing her. She wanted them inside. She wanted more. She prayed for the nerve to ask. "Kellan?"

"Yes?"

"There is something…" She stopped talking as she heard her voice shake slightly. Kellan clearly picked up on it too, because she ceased all movement.

"What's the matter?"

"Nothing, it's just…" She touched Kellan's face but lost her moment of confidence. "Nothing."

"Ash, talk to me." Kellan kissed her fingertip. "I promise there's nothing you can't say. If there's something I'm doing that you don't like, it's okay. You can tell me."

"Oh my God, it's not that. At all. It's the opposite, in fact."

The confusion in Kellan's expression told her she wasn't one hundred percent following. She was going to have to say it. Just rip the Band-Aid off. She squeezed her eyes closed but covered them with both her hands anyway. "I was wondering if you have a strap-on, and if you do, would you maybe want to use it with me?"

She felt Kellan kiss her hands away, dropping soft kisses along her cheeks. She whispered in her ear. "I do. And I do." Kellan found her lips. "Why were you nervous to ask me?"

"I don't know. What if you weren't into it?"

"If I wasn't, I would tell you. As it happens, it's one of my favorite things to do."

"Why didn't you say something?"

"I wasn't sure if you were into it or not."

For some reason Ashleigh felt compelled to disclose the truth. "I'm not sure I am. I've never actually used one."

"Really? All those years with Reagan?"

Kellan's tone was all curiosity and held no judgment whatsoever. It was perfect and it calmed her immediately. She shrugged. "In the beginning we played around with toys. It was fine. Fun, even. We tried a strap-on once, but it wasn't right. I can't describe it." She brushed her fingertips along Kellan's smooth cheeks. "Something tells me it will be different with you. When I think about being with you, I fantasize about it. Is that TMI?"

"Uh, no. That is hot." She kissed her soundly. "Give me one second, okay?"

Kellan dropped a final kiss on her before disappearing down the short hall into the bathroom. When she returned, she had stripped down to a T-shirt and black boxer briefs, barely concealing an obvious bulge. Kellan took the shirt off and slipped under the covers beside her. On their sides, facing each other, Kellan leaned forward and kissed her. With the tips of her fingers she caressed her face so softly that Ashleigh could barely feel the touch. The tenderness was enticing. Soft and precise. It made her crave more. She had chills everywhere.

Kellan read her body, drifting her hand over the outline of her chin, between her breasts, circling her nipples, before she reached lower to her panties and slid them off. "We'll go nice and slow, okay?" Kellan kissed her neck and rolled her on top, so they were in roughly the same position as before. "If you want me to stop, you tell me. Promise?"

She nodded, but in the moment, she couldn't imagine ever wanting to stop. A little breathless, she felt Kellan's bulge press against her. She throbbed against it, certain she was soaking Kellan's boxers over the shaft. She tried to resist riding her too hard. She should probably let Kellan set the pace, but she was dying to feel Kellan inside her.

Kellan flipped them and kissed her hungrily before she made her way down her body. Her tongue was wet and soft and demanding. The contrast made Ashleigh whimper in delight and longing. She absolutely loved the feel of Kellan's mouth simultaneously claiming her and building her up. But then Kellan stopped. She kissed her way back up her body, filling her with two fingers as she asked, "Are you ready?"

It seemed a formality at this point. She was beyond ready and Kellan had to know it, but she nodded assent anyway, biting her lip in anticipation of the unknown.

Kellan hovered over her as she slid off her boxers and eased inside. Holy Christ, it was amazing. She'd been slightly concerned that it would hurt, but all those thoughts melted away, replaced by sheer satisfaction from the fullness of Kellan inside her. Kellan moved slowly, rhythmically, and she spread her legs wider in response. A moan escaped her, and then another. She didn't even care how loud she was. She wanted more. Impossibly, she needed more. She found Kellan's mouth and covered it with hers, the desire to be connected everywhere overwhelming her. Kellan kissed her back. Soft at first, then harder, matching the pace of her hips. She broke the kiss, a little breathless as she dug her fingernails into Kellan's back. She wrapped her legs around Kellan's waist, needing every inch. She was going to explode, and yet release seemed just beyond her reach. She kissed Kellan's shoulder, her neck, tasting her sweat as she clutched her tightly angling for even more depth.

"Kell." She placed her hands on her shoulders, stopping her movement as she spoke.

"You okay? Am I hurting you?" Kellan asked.

"No. You're perfect. Honest." She leaned forward to kiss her, hoping it emphasized her point. "Could I just"—she made a small circle with one finger—"flip over?"

Kellan's grin was sexy. "Yeah. Of course." She withdrew slowly and helped her into position on her hands and knees, before easing back inside.

This.

This was what she wanted. Her muscles tightened around Kellan, igniting mini explosions everywhere. She backed into Kellan over and over, feeling her orgasm build. She was going to come—the wave was cresting. But then she felt Kellan's hands grip her waist tightly, the pace increasing and changing from long deliberate strokes to short staccato ones. Oh my God, Kellan was going to come too. Inside her. From fucking her. How hot was that? The simple knowledge put her over the edge, and she gasped in her release, gripping the pillowcase and breathing a string of expletives into the sheets.

Kellan leaned forward and kissed her shoulder, slipping out of her and sliding into place along her side.

"That was amazing. You are incredible." Kellan kissed her ear as she settled in behind her. Ashleigh was too blissed out for words. She hugged Kellan's arm around her midsection as she nuzzled into the embrace. "Same, baby. Same," she managed to muster in a state of half stupor. Melting into the mattress, she ignored her use of the endearment and the irony of her words, knowing it was an indisputable fact that after what had just happened in this bed, she might never be the same.

CHAPTER SIXTEEN

L et's get ice cream."

"Ice cream?" Ashleigh followed Kellan's attention to the ice cream truck on the corner opposite where they were standing, in the shadow of the High Line.

"Yes. It's summer. It's hot out. I vote ice cream."

"But we're going out to dinner."

"Hours from now. It's not even one. And"—Kellan squeezed their clasped hands—"it's your birthday. That gives you license to do whatever you want."

"Or whatever *you* want." She'd intended it to be playful but somehow it came out naughty. One look at Kellan confirmed she'd caught the innuendo. "That's not what I meant. As if I hold anything back, anyway."

It was a truth she hadn't intended on pointing out so bluntly, but the past three days had been eye-opening, a virtual sexual awakening for her. They'd managed to leave the apartment for short bursts—a trip to the Museum of the American Indian in the Financial District, a tour of the *Intrepid*, where Kellan used her retired military ID to hook them up with a discount. But the vast majority of their time had been spent in bed, on the couch, in the shower, and even once on the kitchen counter.

She discovered that Kellan had a tender spot just below the waistband of her boxers, and when she lingered there, sucking and teasing, it drove her crazy. Likewise, Kellan seemed to enjoy when she tugged her hair, directed her hands, told her expressly what she wanted. And nothing seemed to turn her on as much as when she was loud and vocal. She'd figured out some things about herself too. It was pure bliss when Kellan was inside her, pounding her hard, and she reveled in the way Kellan held her and kissed her so tenderly after she came. It turned out being open and free was an absolute game changer, empowering her with a confidence she hadn't expected. She was comfortable telling Kellan what she wanted, and Kellan was beyond masterful at heeding her requests.

With Kellan, everything seemed smooth and effortless. Right down to the moment this morning when Kellan asked how she wanted to spend her birthday. Ashleigh had purposely left the day open. It was gorgeous outside, sunny and clear, and on the spot she decided they should check out Hudson Yards, a space both artful and luxurious and new to the cityscape.

"So, ice cream, huh?" she said swinging their interlocked hands as they crossed the street.

"Let's live on the wild side," Kellan teased.

"Come on, slowpoke." She tugged Kellan behind her as she followed the sound of the high-pitched jingle to the white and pink Mister Softee truck half a block down. "My treat."

"Absolutely not." Kellan reached for her wallet and touched one finger to Ashleigh's nose before kissing it gently. "Birthday girl pays for nothing."

"That's ridiculous. I know you're going to insist on buying dinner, so let me at least get this."

"No." Kellan's smile could melt her. "What do you want?"

"Twist. On a cone. Chocolate sprinkles."

"Perfect." Kellan turned to the vendor and ordered two. For no other reason than the moment seemed right, she stood behind Kellan and draped her arms over both shoulders from behind, sort of hanging off her back. It was pure PDA, an overtly couple-y way to stand, but she felt Kellan relax into her embrace, and when the vendor served up the first cone, Kellan leaned back and kissed her before she gave it over.

"Thank you."

"You're welcome."

Ashleigh kissed her again simply because she wanted to, and she could. She stepped to the side but held on to Kellan's hand as she licked her cone.

"Miss McAllister. Hi."

Ashleigh wiped her mouth with a paper napkin as three of her honors students formed a semicircle around her. "Hi, guys. How's summer?"

"Great." Salem answered for the group. Made sense, even in this crew of overachievers Salem was the natural leader. She saw Clive and Kelsey exchange a glance and was suddenly hyperaware that she was still holding Kellan's hand. "We just checked out Hudson Yards," Salem continued.

"Oh my God, you gotta see it, Miss M. The *Vessel* is so cool. It's like a giant tessellation. It reminded me the of the M.C. Escher art we studied last year."

"Yes, Clive. Exactly." She didn't hide her excitement at her star math pupil's understanding of the architecture and the geometry involved in creating it. It was half the reason she wanted to see it up close. Genuine curiosity and the unique views the sixteen-story honeycomb-like structure boasted were part of the allure, but she was dying to use New York's latest redevelopment project in her fall curriculum.

"We were just headed that way." She gestured to Kellan, who was making a serious dent in her ice cream. "This is my friend from Colorado." She wiped a line of vanilla melting down the side of her cone. "Kellan, these are my students—Salem, Clive, and Kelsey."

"Hi." Kellan waved.

"Wow, Colorado. Cool," Clive said, giving her a thorough once-over.

"Nice. I hope Miss McAllister is showing you all the fun stuff," Salem said.

"Yes. Ash—Miss McAllister—is a great tour guide."

These were some of the sharpest kids in the city. Ashleigh knew they were picking up on the vibe between her and Kellan. She made a quick circular lick at the base of her cone, ticking her head in the direction of Hudson Yards. "We should be on our way. Enjoy the rest of your break, guys."

"See ya, Miss M." Clive waved as the threesome started backing away.

She hooked her ice-cream free hand through Kellan's arm. "You ready?" But as they started in the direction of the exhibit, she heard the kids call her name, and when she turned around she was met with a trio of smiles and six thumbs up. She shook her head at them but couldn't help but smile at their support. Even her students were Team Kellan.

❖

Ashleigh reached for Kellan's hand as they exited the restaurant into the warm Brooklyn night. "What I love about tapas is that I'm never too full when I'm done."

"What I love about tapas is that it sounds like topless," Kellan joked. "And that is a style of dining I can completely get behind."

"You can't even sleep without a shirt on."

"Fair point." Kellan brought their linked hands to her lips. "But I was more suggesting you naked, me watching."

"Yeah, that's gonna end well."

"I beg your pardon. I foresee a completely satisfying outcome."

She couldn't help but laugh. Everything about today had been perfect. Morning sex with a series of stellar orgasms. Ice cream for lunch. Magnificent pics of the Hudson Yards *Vessel* she would definitely be able to build a lesson plan around come September, and finally dinner at her favorite Spanish restaurant in Park Slope.

"Did you know Casa del Rey was my favorite?" Ashleigh was suddenly intrigued at Kellan's savvy in procuring a reservation at the local hotspot.

"I had a suspicion." Kellan leaned over. "I trolled your Instagram. There were a few pics of you and Shauna from not very long ago. I asked Liam just to be sure. He confirmed what social media only suggested."

"The food is so good. Not gonna lie, part of the allure is that Reagan hates Spanish food. It's nice knowing I won't bump into her and Josh there."

"Do you run into them often?"

"You'd be surprised. For the number of people that live in Brooklyn, this neighborhood feels small sometimes."

"I bet."

"It's a beautiful night out." She did a full three sixty spin and loved feeling Kellan's eyes on her. She knew the sex would be epic the second they got back to the apartment. For an added treat, she wanted to build up the anticipation. "Feel like checking in on Liam?" she asked. "Be nice to have a drink out in his courtyard."

"Sounds great. I bet he'd love to wish you a happy birthday too."

"We don't have to stay long—I promise."

"I'm in no rush," Kellan said. "I have you all night, right?"

She answered with a wink as they entered Connolly's Public House. Ashleigh was thrilled to see Paul behind the main bar, knowing it meant Liam was already out back. She gave him a friendly wave as she led Kellan outside. And stopped dead.

Somebody should've given her a heads-up, but even if they had, there was probably no amount of mental preparation that would have readied her to see a particular party of four standing out from the crowd as they laughed and chatted at a picnic table near the back bar.

Reagan caught her eye first, but the others seemed to notice her simultaneously, a fraction of a second later. Ashleigh wanted to run as fast and as far as possible, but she couldn't. She stood frozen in the moment and then did the unthinkable. Almost on autopilot, her legs carried her forward.

"Hey there." She stood behind Shauna and Mike, a hand resting on each of their shoulders. She lobbed a smile at Reagan and Josh, hoping it didn't look as painful as it felt. "Reagan, Josh."

"Ash. Happy birthday." Reagan was the only one with the nerve to speak, and it looked like she was about to get up and greet her. The situation felt pitiful, and in the moment, she only cared about sparing herself the awkwardness.

"Thanks. Don't get up." She waved her off. "We're going to get drinks."

"Do you guys want to sit? There's room." Shauna scooted over and patted the bench beside her. Ashleigh picked up on a combo of panic and apology in her expression. "Let us buy your round. For your birthday," she added.

"It's all good. We'll just say hi to Liam and come back."

It was a terrible idea and she knew it, but she felt trapped by etiquette and the fact that she shouldn't care that her friends and their boyfriends made up a run-of-the-mill foursome plucked right out of Middle America.

She felt the heat from Kellan's body behind her as they approached the bar and waited for Liam's attention.

"You okay? We can leave." Kellan's voice was soft in her ear, her touch gentle on her back. "We do not have to stay. You don't have to prove anything."

"Nope. I'm fine." She heard the tension in her voice. "No big deal. Shauna and Reagan and Josh are here. At Liam's. Together. On my birthday. Awesome." She felt every muscle in her body stiffen with angst. "Tequila. Immediately," she said when Liam finally made it over.

"Ashleigh, take a deep breath. Let me make you a drink. Something you'll like." She watched his eyes dart past to her table of friends a few feet away.

"Liam. Tequila. Please?" she asked. She couldn't care less about the taste. She wanted to dull the anguish and embarrassment she was feeling. She wanted the courage to face them all, even if it was manufactured. "I never ask you for anything."

He placed two shot glasses in front of her and lifted a bottle of tequila from the top shelf.

Ashleigh knocked back the first one and asked for another immediately. With a somewhat disapproving sigh, he refilled their glasses. She winced away the burn as she felt it go down, the potent liquid warming her chest and her arms almost immediately.

"It's actually not bad," she said, leaning back into Kellan for contact and support. "One more. Please?" She pouted and batted her lashes at the same time. "It's my birthday."

"The puppy dog routine doesn't really work for me," he said. "You're not my type. Do yourself a favor and let those two work their magic for a minute. Then we'll see."

"Do they come here a lot?" she whispered.

"First time." He iced two glasses and loaded a silver shaker with vodka and vermouth. "Shauna and Mike come in once in a while. Reagan's never stepped foot in here, I promise." He gave the tin a hefty shake. "I would've called you. I should have." He seemed genuinely disappointed in himself. "It's just, I knew you went out to dinner. I didn't think…" He filled two martini glasses and delivered them to a pair of women at the end of the bar. "For what it's worth, Reagan seems uncomfortable as fuck. She didn't even order a drink."

"How long have they been here?"

"Maybe an hour." He shrugged.

"Okay. One more for us." She let her head fall back against Kellan's chest, as she was beginning to feel the effects of the first two drinks. "Is that okay?" She directed her question to Kellan only. Her lips tingled and her body buzzed. She let her hand drift to the front of Kellan's pants, even though she doubted she was packing.

"You sure?" Kellan responded with a question, but Ashleigh felt a hand circle her waist, and the expression in Kellan's eyes seemed full of support. Ashleigh nodded.

They kicked back the final shot and Ashleigh had a brilliant idea. "Li, will you leave the bottle and give us four more glasses?"

He answered with a broad smile. "No."

"Why not?" She giggled at his stern yet playful response.

"For one, this isn't a movie. So easy on the leave-the-bottle nonsense." He cleared their shot glasses. "Two, you're getting drunk. Your eyes are already glassy." He wiped the bar where a few errant drops of tequila made it sticky. "If you want to make nice with the straights and Reagan, I'll mix something up and bring it over. Deal?"

"You are a fucking genius and I love you." She reached across and pulled his face close for a kiss. Gathering her semisloshed resolve, she sauntered the few short steps and plunked down next to Shauna, squeezing in close to make room for Kellan.

"So, gang, what's new?" She heard the forced friendliness in her tone and wondered if it was noticeable. Either way the two couples seemed in a collective state of shock at her decision to join them, and no one answered right away. Ashleigh opted to fill the silence herself. "Sorry. You all remember Kellan, right?"

Shauna nodded. "How's the summer treating you, Kellan?"

"It's great. New York is an amazing city."

"What did you do to celebrate today, Ash?" Shauna was clearly the mouthpiece.

"We spent the afternoon at Hudson Yards, and we just had dinner at Casa del Rey."

"Yum." Shauna swatted her arm. "That's our spot, Ash."

"Looks like you have a few spots. Depending on who you're with." It was a low blow, but before Shauna could react at all, Liam was at the head of the table. He lined up seven shot glasses and poured an orangey-pink concoction in each.

"To Ash." He lifted his shot in the air. "Thirty-eight years, baby."

"What is it?" Josh asked.

"Kamikaze passion fruit," Liam said.

"So vodka, right?" Josh pressed.

"Yeah, but not too strong," Liam answered. "And kinda tasty, if I do say so myself."

Ashleigh watched Reagan push her glass slightly to the side, making eye contact with her boyfriend. He nodded, seeming to assume responsibility for its consumption. She didn't know which was more annoying—their obvious ability to communicate without words or the fact that her ex had changed everything about her persona, right down to her affinity for a good cocktail.

"You don't drink vodka anymore?" Ashleigh asked, unable to keep the judgment from her tone.

"I'm just not feeling great," Reagan said.

"It's one drink. You can't have one drink with me?"

"I really can't."

The table fell quiet and Ashleigh watched her friends exchange seemingly knowing looks. It hit her. A thousand seconds too late, but it hit her. With one hand, Reagan covered her belly in case she was still in the dark.

"Oh my God. You're pregnant."

No one said a word. They didn't need to. Ashleigh drained her shot and turned to Shauna. "A little warning might have been okay. Just to avoid, you know"—she faux smiled at Shauna first, Reagan second—"this ridiculously awkward moment." She reached over and grabbed Reagan's kamikaze shot, lifting it aloft before shooting it quickly. "Congrats." The thump the glass made against the wooden table was louder than she expected, but she couldn't help it. She turned to Kellan. "Can we go?"

In some part of her brain she registered the objections of her friends arguing she should stay, as she gathered her purse and walked out. It all seemed like a blur. Her chest was tight, her head spun. She didn't take a full breath until she was on Fifth Avenue, halfway down the block from Liam's. She heard her own laughter in spite of the anger she felt over the situation. Thank God Kellan was there.

She pushed into her and found her lips immediately, kissing her hard, if a tad sloppily. Kellan held her tight but pulled back to assess her. "Are you okay?"

"Yes, I'm okay." Ashleigh wrapped her arms around Kellan's shoulders and reached up to kiss her neck. "I just need you to take me home and make me forget all of this. Do whatever you want to me—

just help me erase this entire night. Think you can manage that?" She slid her hand down the front of Kellan's jeans.

"Let's slow down a little here, okay?" Kellan pulled her hand out. "You're wasted."

"In case you missed it, I'm kind of having a shitty night."

"And I want to help you."

"Good. Because I want you to help me." She reached for the hem of Kellan's shirt, trying for closeness.

Kellan grabbed her hand and held it. "Let's go back to my place. We can talk. Process what just happened in there."

"Fuck processing." She lunged at Kellan, her tongue halfway down her throat before Kellan broke them apart.

"I won't have sex with you like this."

"Excuse me?"

"You're upset. I get it. I want to be there for you. As your friend. As more than that, to be honest."

"But you won't give me what I want?" She folded her arms across her chest and was unable to stop herself from stumbling a little. "Since when are you so righteous?"

"You drank a lot in a very short period of time. Not to mention you're dealing with some heavy emotions. I'm not going to take advantage of you like this."

"I'm pretty much throwing myself at you. That's not really taking advantage."

"Yeah, well, forgive me for not wanting to be your revenge fuck either." Kellan looked right at her, and Ashleigh saw both hurt and anger in her eyes. "I think we both deserve more than that at this point." Kellan rubbed the back of her neck, her anxiety on display, before she held out a hand. Her voice was soft when she said, "Let's just call it a night. I'll walk you home."

Ashleigh walked past her outstretched hand, hating that she was pushing away the one person who was trying to be there for her. But she was too angry to accept any kindness. She wanted to be mad. She needed to be. "I'm good. Bye," she said unleashing it all on Kellan.

"Ash, wait."

"Nope. I'm fine." She pounded down the sidewalk, fully aware that Kellan was following. "I don't need a chaperone. I've lived here my whole life." She held one hand up, simultaneously waving good-bye and dismissing her. But Kellan stayed with her the whole way, and despite the pull in her heart, she didn't allow herself to turn around to say good night when she reached her parents' brownstone. Instead she raced up the stairs and into her bed, sobbing into her pillow, painfully aware her tears were just as much over her fight with Kellan as anything else.

CHAPTER SEVENTEEN

In the back of the rideshare, Kellan's phone buzzed with a text. Ashleigh. She debated opening it. It wasn't that she was uninterested in what Ashleigh had to say, particularly after their street corner argument last night, but she was two minutes from her front door, and even though she was taking a risk showing up unannounced, she believed legit face time was in order.

At a red light, curiosity got the best of her. She rearranged the two hot coffees she was balancing on her knees and opened the message.

Hi. I don't know what to say. I'm embarrassed. You were so sweet to me yesterday, honestly you always are, and last night I acted like a jerk. If you're still mad and don't want to come to my family bbq later, I understand. I've been stressing about contacting you all morning because I know it's not fair and it's pathetic, but I want to beg you not to write me off for the rest of the summer. The things I said, the way I treated you, it's not how I feel. God, I hope you know that. I am so, so sorry.

The note was punctuated with a bright red heart, and Kellan felt her heart swell in response. She thanked her driver for the lift and took the steps in twos, pausing when she reached Ashleigh's front door.

Are you home? It was probably something she should have checked earlier, but Ashleigh's response was immediate.

Yes.

Great. Will you open the door?

Kellan stuffed her phone back in her pocket, just as the heavy door swung open. Face to face with Ashleigh, she was struck by her beauty. Even in sweats and a ratty tee, her skin radiated, and her eyes enticed.

"Peace offering?" Kellan said, presenting a to-go cup to Ashleigh. "You're bringing me a peace offering? I'm pretty sure this should be the other way around."

She ticked her head to the side. "Yeah, well, I'm closer to the Beanery, and I thought you could probably use this right about now."

"You are amazing," Ashleigh said, pulling her inside. Ashleigh took the paper cup and held it close to her face, clearly indulging in the aroma from the fresh brew.

"Are you hungover?"

"Some. I managed to get a lot of sleep. Motrin and a hot shower helped a good deal. This, though..." She took a sip of some coffee that had seeped through the lid. "Oh my God, you made it perfect. Sweet but not too sweet—"

"Light but not too light," Kellan finished. "I have been paying attention."

"Why are you so nice to me? The way I treated you..." She placed her coffee on an ornate table in the hallway. "Kellan." Ashleigh placed a hand on each of her forearms, tracing her tattoos before making eye contact. She looked so serious and distraught that Kellan was tempted to lean in and kiss her, assure her everything was okay between them, but she knew Ashleigh needed to say her piece.

"I am so sorry for last night. You were perfect and kind and I was obnoxious, drunk, and selfish."

"And hurting."

Ashleigh stepped slightly closer, leaning her forehead against her chest, and Kellan hugged her close, kissing the top of her soft blond hair. "None of those things excuse my actions. I know that."

"Hey. We all have our moments."

Ashleigh kissed her chest, and Kellan tipped her head up, placed a soft kiss on her lips, even as she wondered if it was okay to do that here.

"How can I make it up to you?"

"I'm so glad you asked that." She let Ashleigh lead her by the hand into the bright kitchen at the back of the house. Taking a seat at the kitchen table, she sipped her coffee. "Turns out, I have a plan for us today."

"You do?"

"First of all, I got your text on the way here, which was very considerate. But I'm still invited to the barbecue, right?"

"Of course." Ashleigh was moving around the kitchen, and Kellan was touched when she set a plate of scones in front of her. "Eat," Ashleigh said, as she let her hand drift across Kellan's shoulders before sitting down. "I only said that because I was scared you wouldn't want to come, and I wanted to give you an out if you didn't want to see me."

"Party starts at three o'clock?" She took a bite of a scone, the subtle flavors melting into her taste buds. "Holy smokes. Ash, did you..."

"Ha. Don't get excited. That's all Peg McAllister, right there. You see how I got so comfortable here?"

She swallowed another mouthful. "I may move in. Is there a spare room?"

"There's my room." She winked and Kellan felt herself throb. "What were you saying about the party?"

"Well, if I could steal you until this afternoon, I may have gone ahead and made us a reservation at Ax To Grind." She looked at her watch. "In exactly half an hour."

"Wait. The ax-throwing bar?"

"I read an article about it a few weeks ago. It sounds ridiculous and fun. And it seems we both might have some lingering aggression we could stand to get rid of. It's less than a mile from here—did you know that?"

"Is this all in response to my antics last night?" Ashleigh asked with a slight laugh.

At least Ashleigh didn't say no. Not yet, anyway. And she wasn't entirely wrong, but it was more complex than Ashleigh understood.

After arriving home last night, Kellan struggled with a mix of emotions of her own. Some she was willing to face, some not so much. On the surface was frustration over the evening's drastic turn and dramatic demise. Deeper still was the reality that her feelings for Ashleigh went way beyond casual summer fling, a truth that both excited and terrified her.

After talking it over briefly with Blue, she'd decided the best course of action was to ignore it altogether. He seemed to lazily approve as he curled into her lap on the bed while she pulled out her laptop and channeled her energies into a deep dive on Dara Torres, using all the avenues at her disposal. Public records were an amazing thing. She learned that Dara lived in Greenpoint, Brooklyn, and had been officially divorced for an astonishing seven years. Seven years. It made up a decent chunk of the time that they hadn't spoken. On a whim she'd started drafting a message. But it was all anger, it didn't accurately reflect her feelings, and she knew some of it was spillover from the events of her night. She needed to decompress and perhaps sober up before sending the first communication in over ten years.

That's when she'd remembered Ax To Grind. A quick search of the website said there was an opening at ten thirty in the morning, and she booked it on the spot.

"I hope you're not mad." Kellan polished off her scone and washed it down with a sip of coffee. "I just thought, something different. And it's close by, so it won't take up the whole day. We go, we cleanse, we barbecue. What do you say?"

"I think it's wacky. And perfect." Ashleigh stood and kissed her temple, scratching the back of her head in the way she loved. "I'm going to get changed. What does one wear to throw axes?" she asked as she sashayed out of the room.

"Something with covered toes," she called out after her. She heard Ashleigh laugh out loud as she padded up the stairs.

❖

A full two hours later, they stood on the sidewalk in the bright sunshine.

"That was exhilarating." Kellan dabbed the light sweat from her brow with the sleeve of her T-shirt. "Admit it, you had fun."

"At first I was worried I wouldn't be able to do it," she said. "But that fifteen-minute instruction at the beginning was invaluable."

"You had a couple of bull's-eyes. I was impressed." Kellan draped an arm across Ashleigh's shoulders as they started walking.

"You were amazing." Ashleigh slipped a hand around her waist, giving a gentle squeeze. "No surprise."

"Aw. Go on." She waved Ashleigh off in jest. "No, really, go on," she teased.

Ashleigh playfully punched her ribs. "As if you need any encouragement. Your ego is pretty intact, I'd say."

"Yours should be too," she said. "I'll never get where your doubt comes from." She'd said it sort of idly, because she wanted Ashleigh to know she was special. She didn't expect any sort of explanation.

"I think being married for so long and it being so…I don't know. It wasn't bad, our marriage. It was just bland. Mediocre. And then seeing Reagan so happy now." Ashleigh laced her fingers through Kellan's. "It did something to me. Made me feel like a complete failure, for starters. I'm not putting that on her—don't misunderstand me." Ashleigh looked to the sky. "My feelings are mine alone. I know that. Ugh. And now she's having a baby. I don't even know what to make of that."

"Is that something she wanted? That you both wanted?"

"God, no."

Inexplicably, Kellan's stomach dropped. Not because she wanted children. In fact, the opposite was true. For a split second she considered telling Ashleigh everything. The whole Dara story. But what if she didn't understand? What if it changed things between them?

"Sounds terrible, right?" Ashleigh laughed. "You probably think I'm a monster now."

Kellan squeezed her hand. "Hardly." She felt so, so many things for Ashleigh. All she could really think about was how difficult it was to keep her emotions in check.

"Don't misunderstand me—I think kids are great," Ashleigh continued. "I just don't want any of my own. Reagan never did either. You know what it is that gets to me?" She paused a moment like she was contemplating whether or not she should vocalize her thought.

"Out with it. No filters."

Ashleigh let out a frustrated sigh. "In some ways I feel guilty for not letting her go sooner. She's obviously happy with Josh. And I'm not jealous of her. Or him. I want her to be happy. But at the same time, there is an element to all this that makes me feel somehow erased from the narrative. Like everything we shared wasn't real. Or didn't matter. We were together for seventeen years. That should count for something."

"Do you honestly think she doesn't care about what you think?"

"I don't know anymore."

"She cares about you. Genuinely, I'd say." She didn't know why she was offering an opinion, other than it seemed Ashleigh needed to hear it. "It's obvious how much you matter to her." Ashleigh touched her fingertips gently and Kellan wondered what she was thinking. On the walk signal, they crossed Eighth Avenue, and Kellan was positive they had overshot her house.

As if reading her mind, Ashleigh said, "Is it okay if we stroll through the park for a bit? There's still plenty of time before we're expected home. And it's actually insane that we haven't been in Prospect Park yet."

"Definitely," she said. There was still a lot she wanted to say, and she hoped the tranquility of the park would give her the courage to do it. "Getting back to Reagan for a second," she started. "I know you probably didn't notice last night, but she cares about your opinion. I don't know if she wanted your blessing or what, but she was basically hanging on your words. I saw it the day we ran into them at the food fest too. It makes me so jealous." It was cathartic and refreshing to admit out loud, but still her head clouded with stress. There weren't supposed to be any feelings. Not ones like this. Desire and longing, yes. Even regret for the days they didn't see each other could be rationalized as wanting to capitalize on the brevity of summer. Pure jealousy of an ex was something altogether different. She knew exactly what it was, and it scared the hell out of her.

"It makes you jealous?" Ashleigh asked.

"Yes." She lowered her arm from Ashleigh's shoulder and stuffed her hands in her pockets, self-conscious over the fact that she was divulging to this extent. "I hate that she gets under your skin. I hate that it bothers me so much."

"Kellan, it's not like that. I swear." Ashleigh folded her arms across her chest. "With Reagan, it irks me that I came out looking like a fool. Like my life, our life, was some kind of joke. I know that makes me self-centered and shallow. I don't even like to say it out loud because it's so unbelievably pathetic. Logically, I know our relationship was real and valid, but I see her and I just feel…ridiculous." She stepped forward and put her hand on Kellan's chest. "I want you to know, I need you to know, I have no lingering romantic feelings for Reagan. None, whatsoever. I spend just about all of my time thinking about you."

"For real?" Kellan knew she sounded desperate, but in this moment, she needed reassurance.

Ashleigh nodded and the sentiment in her eyes said she was telling the truth.

Kellan swallowed hard, channeling her courage. "Look, I know we've said this—us—is, you know, just for fun. Nothing serious." She hoped her words wouldn't scare Ashleigh away. "But I'd be lying if I didn't admit to some major feelings right about now." She pulled at the back of her neck, feeling the tightness around her chest as her heart pounded like crazy. "I'm sorry if that's not what you want to hear."

"Why would I not want to hear that?"

Kellan took a step closer. "Because I know this is supposed to be a no-strings-attached kind of arrangement. And here I am, adding strings. Making it complicated."

"I hate to be the one to tell you this, but I have some serious feelings of my own."

"You do?" She'd hoped, but the confirmation sent a chill through her body.

"Of course, I do. Kellan, you're basically the first person I talk to in the morning and the last person I talk to at night. We spend most days together. You make me smile. I tell you, God, everything." Ashleigh covered her face the way she did when she was shy. "It's so stupid, but I miss you when we skip a day."

"It's not stupid." She took Ashleigh's hand away from her face, stealing a kiss. "I hate the off-days."

"So let's not have any more."

She looped her arms around Ashleigh's waist. "That's all you. You're in charge of the schedule." Kellan watched Ashleigh smile and was happy she knew she was teasing. She swayed them a little. "But I'm leaving in a month—"

"Shh, shh, shh, shh." Ashleigh covered her lips with one finger. "Uh-uh. We're not talking about that."

Kellan smiled in spite of the playful scolding. "So what do we do now?" she asked, still referencing the elephant in the room.

"Now…" Ashleigh stood on tiptoe, wrapped her arms around her neck, and spoke through a string of sweet kisses. "Now, we go eat burgers. I introduce you to my sisters. Granny will no doubt embarrass me." She rolled her eyes but smiled. "Ooh, there'll be cake. And"—she finished with a final kiss—"when no one's looking, I'm going to swipe the leftover icing." She wiggled her eyebrows. "For later."

"Later?" She played dumb even though she knew exactly where this was going.

"Later." Ashleigh's smirk was coy. "When we go back to your place and you're inevitably hungry, maybe I'm gonna be the treat."

"Now that's a plan I can get behind."

"Yeah, you will." Ashleigh's eyes held both heat and spirit, but beyond the surface was something deeper.

Kellan knew exactly what it was. Because she felt it too.

CHAPTER EIGHTEEN

I owe you an apology," Ashleigh said.

She slid into the chair across from Shauna. Almost a week after her meltdown at Liam's, she asked her best friend for a brunch meetup at their favorite spot near the park. Shauna had texted her daily since their encounter, but she'd mostly avoided the messages, answering with a chilly request for time. This morning she'd woken with a sense of calm and the knowledge that things would only get more awkward the longer she avoided contact.

"I think it's the other way around."

"I don't know, Shauna. I acted pretty immature." She pushed her hair behind her ears. "Seeing you guys there. The four of you. And then Reagan with the baby bombshell. The whole thing just blew my mind. I was not prepared for any of it."

Shauna covered her hand on top of the small table. "I'm so sorry, Ash." She squeezed her palm a little. "Please know that I never meant to hurt you."

"I know."

"We don't even hang out that much." Ashleigh shot her a look that said she doubted the truthfulness of the statement, and Shauna hesitated. "The guys get along. Obviously, I'm still friends with Reagan. So, sometimes. It was never meant to be behind your back. Being at Liam's on your birthday…" Shauna shook her head at herself. "It was inconsiderate. And completely my fault. Mike loves this one craft beer that Liam has on tap. Reagan was dead against it. But I knew you were going out with Kellan, I figured there was no way you'd be there."

Ashleigh felt her stomach tighten at the memory of seeing them laughing and smiling so easily. At the same time she heard genuine torment in Shauna's tone.

"It's okay. I can't lay claim to the whole neighborhood." She felt forgiveness coming through. "I bet Liam was thrilled to see you guys."

"Not really the point."

"A little bit it is, though. He's trying to make his restaurant profitable. We're his people." It was the truth and she knew it. "Why would any of us give our business to his competitors, right?"

"You're too good."

"Ha!" She slapped Shauna's hand. "The voodoo doll of you I've been sticking for the past few days would beg to differ."

Shauna rubbed her back. "I knew these pains weren't psychosomatic." Her smile was contagious. "Can we hug already?"

"Yes."

Ashleigh stood and their embrace was so heartfelt, she was choked up when they parted. The arrival of their waitress broke the moment.

"Ladies. Coffee, juice, Bloody Marys. What can I get for you?"

"Coffee for me," Ashleigh said, dabbing an escaped tear away.

Shauna ordered the same, and they perused their menus before they decided to split a salad and a spinach quiche. Their server talked up the hotspot's signature mini muffins and homemade strawberry butter, and they exchanged a knowing glance before they heartily agreed. As the waitress applauded their choice and walked away, Ashleigh looked at Shauna.

"You can afford the extra calories anyway. Since you double-date at CrossFit now." She stuck her tongue out.

"Ouch." Shauna covered her heart but laughed. "I suppose I deserve that."

"You don't." Ashleigh smiled, knowing things were back on track. "But it was right there, and I couldn't resist."

"Ash, about Reagan. I should have told you. It's just…baby news is so weird. It's like, at first, it's all, nobody wants to jinx it." Shauna waved her hands emphatically to make her point. "And then they wanted to tell their families first. Honestly, it never felt like it was really my news to share. Reagan wanted to be the one to tell you. I think she just didn't know how."

The explanation made sense and she realized she wasn't mad at either of them. "I know it's not my business, and I'm not looking for gossip." She felt curiosity besting her. "Were they trying to have a baby?"

Shauna's expression said it all, but she gave an answer anyway. "God, no."

The knowledge should have soothed her, but it did the opposite. While it was nice to know Reagan hadn't completely changed who she was, that small comfort was outweighed by the reality of what the truth meant. Reagan and Josh had gotten accidentally pregnant. It implied a neediness and desire for each other that had led to carelessness. Her stomach turned on the spot.

"Ash, she was so scared when she realized." Shauna toyed with her fork. "When she told me, I honestly think she wished she was talking to you."

"Stop. Reagan loves you."

"No, I know. But what we have, it's not like what she had with you." Shauna chewed her full lips, seeming to search for words. "What I mean is you two have a connection. I think she misses that."

"I know," she said. It was the truth and she realized it in this moment in a way she hadn't understood before. She missed Reagan too. Not the romantic part of their union, but the loss of everything else hurt just as much, if not more. The years of friendship and closeness, the comfort of being with someone who genuinely cared about you even after they knew all the flaws. It was a trust true and deep and hard to come by. She knew how Reagan stressed about the unknown, how she panicked at the beginning of every school year, listing her own perceived shortcomings as a teacher. She imagined Reagan might be something of a basket case at the thought of motherhood.

"She's got this. She'll be a great mom." Ashleigh said it with pride, knowing the message would make its way back to Reagan. "She's kind and patient. And she's far and away the bravest person I know."

"You mean it, don't you?"

Ashleigh nodded. For the first time in ages, she didn't feel anything but pure happiness for her ex.

"How's things with Kellan?" Shauna asked, obviously attributing her change of heart to the summer romance.

"Great." She knew she was beaming. She didn't even try to hide it.

"Girl." The word curled from Shauna's mouth. "You better be ready to dish."

"What?" she teased, sipping her coffee.

"Don't you *what* me. Tell me everything."

"You don't want to talk about your wedding? It's right around the corner."

"What's to talk about? I love Mike. The man is a saint. He puts up with me and my family, who are driving me batshit crazy. Aside from that, baby Jesus better give me some good weather. Done. Now you."

She laughed at Shauna's boiled down assessment of her big day. "So, me and Kellan." She loaded a tiny cranberry-orange muffin with strawberry butter. "Things are good. Kellan's great. Funny. Thoughtful. The other day we were in the subway coming back from somewhere. I forget exactly." She paused trying to remember if it was the Frick Museum or the 9/11 Memorial. "Anyway, this woman was struggling with her stroller, you know, getting up the stairs. Right away Kellan just carries it for her. Like, without even thinking about it. It was sweet. She's constantly holding doors, being chivalrous. It's really nice."

"Yeah, yeah, that's great." Shauna took a sip of water. "She's a knight in shining armor. Got it." She rubbed her hands together expectantly. "Now, give me the good stuff."

"Like?"

Shauna answered her with a look.

"So you only care about the sex?" she teased. "You're such a dude. Not even interested in my feelings?"

"Wait. There's feelings?"

"Hmm. Now you'll never know." Ashleigh knew her face probably showed the depth of what she was starting to feel for Kellan, but she gave Shauna a full toothy grin, knowing it would drive her crazy that she wasn't admitting anything just yet.

"Well, hold on now," Shauna countered. "I am one thousand percent interested in every lewd detail of what happens in the boudoir. But are you saying there are feelings too? Because if that's the case, you better spill."

Ashleigh speared a cucumber from the salad and held it aloft. "There might be."

"Mutual feelings?" Shauna sounded tentative, as though she didn't want to assume.

Ashleigh didn't want to go overboard, but after their conversation in the park, she was pretty sure they were on the same page. "I think so."

"Wait. You guys don't...I mean do you...are we talking the big *L*?"

"God, no. Let's not get crazy. But we did have a talk the other day. And then, Shaun, she came to the house for my birthday. My parents had a little barbecue and a cake—"

"She met your parents?"

"Actually, it was the second time she met them. We all had dinner at Liam's one night before that." She looked at the bright sky, remembering the small party. "She bought me this gift. It was so sweet."

"Tell me."

"It's no big deal. But we do coffee almost every day at this place by her. So she got a pound of my favorite Ecuadorian roast. And then"— she covered her heart remembering the sweet gesture—"she got me this mug. It's nothing really, and it probably sounds stupid, but it was personalized to include all the places we've visited together in the city. Inside at the base, she signed it with a heart and her initials." She felt her heart swell at the memory. "I know it's no big deal, but it was just so thoughtful."

"And super shmoopy."

"I know you think it's cheesy."

"I don't." Shauna shook her head. "I think it's the kind of gift you buy your girlfriend when you're falling in love with her in the greatest city on the planet."

"Let's not get ahead of ourselves." She swallowed the last of her coffee. "She's still leaving at the end of summer."

"Why, though?"

"Because she has a job, and a life, in Colorado."

"Look, it's none of my business. And if you want to tell me to shut it, go ahead. But you are sitting in front of me swooning over a mug."

Ashleigh scrunched her face knowing she was right. But she didn't feel like addressing that truth. She whacked Shauna's fork with her own. "I'm not swooning."

"You are. I'm not even making fun of you. Honest. It's really cute." Shauna pulled off a piece of the quiche's flaky crust. "It's nice to see you happy."

"It's good to be happy."

"What if it's not for the summer? What if when Kellan goes home, you try long-distance?"

"You sound like Granny."

"Only the smartest lady I know."

Ashleigh pushed the salad around on her plate, considering the option of a cross-country romance. "I don't know how it would work."

"You visit there. Kellan comes here. Weekends, school breaks. We get plenty of them. It's not impossible. People do it."

"I guess," she said, idly wondering what Kellan would make of the idea. "Think about it, though." She watched Shauna's face to assess her reaction. "Imagine you only saw Mike on weekends and holidays. Seems crazy."

"It took me forever to find Mike. I'm talking years of dating guys who were jerks, or not ready to commit, who were intimidated by a woman who is smart and has confidence." Shauna half frowned. "Mike is none of those things. He gets me. He has from day one. Let me tell you, if I had met him five years ago on vacation in DR or Grenada or anywhere else, and that's where he lived, you bet your butt I'd have figured out a way to make long-distance work."

"You guys are getting married in less than two weeks. Maybe comparing to you two is a bad example."

"Maybe. Maybe not. I can tell by the look on your face and the way you sound that this is more than some passing thing. You like Kellan. A lot. Not for nothing, but isn't that how relationships start?" Shauna's question was clearly rhetorical as she continued talking. "You don't have to say anything right now, but you should think about it. If all this"—she waved over Ashleigh's body—"is because of whatever you have with Kellan, I think you should at least consider it. And talk to Kellan. Life is short. Figure something out."

She sat all the way back in her chair, letting the weight of Shauna's words sink in even as she wondered how or if she would broach the idea with Kellan. In spite of their talk in the park, she feared that saying something might ruin the perfect vibe they had going. Perhaps part of the allure was the transient nature of their union. She swallowed back the thought, knowing with absolute clarity that even if that had been true at some point, her heart was in it for real by now. And she had every reason to believe Kellan's was too.

"Now." Shauna broke her train of thought. "What are you wearing to the wedding? Please tell me it's something skimpy and sexy that Kellan's going to rip off you the second she gets the chance."

CHAPTER NINETEEN

O h my God. Right there. Just like that."
Kellan listened to Ashleigh's smooth breathy voice and watched as she writhed on top of her. She could feel the subtle stirring of her own orgasm starting to build and knew she only had a few more seconds before she gave in completely. She gripped Ashleigh's hips tight as she thrust inside. Ashleigh answered with a soft moan, a sound she recognized as approval. Ashleigh was on top of her, straddling her, riding her. The image alone was almost enough to make her come. But the way she moved, the little noises of pleasure, the overt demands to be taken harder and faster contrasting with the shy way she asked for what she wanted...it sent her over the top. Every. Single. Time.

As if she was tuned in to the same frequency, Ashleigh whispered, "Are you almost there?"

Kellan was holding back with every ounce of restraint, but she managed a nod in response.

Ashleigh rested her weight on her torso, and with the slight movement Kellan felt the strap-on slide infinitely deeper. Ashleigh sat back up and moved steadily on top, the base pressed up against Kellan, the friction driving her crazy in the best way. She touched Ashleigh's clit and started to massage it gently.

"Christ," Ashleigh breathed out. "Don't stop. Do not stop," she ordered as Kellan pounded into her while making small circles with the pad of her thumb. Ashleigh closed her eyes and let her mouth drop open. Kellan was in awe of the way Ashleigh looked and sounded and moved when they were together. Even though it was cliché, she couldn't get over how breathtaking it was when Ashleigh let herself go completely. Despite her best efforts, Kellan felt it in her heart when she let the rhythm of her own body take over so they could climax together. Looking absolutely sated, Ashleigh settled in alongside, facing her. She drifted her hand across Ashleigh's gorgeous curves, the softness of her skin immediately heightening the aftershocks still coursing through her body. Leaning in for a kiss, she felt Ashleigh caress her face and smile against her mouth.

"That was freaking amazing," Ashleigh said. "I love that you can come from that." She looked slightly bashful as she spoke.

"You sound surprised."

"I am, I guess." Ashleigh pulled her in for another kiss and her center throbbed when their tongues touched briefly. "I'm not complaining. I suppose I just don't understand how."

She smiled, thinking about their connection moments ago, and wondered how to describe what she was feeling without scaring Ashleigh away. "It's pretty simple, I think." She decided to go with pure honesty. "For one, there's a gorgeous woman on top of me. Your body is beautiful. And Ash"—she trailed her hand lightly over Ashleigh's skin, delighting in the feel of her smooth skin as she spoke—"the way you move." She rolled onto her back, remembering everything in detail. "By now I can tell when you're going to come. That kind of does it for me," she admitted.

Ashleigh snuggled closer, and Kellan lifted her arm so Ashleigh could rest her head on her chest. She was getting used to this. Too used to it, maybe. She blocked it out and concentrated instead on Ashleigh against her, quietly drawing designs on her stomach with the tip of one finger.

"Are you okay?" she asked, dropping a kiss on Ashleigh's forehead.

Ashleigh tilted her head to make eye contact. "Are you kidding me?" she asked, obviously being rhetorical. "I am so much more than okay right now." Ashleigh kissed her bare chest. "I do worry you've ruined me for good, though."

"Wha…?" She answered playfully sensing the spirit in Ashleigh's tone. "What does that mean?"

"This," Ashleigh said. "All of this." Ashleigh waved between their bodies. "Sex has never been this good. And now you're going to leave at the end of summer. And I'm doomed." She hung her head, likely for dramatic effect. It touched her anyway.

"You'll find someone else," she said, thankful her voice didn't crack and give away what she was really feeling. "You really are special. I wish you could see what I see." She was venturing into dangerous territory but was unable to pull back. "You're kind and sweet. So smart. Seeing New York, being with you. This summer has been the best of my life." She felt herself choking up but knew she had to be brave. "The second you put yourself on the market, they'll be lining up at your door."

"My parents' door, don't you mean?"

"Like it matters one iota where you live." Even though she knew Ashleigh was being silly, she wasn't ready to let go of the moment. "The fact you live with your mom and dad didn't slow me down for one second. I was interested from the first time I met you."

"See, then you do that." Ashleigh pouted.

"Do what?"

"You make me all mushy."

"Mushy?"

"You know what I mean." Ashleigh sat halfway up and looked at her. She bit her bottom lip and paused like she was going to drop something serious. But then it seemed as though she thought better of it as she shook her head a little. "Even if I do. Meet someone, that is." Her shrug was somehow suggestive and impish. "What if they can't do all this? The way you do? The way I like it."

She swallowed hard, knowing she couldn't really be annoyed that Ashleigh was considering other people. At least she'd buried that truth in a compliment of sorts. Still, the reality of their situation crept under her skin. Throwing back the covers, she reached for her shirt and boxers from the floor.

"Ash, sex is about communication. Not moves, or strap-ons, or even the real thing, for that matter." She pulled her shirt over her head and sat on the side of the bed as she slipped into her boxers.

"I hate that you're getting dressed."

"You know I'm not going to hang out naked, particularly when we're talking about your future dating prospects."

"Oh my God. Are you mad?"

Mad wasn't the right word, but she'd heard the tension in her tone, and clearly Ashleigh had picked up on it too. She rubbed the tops of her knees, hoping to channel some inner calm and say the right thing. "Just...find someone who's good to you and don't be afraid to tell them what you want." She leaned back, intending to place a soft kiss on Ashleigh's lips in a sign of support, however difficult it was.

Ashleigh didn't let her go. She held her face and kissed her over and over before she stopped to talk. With their foreheads touching she said, "Do you get that I've never been like this with anyone?"

"I know."

"No, I don't think you do." Ashleigh's hand brushed over her face, as though she was memorizing it with her fingertips. "There is something about you. About us. I can't really put it into words. Being with you is amazing. I tell you, God, everything." She stared right at her and took her time before she said, "I trust you. In a way I haven't trusted anyone."

Kellan wanted to believe her words were true, but she had some internal doubt at the statement. To her credit, Ashleigh read her expression without fail. "Reagan was different."

"How is that possible?" She couldn't keep herself from asking.

"We've been platonic for so long now, it's hard to remember what it was like before. But even then, it never seemed as easy as this." Ashleigh studied her with intensity. "Maybe it's your eyes. They're unbelievable."

Kellan looked down, embarrassed that she could feel herself blush.

"Look at me. Please?" Ashleigh asked. Kellan obliged the request and they stared at each other for a long second. "It was the first thing I noticed about you. The shade of green is almost indescribable. Kind of mossy, almost gray sometimes."

"My dad's are the same."

"For real?"

Kellan nodded.

"Can I see a picture?"

Kellan reached for her phone from the end table and pulled up a pic with her dad. She handed the phone to Ashleigh.

"Wow." Ashleigh looked back and forth from the image, obviously assessing her. "You do look alike. The eyes are the same for sure." She placed the phone back in its spot. "Can I say something without you freaking out?"

It was a loaded question but she was dying to hear. "Of course."

"The thing about you, about your eyes, specifically." Ashleigh took her time, as though she was choosing each word with care, and she could feel her heartbeat going insane with anticipation. "It's not just the color. Or your amazing long eyelashes. There's something so much more. It's hard to explain." Ashleigh broke eye contact and caressed her forearms. In the silence, she didn't know if she was supposed to respond or if Ashleigh was still trying to put her thoughts together.

"Ash—"

Ashleigh cut her off with the subtle shake of her head. "Just give me a minute," she said. She tipped her head back as if allowing herself permission to emote. "It's just that I felt immediately comfortable with you." Ashleigh looked right at her, touching her face and bringing it close to hers. "It was like I could see in your eyes that you wouldn't hurt me."

"I would never—"

"I know. I could tell. Right from our first coffee together at the Beanery. I felt, I don't know, safe. I know that sounds corny. Maybe even a little crazy." A nervous laugh accompanied the words and she broke eye contact but continued to talk despite any nerves she might be feeling. "So tell me, how am I supposed to find that with someone else on some dating app?"

It should have made her happy to hear Ashleigh profess the depth of her feelings, however roundabout the admission. But inside, she felt something else. Something foreign, and she didn't know how to make sense of it.

"So don't," she said without filtering.

"Don't...what? Date?" Ashleigh asked. "You literally just told me to find someone nice."

"Forget what I said." She pulled her shirt off and slipped back under the covers. "I'm an idiot."

"No, you're not." Ashleigh moved close as she lay down next to her.

"I think..." Kellan rolled so she was on top. She held Ashleigh's arms over her head, taunting her with a string of lingering kisses across her chest and neck. "I think you should hold out for me."

"You do?"

"I do." She continued to kiss her everywhere, letting go of her arms so she could use her hands. She cupped Ashleigh's breast tenderly, dancing her tongue across the nipple.

Ashleigh spread her legs wide in response and Kellan reached down, unable to stifle the gasp at feeling how wet she was already. Ashleigh must've felt her shudder, because she held her face with both hands as she said, "You do that to me. Only you."

Kellan kissed her hard, feeling herself throb with desire. She moved against Ashleigh's center, knowing she'd be able to come from the slightest contact. "I want you in my mouth," she whispered, before starting her descent.

But instead of encouraging her, Ashleigh held her in place. "Okay. But why do you get to have all the fun?"

She paused, confused, but Ashleigh just smiled. "Lie on your back," she said.

Kellan grinned as she lay back, flat on the mattress. She watched in excited awe as Ashleigh turned and got into position on top of her. Her bottom was soft and gorgeous as she brought her close to her face, and she felt Ashleigh's tongue on her at exactly the same time she tasted her sweetness. Their bodies touched everywhere, moving together perfectly. It had been ages since she'd done this with anyone, and she'd forgotten how good it felt. Almost as the thought hit her brain, she altered it on the spot.

It was Ashleigh.

Even normal, run of the mill activities were heightened when she was with Ashleigh. Walks were fun and exciting, dinner was an event, their trek across the city was filled with laughs and memories. Fuck, even her coffee tasted better when they were together.

She let go of the internal tension she'd been subconsciously holding for weeks, simultaneously giving in to her orgasm on the spot. Her heart pounded out of control and crashed against her chest, knowing in that precise, bizarre moment what it all meant.

Kellan opened her eyes to Ashleigh playing on her phone and cuddling Blue next to her on top of the covers. "I can't believe I fell asleep."

Ashleigh leaned down and kissed her temple. "Naked too." She raised her eyebrows, seemingly giving herself credit for the anomaly. "What are you doing to me?" She rubbed her eyes. "Passing out? And without clothes. This is a first."

"Relax, killer. You were only out for twenty minutes or so."

Kellan searched through the covers for her clothes. "Did you sleep?"

"Nope. I hung out with this guy." Ashleigh scratched between Blue's ears, and his purr was so loud they both laughed.

"He does love you." She reached over to touch him, but her hand brushed over Ashleigh's instead.

Ashleigh smiled at the contact and laced their fingers together. "I love him too."

Her voice was so soft and sincere, and she hated herself for being jealous of the cat. "I think he's going to miss you."

"Is that true, Blue? You gonna miss me?"

Out of nowhere, Blue leaped up and hopped off the bed, and Ashleigh laughed. "Guess not."

"Are you kidding?" she said. "He's so distraught he can't even talk about it." Kellan scooted herself upright and found her shirt and shorts. She hugged her knees close and thought for a second. "You know, I've been thinking."

"Oh yeah?" Ashleigh turned to her and her eyes were so full of contentment it made her warm all over. "What about?"

"What if..." She reached forward and hooked a strand of hair behind Ashleigh's ear. Ashleigh kissed her hand in thanks. "What if I come back next summer. We'll send Aunt Holly off to a new locale. You and Blue can get your fix in. And you and I can see all the things we don't get to this summer." Ashleigh was clearly listening, but in the dim light she couldn't read her expression and she panicked. "This will also help with the dating dilemma you mentioned earlier."

"I'm supposed to wait a whole year?"

A nervous laugh escaped her. "No. No. That's not what I meant." Fuck, she was making a mess of this. She took a deep breath and spoke from the heart. "Come visit me. In Colorado. I'll teach you to ski, like your grandmother wants."

"Are you serious?"

It was the closest they'd come to talking about the future, and while it wasn't a subject she'd planned on broaching, she wasn't ready to say good-bye either. "I've been thinking about it a lot, honestly. I mean...what if I stayed? Not forever, obviously." She heard her voice shake and she got up just to alleviate some of her anxiety.

She walked into the kitchen and leaned across the island. "I don't want to scare you. Or pressure you." She picked at her fingers nervously. "I just haven't felt this way...about anyone...in a long time." Or ever. One step at a time, she reminded herself. "If I stayed for a bit, we could see where this goes." Her throat was cotton, her tongue dry as the Sahara. She looked up to check Ashleigh's reaction.

"Kellan." Ashleigh tossed the covers aside, and Kellan caught a glimpse of her light pink panties. Ashleigh bent down and picked up an old Army tee that was enormous on her small frame as she sauntered over. Ashleigh touched her cheek gently. "I would love it if you stayed."

She was thrilled at the response, and she hugged Ashleigh tight before lifting her onto the island to kiss her. "I know you'll be busy with school, but there's this friend I've been meaning to look up anyway."

"It will be nice to have you around. The beginning of the school year is hectic, but we'll figure it out. Will you stay here? With your aunt?"

"I don't know. I guess I hadn't thought that far." She chuckled in relief and reached over to welcome Blue, who had jumped up to celebrate with them. "Hear that, Blueberry, you may be stuck with me a while longer."

Ashleigh reached over to give him some love. "That means me too," she said before giving her attention back to Kellan. "What about your friend?"

"What about her?"

"I meant, would you crash with her?"

"Um, no." At this point her only hope was to tap into the connection she and Dara once had, but they were light years away from that kind of milestone. "Most definitely not."

Kellan leaned in to kiss her, but Ashleigh pulled back. "Hold on. Who is this friend? An ex?"

"No. Nothing like that." Even though it wasn't a lie, this seemed like the wrong time to break down the details.

"Who is it?"

"Her name is Dara. We were friends in the Army. I've been meaning to reach out to her, but it just so happens I'd rather spend every waking moment with you." Technically the truth, but she hoped it came off as cute.

"What am I going to do with you?" Ashleigh pulled her in close, kissing her face repeatedly before she found her lips.

"Honestly, whatever you want."

The kiss that followed was deep and soft, and they were both a little breathless when it ended.

"We should eat something," Ashleigh said. "Since we lounged the afternoon away."

"Are you upset we didn't do anything exciting today?"

"For the record, I completely disagree." Ashleigh kissed her lightly and slipped under her arms, hopping off the counter.

"I never asked how things went with Shauna at brunch. Are you two all made up?"

"Yep. We good." She opened the pantry cabinet to assess its contents. "Speaking of Shauna…" She closed the cupboard. "Her wedding is a week and a half away."

"I know. Is she excited?"

"She's ready. You're still going to come with me, right?" Ashleigh shuffled back and forth, like she was nervous. "I know I asked you a while back, and I should have brought it up again before now."

"Of course I'm coming with you. If I remember correctly"—she tapped her chin in jest—"there was a promise I'd even get lucky."

Ashleigh rolled her eyes but clearly enjoyed the banter. "I was wondering how you'd feel about going out a day or two early. The vineyards are supposed to be beautiful. I've been out there before, but mostly to the Hamptons. I've never been to the wine country. I'd love to see it with you. The place where Shauna's getting married looks amazing, and I could book a few extra days."

"That sounds awesome."

"Great. I'll make us a reservation later. Now, what are we going to eat?" She sauntered to the fridge and bent over to look in. Kellan took one look at her ass on display covered by the scant pink fabric and came up behind her.

"I have no food," she whispered as she held Ashleigh's hips and pressed against her bottom.

"I see that." Ashleigh leaned all the way back, giving her access to explore her body. She reached behind her and pulled Kellan into a searing kiss. "Why don't you order us some Thai and meet me in the shower." Ashleigh held on to her hand as she started backing away.

"Thai does not take that long to get here."

Ashleigh took her shirt off and dropped it to the floor. Her eyes held devious invitation. "I guess we better be fast then."

Chapter Twenty

New York in August was a hot, humid mess.

Ashleigh swore it was a heat wave that would pass, but four days of ninety-plus temps, and Kellan was ready to send up a white flag to Mother Nature. The last few trips to Manhattan were soupy at best, leaving them vying for the shower the second they made it back to her apartment. Today they'd opted to stay local, chilling in bed until midday before a leisurely walk in the park. Kellan won the coin toss and was sitting on the sofa freshly showered and cooling off when Aunt Holly's video call came through.

"Aunt Holly. So good to see your face. How's…London?"

Kellan furrowed her brow, all but admitting she forgot which city her aunt was currently residing in. Despite frequent communication about Blue, the apartment, and Aunt Holly's travels, in the moment she drew a blank.

"I'm actually in Dublin right now."

"Damn. I was close."

"I think the people of Ireland might disagree with that statement."

Kellan held one finger up. "Good point." They laughed together and Kellan adjusted the angle of her phone, so Aunt Holly could see her fur baby perched on the back of the couch not far from her head. "Hey, Blue, you see Mommy?"

"Hi, baby Blue. I miss you so much," Aunt Holly crooned and pouted at the same time. Blue licked his paw and rubbed his face with it.

"He misses you, I swear."

"I'm sure." She shrugged. "You're probably spoiling him rotten."

"Like you don't."

Aunt Holly winked in response. "He's so perfect. It's hard not to."

"Agreed. He's a good little guy." She reached back and was happy when Blue let her pet him. "Did you get my message the other day? About Blue and going away? I don't want to do anything you're not comfortable with."

A day earlier she had emailed Aunt Holly, explaining about Long Island. It would mean leaving Blue home from Friday to Sunday morning, and while she was confident Olivia across the hall would be willing to pick up the slack, she didn't want to do anything without her aunt's express permission.

"Oh, honey, it's all worked out already." She gave a dismissive wave. "I talked to Olivia yesterday. She's crazy for Blue, and let me tell you, the feeling is mutual. You think we spoil him? He's probably going to eat nothing but treats for two days."

"Are you sure, Aunt Hol?"

"Of course. Tell you the truth, Olivia was my backup plan for the entire summer. But when your mom offered your services, I jumped on it." In the background Kellan heard the shower water shut off and knew it meant Ashleigh would emerge soon. "So, tell me, how's the summer going?"

"It's good."

"You seeing some of New York?"

"Yeah. For sure."

Ashleigh tiptoed past in a towel, putting a finger over her lips, signaling she realized Kellan was on a call.

"So your mom says you have some hot girlfriend who's showing you all around."

Out of camera range, Ashleigh obviously overheard and did a little dance that included a cheer for herself.

"She tells you everything, huh?"

"We're sisters, so yeah."

Kellan tried hard to keep her focus on the camera and not naked Ashleigh in the background. Ashleigh seemed intent on torturing her and gave her butt a wiggle, then turned around and flashed her. Kellan stifled a giggle at her antics. Aunt Holly's lips were still moving, but she hadn't heard a word.

"Sorry, what was that? You froze for a second," she lied.

"Willow said this is some woman from the Army you knew. That you had a big mysterious falling out with? Is that right?"

"No, no, no." Leave it to her flaky aunt to get the details wrong. "This is somebody different."

"Ooh, a summer fling. That sounds exciting. It almost makes me miss dating," she said offhandedly. "Anyway, what's going on with the Army woman? Your mother seemed to think she was pretty important. She even went so far as to say she thought that might be the reason you were so eager to come to Brooklyn. I told her it was to avoid her hovering over you." She was cracking herself up overseas, but Kellan only registered Ashleigh hearing every word loud and clear across the room.

"Uh, nothing is going on with Dara. I haven't gotten in touch with her yet."

"Kellan! What are you waiting for? I'll be back in a few weeks. I'm not kicking you out. Obviously. You're welcome to stay as long as you want. But your mom seemed to think this Dara person was pretty special. I'm sure you'd like some time to really reconnect and not feel rushed. Life is scary, believe me, I know. Take the risk."

Aunt Holly and her mother were two peas in a pod, always seizing the day and living in the moment. Little did they know, she was actually following their mantra. Only with Ashleigh.

"Yeah. It's on my list. Promise."

"Okay. Well, don't wait too long."

She nodded but a few feet away she saw Ashleigh's face fall.

"Oh, and Kellan, don't worry about giving Olivia a key. She's already got one. Have a fantastic time at your wedding."

"Thanks, Aunt Holly." She mustered a smile. "I'll talk to you soon."

"Okay, kiddo. Give my boy beaucoup kisses for me."

"I will."

"Bye, honey."

She waved good-bye and ended the call with a click. When she stood up from the couch, she saw Ashleigh stuffing her clothes into her overnight bag with attitude.

"Hey, hey, hey." Kellan came up behind her and looped her arms around her waist, but Ashleigh pushed her away. "I can explain those comments."

"You mean how there's this super-special person in your life that your whole family knows you came to New York to reconnect with?" Ashleigh took a step away and faced her. "Are we going to talk about how we share just about everything, but I'm in the dark here?" She zipped her bag angrily. "No thanks."

"Sit down. Calm down."

"No." She hooked her bag over her shoulder. "I think I should go."

"Ash, please?" She reached for her hands, wanting so desperately to touch her. "Please don't run away from me. It's not what you think. Aunt Holly is confused."

"Is she, though? From the sound of it, your mom also thinks Dara is the greatest thing since sliced bread. You must have said something that made them think she's so important to you."

"She is." She looked up at the ceiling fan and took a deep breath. She touched Ashleigh's hips with her fingertips. "Come sit with me?"

Ashleigh put her bag down and took her hand, her defenses seeming to drop. "I will if you talk to me. Tell me what this woman is to you. Because right now, I'm feeling pretty out of the loop." Kellan sat on the couch and rubbed the tops of her knees, trying to figure out exactly how to start. Ashleigh reached over and held her hand. "It's okay. Just be honest with me."

"I haven't lied to you. I swear," she started. "I met Dara when I was young. Maybe twenty, I guess." She calculated the years in her head. "The Army was an interesting place. Great people. Some real jerks. I guess a mirror of the world, really. Our units were stationed in tandem for a long time. Even though she's a bit older than I am, we clicked." She shrugged. "I don't really know how to describe it." Kellan racked her brain trying to come up with good examples, but nothing popped in her head. She wanted Ashleigh to understand their connection. She needed her to. Instead of continuing to overthink it, she went from the gut and hoped it made sense. "Dara and I had the same mindset. The same humor. Being away from home for so long can be lonely. I didn't feel alone when she was around. We talked about everything. Our lives, our families, our dreams. I don't know how to describe it better than that."

"But it wasn't romantic?"

"It wasn't. I promise."

"Was it like having a sister?"

"Not having a sister, I guess I can't honestly say. But it did feel different than a family connection. Dara felt like the other half of me, if that makes any sense."

Ashleigh nodded, seeming to take it all in. "So what happened that you two stopped talking?"

How the fuck was she going to explain this without giving all the particulars? She chewed her lip, searching for the most honest account. "Let's see. Dara's husband is an asshole. Her ex-husband, I should say." That was one hundred percent true. *Stick to facts*, she reminded herself as she continued. "I had a detail in the States. Twelve years ago. I was in DC, and we got some leave time. I drove up here to see her."

"And?"

"We had a nice visit at first. She had a little girl who was about a year old at the time. But she and her husband were having problems. That much was obvious."

"Because of you?"

"No. I mean, not really. Although my being there didn't help any. Ronnie never liked me. He was always threatened by the closeness Dara and I had, even though there was no reason to be."

"Are you sure?"

"Please don't be like that, Ash."

"I'm sorry. I'm sorry." Ashleigh held a hand to her forehead and seemed legitimately stressed. "It's just, what if it wasn't romantic for you, but it was for her? I see the way women look at you. Half the time I can't even believe you're with me. And you just said she's divorced now. And your whole family is rooting for her."

Kellan couldn't help but smile despite the seriousness of the conversation. "My family doesn't even know her. And trust me, they're going to love you." Kellan already knew she did, and if the timing hadn't been so awkward, she would have said it right then and there.

"So what happened? With you and Dara and the husband."

"It was a mess." She rubbed her face, reliving the stress from the weekend over a decade ago. "They were in a bad place. Ronnie pulled me aside. He basically asked me to leave. Like, walk out of Dara's life. He even offered me money."

"What do you mean?"

"He gave me some nonsense that as long as I was around, he would never live up to Dara's expectations. He wanted to make their family work. They'd tried for a very long time to have a baby. That had finally come to fruition. He wrote me a fat check to go away."

"What?"

"I didn't take it. Obviously. But I thought, here's a guy who is so desperate he's willing to pay me to be gone. And it was a lot of cash. So much that I wondered if Dara knew about it and if she felt the same. I don't know. None of it made sense."

"And you haven't talked to her since then?"

"She reached out to me a few times. Early on. I avoided her. I know it sounds crazy. I wanted whatever was best for her. What if she was too afraid to tell me to go? I wanted to spare her that pain. And even though none of us understood it, she was head over heels for Ronnie. She had to want her family to work. I guess there was a part of me that wondered if Ronnie was right. That I was in the way. I realize it's stupid now." Talking about it reopened the wound, and she realized that over the years, she'd even avoided thinking about their rift, as kind of a self-defense. "My unit went back overseas, making it impossible to see her anyway. I still missed talking on the phone, Skyping, emails, all of it. I learned to cope."

"Did you come to Brooklyn to find her?"

"I was coming anyway, once my mom asked me to pitch in. But yeah, it factored into my decision for sure." There was no denying it. And she didn't want to lie to Ashleigh, even if she wasn't giving every last detail. Deep down she knew there were parts of the story that simply weren't hers to tell. So she chose to be honest by revealing the truth of what she felt. "I miss her. And if she misses me even half as much, with so much time having passed, I thought we could maybe give our friendship another chance."

"And now she's divorced. I bet that helps." Ashleigh leaned close and rested a hand on her thigh.

"I didn't even know that until Liam told me a few weeks ago."

"Why haven't you called her?"

She reached down and held Ashleigh's hand. "It's a combination of things, really." She touched Ashleigh's smooth pink nail polish. "I guess part of me is scared. But also, as important as Dara is to me, I didn't want to lose any time with you."

"Do you want to stay in Brooklyn because of her?"

Kellan laughed—she couldn't help herself. She looked right at Ashleigh, hoping her courage would hold up. "I'm staying for you. I love you. I know it hasn't been long, but I never felt this way before. Never. Not with anyone. So I'm sorry if I'm saying it too soon, or not being chill about it, but this never happened to me before—"

"Shut up." Ashleigh held her face.

"It's just—"

"Stop talking."

"I'm sorry."

"Stop apologizing and kiss me already."

Kellan leaned forward and met her lips, trying to put every ounce of what she was feeling into the small action.

"I love you too, you know."

"You do?" Kellan grinned against her mouth.

"You know it. You can't even pretend." Ashleigh scrunched her face in a fake grimace.

"I hoped. I didn't know."

"Well, now you do."

Kellan leaned in again, but this kiss lingered with the heat and emotion between them. Ashleigh was the first to pull away. She pressed their foreheads together, and Kellan felt her hand caressing the side of her face.

"God, I was so worried I was the only one feeling it," Ashleigh said, as she wiped a tear. "Thank you for saying it first. I love you, Kellan." She kissed her again. "But I was so scared you didn't feel the same way. And it's so soon and it's crazy. People are going to think we're nuts." She laughed as she smeared another tear away. "I don't even care."

"So what do we do now?"

"Now…" Ashleigh peppered her face with baby kisses as she spoke. "I go home and put in some face time with my family. You should come. They'd love to see you. Plus they'll feed us." Ashleigh looked her right in the eye. "We'll make the rounds. Say hi to Liam."

"I like this plan."

"In a few days, we'll head out east for Shauna and Mike's wedding." She scrunched her shoulders up, as if reveling in the thought. "And our own romantic getaway."

"I can't wait." It was the truth. Even though they hadn't spent a night apart in weeks, something about a weekend away together felt like validation of their status.

"But you're not off the hook." Ashleigh dotted a kiss on her nose. "Once we get back from Long Island, you're going to get in touch with Dara and get your friendship back on track. You can be scared all you want. I'm here to help you any way I can."

Kellan kissed her with everything she had, hoping that Ashleigh would feel it as deeply as she felt it. "Did I tell you how much I love you?" she asked, pulling away slightly.

"You did. But you can keep saying it. It honestly doesn't get old." Ashleigh stood up and pulled Kellan with her. "Come on. Let's go see Bill and Peg McAllister. We can continue this lovefest later."

"You bet we can."

Chapter Twenty-one

"What's in the bag, bro?"

Kellan hoisted her duffel onto a stool and leaned up against the bar, greeting Liam with a standard fist bump. "Clothes for the weekend. Shauna's wedding is tomorrow. Ashleigh and I are planning to make a weekend of it."

"Nice." Liam continued his bar chores. "I know it's early, but do you want a drink or anything? Juice, iced tea? I actually just made a fresh pot of coffee."

"Nah, I'm good." She looked around the empty bar. "I'm actually surprised you're open this early."

"Technically, I'm not." He laughed. "There's always something that needs doing here. Since I live right upstairs, I spend most of my waking hours here. Mornings included."

"How is it going? You seem to keep a crowd most days."

Liam nodded, his pride in his business evident. "It's going great. And you know, I know I talked about doing this, as like a dream of mine, but I wasn't sure it would work or that I would like it."

"But you do?"

"Dude, I freaking love it. It's ten o'clock in the morning, and I'm down here by choice. How many people get to say that about their jobs?" He fiddled with a tap. "Anyway, I'm sure you didn't come in here to hear me wax on about the bar business. What gives?"

It was amazing how well he could read her. "So, you know that things with Ashleigh are going pretty good."

"I gathered. A weekend away and everything. That's awesome."

Kellan smoothed the wooden lip of the bar to keep grounded. "I'm thinking of staying here for a bit. Like, even after my aunt gets back."

"No way. It's that serious?"

"It's that serious." She looked up at him, knowing it was absolutely true.

"Holy shit." Liam's smile spread from ear to ear. "Wait. Is she…I mean, does she feel the same?"

Kellan nodded. "Think so."

"This is fucking great." He touched his fingers to his temples, clearly mind-blown, but in a good way. He scooted around the bar, waving her toward him. "Get the fuck over here and hug me already," he ordered.

"You got it, Sarge," she said. His excited energy was contagious and she knew she was beaming as he hugged her tight.

"This is the greatest news. So this means you're going to stay in New York?" he asked.

"For a little while. Until we see where this goes and figure it all out." Kellan released from his embrace and hopped up on a stool. "That's sort of why I'm here. I guess I was wondering if you had any shifts open. Bartending, waiting tables. Fuck, I'll even clean your bathrooms. I have the pension check, but some extra cash would be key. If not, no big deal, I'll find something."

"Dude, I have so much work here. Andy, my bar back, is going off to grad school in a few weeks. One of the other guys just gave notice because he's getting ready to study for the Series 7, so he can be a stockbroker. Paul calls out every time he meets a new guy. Trust me, I have slots to fill."

"Are you sure? I don't want to put you on the spot. I just figured it was worth asking."

"No. It's done. You tell me when you're ready, and I'll put you on the schedule."

"Thanks, Liam."

"What are you doing about housing?"

"I don't know." She let out a low laugh. "Sort of tackling one thing at a time."

"Well, it so happens I have the solution for that too."

Kellan raised her eyebrows, truly at a loss over where this might be headed.

"Turns out, I live upstairs by myself, in a two-bedroom apartment."

"No, Liam, I couldn't do that to you." She was appreciative of the gesture but waved him off just the same.

"Kell, rent around here is fucking astronomical. I literally have a spare bedroom. Bunk with me until you and Ashleigh figure your stuff out and see where it goes."

"I mean, if you're sure?" She was overwhelmed with gratitude, but she truly didn't want to overstep the boundaries.

"Dude, would you do the same for me if the situation was reversed?"

"In a heartbeat." The answer was so natural, the words seemed to come out on their own.

"Settled, then." He zipped back around the bar. "I don't know exactly what your plans are for the rest of the morning..." He let his sentence linger, and she knew he was waiting for her to fill in the blanks.

"I was headed up to Ashleigh's." She gestured in the general direction with her chin. "She's borrowing her parents' car so we can drive out to the vineyards in Long Island. To the North Fork, whatever that means." She smiled, pretty sure she knew where this was going.

"Excellent. Can we please arrange for her to meet you here? Cause I'm going to need to hug her ASAP."

"Already on it," Kellan said as she thumbed out the message to Ashleigh.

❖

"Do you get stressed about school starting up?" Kellan asked.

After reaching Riverhead at one, they spent the afternoon hand in hand, window-shopping antique stores in the quaint town before checking in to the boutique hotel on the grounds of the winery where tomorrow's nuptials would take place. Not that Kellan had any real expectations, but the venue was sheer beauty, the perfect mix of classic chic and rustic elegance, and she was thrilled to be outside exploring as the day faded into evening.

"God, no. In case you hadn't figured it out by now, I'm a huge nerd."

Kellan squeezed her hand. "Kinda dig that about you."

"You may not feel that way in a month. When I talk nonstop about curriculum and math club and class projects. Confession time," she whispered. "I love school." Ashleigh hooked her free hand through the crook of her elbow and pulled their bodies closer. "Now you," she said.

"Now me, what?" Kellan asked.

"That's my big secret. What's yours?"

"Ash." Kellan dropped her voice a register, matching the serious tone as she brought her lips close to Ashleigh's ear. "I don't want to hurt your feelings, but that's not a secret."

"I hate you." Ashleigh pursed her lips, but the smile underneath came through.

"Uh-uh. I don't think you do," she teased. She stopped walking and kissed Ashleigh sweetly. "I think you love me." She held Ashleigh's face in her hands and dotted soft kisses everywhere. "Which is perfect. Because I am so in love with you." She found Ashleigh's beautiful full lips and kissed her with everything she had. It was only when she pulled away that she noticed the sky behind them.

"Turn around," Kellan said as she took in the layers of pink, orange, lavender, and azure contrasting with the acres of green grapevines stretched out before them. "It reminds me of the night we went to Fire Island."

"What a night." Ashleigh pointed to an ornate gazebo a few yards in the distance. "Let's stop for a minute."

"Sure."

Kellan guided them up the worn wooden stairs and led them to the far edge of the pavilion where they could truly enjoy the view. She held Ashleigh from behind, as they silently watched the sky change color. Kellan was high on life, intoxicated by fresh air, the scent of summer, the fragrance of Ashleigh's skin, her hair, her perfume, the very essence she'd grown so accustomed to in such a short time.

"Look at those amazing colors." Ashleigh caressed Kellan's hands leaning the weight of her body against her torso.

"Safe to say you're more sunset than sunrise?"

"You know, I don't know," Ashleigh answered, seeming to think about it on the spot. "Sunrise is beautiful. But there's something romantic about a summer sunset." She shrugged. "Although I wonder if I only think that now, because of you." Ashleigh shifted position until their gazes met. "Can I ask you a question?"

"Always."

"Best part of the summer?"

"This, of course." She hugged Ashleigh tighter.

"I mean if you had to pick one day above all the others. What would it be?"

"Fire Island."

"For real?"

"Everything about that day was perfect. Start to finish." She felt herself almost choke up at the memory. "Sometimes I still can't believe you came over that night." She kissed Ashleigh's cheek.

"I know." Ashleigh closed her eyes, and Kellan wondered if she was reminiscing. "I was so nervous."

"Me too."

"You were not." Ashleigh swatted her forearm playfully. "You were all big dick energy, full of swagger."

"Guess it's a good thing I came through on that front." She buried her smile in the crook of Ashleigh's neck, delighting in the playfulness of their affectionate moment, so perfectly representative of their blossoming relationship.

"You're so bad." Ashleigh shook her head, but Kellan heard sheer pleasure in her tone.

"I'm just kidding." Kellan felt suddenly serious. "Honestly, the crazy part about all of this—everything—is that I never felt nervous. Or uncomfortable. Or like I need to be anything other than what I am."

"Is that new?"

"I know it sounds dramatic, but it is true. I'm so myself with you. Since right from the very beginning. No pretense, no nothing. I think that's why it all happened so quickly for me. Well, aside from the fact that you're amazing and sweet and smart. And thankfully willing to settle for me."

Ashleigh turned around and faced her. "I'm not settling, though. That's just it. I didn't expect this to happen either. When things went south with Reagan"—she fingered a button at the top of her shirt—"I just assumed I would never find anything like it again. And I didn't, if I'm being honest." Ashleigh made eye contact again. "What we have is light years from that. That's not a dig at Reagan or our marriage. It's more…I didn't know what I wanted, what I really needed, until you. I don't walk on eggshells with you, and I don't worry that you'll judge me or leave me, or keep things from me. I think I'm the best version of me when I'm with you. It's like I didn't even know this person was in here."

When they kissed, Kellan let her touch linger for a second. She was more than turned on by the conversation, the company, the gorgeous woman in her arms. Ashleigh moaned into her mouth, and Kellan knew she was feeling it too, but they were dressed for dinner with reservations at the on-site restaurant in a scant few minutes.

"We should go to dinner," she said, knowing her eyes revealed the real hunger she felt.

"Okay." Ashleigh sucked her lower lip in, a move that was pure seduction. "But don't hold back. I'm going to need you at peak energy later."

"Roger that."

"I didn't even tell you the best part of my conversation with Liam." Kellan speared a julienned carrot from her entrée.

"I thought working down the block from where I live was the best part," Ashleigh countered.

Kellan didn't fight the grin she felt spreading. "This kind of goes hand in hand with that." She took a small bite and chewed quickly, ready to drop the news. "In addition to hooking me up with a job, Liam offered me a place to stay for a while."

"Oh my God, you'll be living with Liam?" Ashleigh put down her fork. "That's like steps from my parents'."

"I know." She paused wanting to assess Ashleigh's reaction. "Too close?"

"Not at all." Ashleigh took a sip of her drink and her eyes danced in the dim restaurant light. "I actually think it's perfect," Ashleigh continued. "I'll get to see you a lot." She smiled. "I'd be lying if I didn't admit to having wondered what we were going to do if you were crashing with your aunt and I was living with my parents."

"Look at you. Only interested in one thing," she teased.

"You know that's not true." Ashleigh froze, her fork hovering over her plate. "You do know that, right?"

She knew it. Without a doubt, she knew it. "Of course I do." She tossed Ashleigh a wink. "I was just playing with you."

"Playing with me, huh?" Ashleigh reached over the small table and took Kellan's hand. She glanced around, perhaps to make sure they didn't have an audience, before she guided Kellan's hand along her thigh under her dress. "If you really want to play with me..." Ashleigh's expression was enough to get her going, but she seemed intent on raising the stakes. She spread wider and Kellan followed the heat emanating from between her legs. "I'm going to be all yours. So soon."

Kellan let her fingers graze over Ashleigh's center, feeling how wet she was already. Her heart pounded at the sensation that was only heightened by the full flush of color in Ashleigh's face. Ashleigh's eyelids hung heavy and her lips parted slightly.

"We should get going." Ashleigh's voice was breathy and hot.

"You think?"

"Yeah." Kellan was hard and throbbing and dying to be inside Ashleigh. "Let me just grab the check," she managed to say.

"While you do that, I'm going to run to the ladies' room."

Kellan couldn't take her eyes off Ashleigh as she walked the length of the restaurant to the restroom. Tonight was going to be off the hook. She scanned the floor for their server, finally making eye contact after he delivered cocktails to a nearby couple. Waiting for the bill, she closed her eyes and rolled her neck, trying to temper the anticipation.

Ashleigh returned in the middle of her stretch, placing a hand softly on her shoulder, and she bent down to kiss her cheek delicately. "These are for you," she said as she dropped something in her lap.

"What's—" Kellan started to examine the item before realizing the teensy bit of black fabric was Ashleigh's panties. Holy fuck. "Um, Ash...did you...are these...are you..." She couldn't even make a sentence.

Ashleigh drew in her bottom lip and nodded. "Ready?"

Hell, yeah, she was ready. Ready. Willing. Able. Jacked. Also smitten, swooning, and head over heels in love...just in case anyone was keeping score.

CHAPTER TWENTY-TWO

Ashleigh took out her phone and snapped a few stills of the arched trellis where Mike and Shauna had exchanged vows less than twenty minutes earlier. While the bride and groom were having official wedding photos taken, she wanted a few keepsakes of her own. She already had an idea for a Christmas gift for Shauna, and the more images she grabbed, the better. Last year, in the midst of her divorce, she'd dreaded this day. Out of the blue she found herself idly wondering if she'd ever get married again. Three months ago, she would have vowed never. But that was before the summer, before Kellan. Now, she wasn't so quick to dodge the idea. She spied Kellan at the bar getting their drinks and snuck a candid in her dapper wedding attire.

"You should let me take a picture of you two together, when Kellan gets back over here. You're a great looking couple."

Reagan's voice next to her took her by surprise more so than the compliment itself. She'd been so caught up in her own weekend she'd actually forgotten all about Reagan and Josh being guests.

"Thanks. That'd be nice," she said. "Where's Josh? I didn't see you guys at the ceremony." Ashleigh half wondered if she'd missed their arrival.

"We just got here. Traffic," she explained with a sigh. "He's over at the bar too." Reagan gestured with her chin in the general vicinity.

"Is it hard not being able to have a drink on a day like today? I know you enjoy a glass of wine."

Reagan touched the belly that was just beginning to pop, and Ashleigh wondered if it was maternal instinct or reflex on display. "I deal." She shrugged and frowned. "Small sacrifice in the long run."

"How are you feeling?" she asked, genuinely curious.

"Mostly okay. Thanks." Her smile revealed she was grateful for the concern. "I'm sorry about your birthday. I should have been more considerate."

"Eh, water under the bridge." Reagan's belated apology was thoughtful and it touched her, but she didn't want to harp on it. Instead, she pointed a manicured finger at the tiny baby bump. "Do you know? Boy or girl? Or are you not telling people?"

"Boy." Reagan smiled and patted her stomach. "I'm going to be outnumbered."

"You'll be fine. Great, actually." She touched Reagan's forearm for reassurance. "You were meant to be a boy mom." She didn't really know what that meant, but it seemed her ex could use some positivity. The look Reagan gave her was full of appreciation, but anything she might have said was cut off by Kellan's arrival.

"Ladies." Kellan sported a beer for herself and two sparkling waters with lime. She handed one off to each of them. "Josh needed to use the men's room," she said by way of explanation.

"He's going to check the score of the Yankees game," Reagan said with a snort. "Nice effort, though. I hope he at least paid for the drinks since he tried to rope you in to his cover-up."

"Open bar." Kellan's smile was conspiratorial, and Ashleigh couldn't help but find it absolutely endearing.

"Can you believe they're in cahoots already?" Reagan turned to Ashleigh, clearly expecting lighthearted support in opposition to their dates' collusion.

Ashleigh shook her head and shrugged dramatically. "We're doomed." She was teasing, of course, and truthfully all she felt was absolute elation at how normal and natural this all felt. The irony of holding hands with her new love as she joked with her pregnant ex-wife about the boundaries of relationships and significant others was kind of a mind bender, but she went with it. Life, always with the surprises.

"What'd I miss?" Josh entered the conversation like a bear, as though he'd been in a rush to make it back to cocktail hour.

"Not the box score, that's for sure." Reagan called him out on the spot, but her tone was all jest and he obviously knew it.

"I'm sorry, babe." Josh kissed her cheek. "They're up three–nothing, if anyone's interested." He cringed in a kind of apology to the small group, and when Ashleigh caught a glimpse of him rubbing Reagan's back, she felt nothing but happiness for both of them.

"Now this is a moment to capture." Shauna was suddenly upon them, her photographer a mere few steps behind. "Hey there, gang," she said, inserting herself between the two couples. She orchestrated them into an impromptu group pose yelling, "Smile!" as the cameraman snapped at will. When he'd finished, Shauna faced them. "How are we all doing here?" she asked.

Ashleigh scanned each of their faces, taking stock of the unlikely foursome's chill vibe. "Great, actually." She took a sip of her drink. "You look beautiful, Shauna. Mike too," she added. "But I'm biased."

The rest of the group chimed in with compliments and well-wishes, and Ashleigh was enjoying the natural flow they all seemed to have together. She was consciously aware of Kellan's hand around her waist or on her back, and she reveled in it, stealing more than one guilty pleasure glance at her handsome face. Finding Kellan's hand, she laced their fingers together and squeezed gently, loving the wordless communication when Kellan returned the gesture and looked deep in her eyes. It wasn't like anyone noticed their PDA—Shauna was holding court with a hilarious story about her warring grandmothers. Ashleigh was only half paying attention, so caught up in her own perfect world at the moment.

"Kellan? Oh my God. Kellan."

Ashleigh's gaze went to the woman whose arrival interrupted her thoughts, then looked at Kellan and registered utter disbelief on her gorgeous face. But before she could ask what was happening, Kellan filled in the blanks.

"Dara?" she said, immediately releasing Ashleigh's hand. Kellan stammered more than she spoke, but it seemed like she was trying to make sense of what was going on.

"What are you doing here?" Dara looked from Kellan to Shauna, waving a finger between them.

"Kellan, you know my cousin Dara?" Shauna picked up the slack.

"Um, yeah. We were in the Army together." Kellan shook her head, clearly blown away by the turn of events. "But I had no idea..."

Dara took a step toward Kellan. "Get in here already." She threw her arms around Kellan's neck and pulled her in for a serious hug. "I missed you too much."

Ashleigh patiently waited for an introduction as she watched Kellan sway Dara in her arms, feeling herself shrink smaller by the second as they all watched the heartfelt reunion in silence. When Dara pulled away, she was wiping tears from her cheeks.

"I'm so sorry to interrupt you all." She sniffled and fanned at her waterworks. "It's just, Kellan and I haven't seen each other in a very long time." She bit her lip and covered her mouth, her emotions on display as she wrestled with the surprise and whatever else she might have been feeling. "Shaun, I can't believe we didn't put this together in all these years."

"I just met Kellan at the beginning of summer." Shauna gestured to Ashleigh, but Kellan spoke up.

"I'm here with my girlfriend," Kellan said. "I'm sorry." Kellan was obviously flustered. "This is Ashleigh."

Ashleigh bristled slightly when Kellan touched her back, but she forced a smile and extended her hand. "Nice to meet you. Shauna's my best friend," she said, completing the explanation of the wild circumstances.

"Ah, gotcha. Gotcha," Dara said with a nod, seeming to file everything away. "Again, I didn't mean to crash your conversation." She rested her hands on top of Kellan's shoulders, and Ashleigh felt a pit in her stomach at the familiarity of the action. Logically, she knew her jealousy wasn't warranted. They were friends. Kellan had even introduced her as her girlfriend. But still she felt as though there was something deeper between them as she watched Dara stare into Kellan's eyes. "I just can't believe it," Ashleigh heard her whisper over and over.

"See, Mommy, I told you. I knew I was right!"

Everyone's attention turned at the squeal of a teen in a fancy dress as she approached the group with a mix of excitement and attitude.

Dara turned to the girl, who was almost her height. "You were right," she said, pulling her close to her side and draping an arm across her shoulders in full motherly pride. "This is Zoey," she said, seeming to almost present the young woman to Kellan.

As stunned as Kellan might have been, it was nothing compared to the shock Ashleigh felt barreling through her. One look at the girl's remarkable green eyes said it all. There could be no disputing it. Ashleigh had looked into those same eyes nearly every day for the past six weeks. She felt her breath catch as she noticed the girl also had the same strong chin and perfect nose as Kellan. Even the smile was a mirror image. Holy Christ. Without a doubt, Zoey was Kellan's. Why or how, she had no idea, but it was undeniable. Her heart stopped as she registered the three of them staring at each other, taking it all in. She prayed for composure as she internally thanked Reagan and Shauna and Josh for pretending to be interested in whatever conversation they materialized just to avoid watching her internal meltdown.

"Do you all…I mean…do you want some time alone?" Ashleigh didn't know what she was even offering. They were in the middle of a wedding reception. All she knew was her world was falling apart and she didn't know what to do.

"No, no, no." Dara put a hand on her forearm, and Ashleigh wondered if she was reading her face. "We should let you two enjoy the party." She turned to Kellan. "Are you in New York now?"

"Yes. Sort of. It's a long story." Ashleigh felt Kellan's eyes on her but couldn't bring herself to meet them. "I'm staying at my aunt's in Dumbo."

"Swanky," Dara said with a tense laugh. "I have to make the rounds with my relatives in from DR." She nodded toward a crowd on the far side of the pavilion. "We live in Greenpoint. Could we get together? For lunch or something?"

"Please?" Zoey chimed in.

"She's got some questions." Dara patted Zoey's shoulders. "And I'd really like to catch up." Dara shifted her attention to her, and her eyes seemed to offer an apology. Ashleigh felt her throat burning, nonetheless. "I'm sorry to have intruded. Really, I am. Come on, Zo. Let's get back to the fam."

Ashleigh was waiting for them to walk away before she said anything, and in truth, she didn't have a clue what was going to come out of her mouth.

"Ash, before you freak out, I can explain."

"Before I freak out," she echoed. Her voice was low and composed, in absolute contrast to what she was feeling inside. "Kellan, I can't…I don't even know what to feel right now." She headed toward the bathroom without another word.

Kellan caught her arm just before she went in. "Please talk to me."

"About what?" She took a few extra steps past the ladies' room, out of the public view, where there was privacy. She wrenched her arm free when Kellan tried for her hand. "Are we going to chat about the child you have? You know, the one I just met?"

"Stop."

"Me, stop? How about you stop. Stop lying to me. Maybe start telling me the truth." The tears were coming, despite her best efforts to keep them inside.

"I didn't lie to you."

"Oh no?" She paced the small area, knowing there was no real escape. "So I didn't just meet the most significant person in your life? A person you obviously had a baby with."

"It's not like that."

"You know what, Kellan? I don't care." It wasn't the truth, but she was angry and hurt and heartbroken. She just wanted it all to be over.

"You do care. And so do I. Just talk to me."

Kellan came up behind her and wrapped her arms around her. Against her will, she felt her blood pressure regulate at the touch, and she hated herself for it. Even now when she was furious, Kellan still managed to worm her way into her heart. How did she do that? She forced herself away from Kellan's embrace, hoping distance would bring her to her senses.

"No. Not now. Not here." Ashleigh shook her head in defiance. "I'm not going to make a scene at my best friend's wedding. This is Shauna's day. Let's not ruin it." She took a deep breath, trying desperately to pull herself together. "I have to use the ladies' room and not look like I am completely falling apart."

She started to walk back inside, but Kellan found her hand and brought her in close. Kellan kissed her softly and whispered, "I love you." Ashleigh let herself feel it, but when she looked up into Kellan's eyes, instead of the solace she so typically found there, she was triggered right back to the incident that had just unfolded.

If this was love, why did it feel like betrayal?

CHAPTER TWENTY-THREE

"You have to talk to me sooner or later."

"I actually don't."

"Come on." Kellan stared out the passenger window as they cruised along the highway back to the city. "Let me at least tell you what's going on."

"Now you want to come clean? It's a little late for that."

"Ashleigh, please. I'm begging."

"Why, though? You had a million chances to talk to me in the last month and a half. This is obviously something you didn't want to share. I'm going to go out on a limb and say that if we hadn't literally bumped into your clone last night, I'd still be in the dark."

The statement itself was true, if fundamentally inaccurate in what it implied. Yet Kellan didn't quite know how to defend it. They'd survived the wedding. But it was a series of going through the motions, and even when she'd convinced Ashleigh to dance, Ashleigh refused to make eye contact. When they got into bed, Kellan tried for a cuddle, hoping closeness would permeate the wall Ashleigh was clearly intent on putting up, but when she reached out, Ashleigh pulled away. This morning they'd packed up and left in silence, skipping Shauna's day-after brunch, with Ashleigh blaming their need to get home early on Blue. Forty minutes into the drive and they'd not even scratched the surface.

"It's not that I didn't want to tell you." Kellan pressed the base of her hand to her forehead. "I almost told you a hundred times."

"Why didn't you?"

"I don't…" She let her sentence fade away before trying again. "It's just not that simple."

"You have a kid, Kellan. That's a pretty serious omission."

"Ugh." The assumption in Ashleigh's tone annoyed her. It was as though she'd already made up her mind about the whole situation without even bothering to understand the details. "It's not even like that. I don't have a kid. I mean technically, I guess. But see, you're twisting it."

"I'm twisting it? I'm fucking twisting it?"

She saw the spit fly from Ashleigh's lips and registered her anger. She needed to de-escalate and start over. "Can we stop?"

"Oh, I think we're done."

"I meant stop the car," she said in a low voice, the finality of Ashleigh's statement hitting her full force. "Please don't call it quits over this. Not without knowing the full story. You've got to be curious what the hell is going on. Ash, I want to tell you. Let me talk. Please?"

Ashleigh was quiet, but she put on her directional signal and took the exit ramp into a shopping plaza off the highway. She pulled into a space at the far end of the deserted lot and slammed the car into Park, squaring her body against the door and crossing her arms over her chest. "I'm listening," she said.

The defensive body language was unmistakable, but it just made her long to reach across the console and touch Ashleigh. Instinct told her it was a bad idea.

"I know it looks like Zoey is my kid," she started.

"Um." Ashleigh hitched her shoulders high in a kind of challenge.

"I suppose it's true. But only in the most technical sense. Like, the biological sense."

"Is there any other way to be a parent?" Ashleigh countered.

"Yeah, like a thousand ways. There's adoption and fostering." She shook her head at the naivete of Ashleigh's argument. "Also actually being a presence in someone's life. In my opinion, that's what makes you a parent."

"Is that what happened here? Dara adopted your baby? That's the special bond you two share?"

"No. Ash, no." Her head was spinning. "That's what you think is going on?"

"Kellan, I have no idea what's going on. Because you chose not to tell me."

She collected her thoughts for a minute, trying to figure out where to go from here. In the hours that had gone by, she'd been so overwhelmed that even though she asked for a chance to explain, she hadn't really planned out what to say.

"Zoey isn't mine because she never was." She picked at a loose thread from the ripped knee of her jeans. "Dara tried for years to have a baby, but she had a specific fertility problem that stemmed from her eggs being low quality or small or...something. I don't remember the medical term. Bottom line, she couldn't get pregnant with her own eggs. So I gave her mine. It's not like I was going to use them anyway."

Ashleigh looked through the windshield, seeming to take it all in. "You were her egg donor."

"Yes. It made complete sense to me. Dara was my best friend in the world. I would have died for her on the battlefield a hundred times over. And she would have done the same for me. I know that for a fact." She felt her throat tighten with heaviness at the statement but forced a cough to keep it at bay. "She happened to have a medical problem that I could help with. If she'd needed blood or a kidney, I wouldn't have thought twice about it. I didn't see how this was any different at all."

"Zoey is your baby with her husband?"

"Zoey is Dara's child," she corrected. "Conceived with my egg and Ronnie's sperm," she said, spelling it out in the most sterile language.

"I'm sorry. That's what I meant." Ashleigh pressed her fingertips to her temples as though she was trying to understand it all.

Kellan reached for her hand, and for the first time in twenty hours, Ashleigh didn't immediately pull away. "I know this is a lot to process—"

"Why didn't you talk for so many years? You told me you hadn't talked in twelve years. Why?"

"I told you why." She looked at Ashleigh's delicate hand as she caressed her slender fingers. "Ronnie asked me to back away from the family unit they were trying to build. It hurt. Obviously. But I thought maybe it was a decision they'd come to together. I opted to respect their wishes."

"It's clearly not the case," Ashleigh said, withdrawing her hand

and looping a strand of hair behind her ear. "He's not in the picture anymore, and she couldn't stop staring at you all night. Both of them, actually."

Kellan had noticed the looks too. Even though she'd only interacted with Dara for a brief minute to exchange contact information, Kellan had been aware of their eyes on her all night. Zoey seemed especially interested, and Kellan couldn't blame her. The curiosity was mutual.

"She looks so much like you. I can't get over it."

It was the truth, but in the moment, Kellan wondered if Ashleigh's statement was just a use of the cliché, or if that was how she really felt.

"I bet that's why her husband couldn't take you being there," Ashleigh said. "I'd be shocked if that kid got any of his genes."

"Trust me, it would be a blessing if she didn't."

There was silence as Ashleigh stared out the window, and Kellan wanted to know what she was thinking. But she was too scared to push any further than they'd already gone. When Ashleigh looked over, her expression was serious and pained.

"Why didn't you tell me any of this?"

If that wasn't the million-dollar question. Kellan knew her reasoning and she believed in it still, even in light of how things were unraveling. She licked her lips and spoke directly from the heart.

"I wanted to. I hope you know that. Even though I've always thought about it as simply a medical procedure, it is something that crosses my mind often. Not because I have regrets or wanted more involvement or anything like that." She wiped her hands against her jeans. "Mostly because I missed Dara so much. Our friendship was so important to me. You were the first person I ever really wanted to talk to about it. It actually hurt to keep it in."

"But then—"

"It's all so linked together. I told you about Dara, or what I could, anyway," she said even though she knew she'd downplayed it. Her stomach turned from both hunger and stress. "The rest of it, the Zoey part…" She stared out the window, knowing full well her future hinged on her explanation. "I fundamentally believe it's not my story to tell."

"But it was your body. Your DNA out in the world. How is that not your business?"

"I hadn't talked to Dara in years. I didn't have a clue what she'd shared with people." Kellan felt her anxiety skyrocket. "I mean, knowing her like I did, I thought she'd probably be the kind of person who'd tell it like it is. Be open that she used a donor and all that. But Ronnie was so freaked out by it. And I never really asked Dara what her intentions were. Honestly, it was none of my business. Those were their choices to make."

"She obviously knows, though. Zoey is literally the one who saw you first. I mean, you heard her. She picked you out of the crowd. It seems she knows all about you."

"I know." Kellan had been fixated on the same piece of information since yesterday. She saw a seagull coast into the distance and wondered how far away the water was. "Ash, I didn't know that until yesterday. I swear to you."

Ashleigh nodded, and Kellan wondered if she believed her and if it made a difference at all. She could feel her chest tighten, and she just wanted to know that everything was going to be okay. That this was just a hiccup. She reached over and touched Ashleigh's thigh gently.

"Tell me this doesn't end us." It wasn't a question so much as a plea, and she heard her voice crack with doubt. Ashleigh covered her hand and the contact soothed her.

"I don't know." She watched Ashleigh lean her head all the way back and cover her eyes. Kellan was sure she was crying, but she didn't know how to fix it. There was no undoing the past. Not the decision she'd made fourteen years ago, nor the way she'd elected to handle that information presently. "It's a lot to think about," Ashleigh said. "Right now I'm just trying to get through today."

Kellan agreed with a subtle nod, even though she didn't really know what that meant.

"Do you want coffee or anything?" Ashleigh's voice was flat as she pointed to Starbucks at the end of the strip of stores. "I know I rushed us out this morning. I'm sure you're starving."

For the first time in forever, Kellan couldn't even think about putting anything in her stomach. Her head was beginning to pound, and the lack of caffeine was probably a contributing factor, but even coffee had no appeal.

"No," she managed. She wanted to say more, to beg for Ashleigh's understanding, her support, her love. But the emptiness inside told her there were no words that would make a difference. She stayed quiet as Ashleigh pressed the ignition and pulled back out onto the parkway.

❖

Three days into their hiatus, and Kellan was going crazy. Ashleigh had asked for time. To think, to deal, to adjust. To be honest, she wasn't really sure what Ashleigh was doing during the separation. All she knew was seventy-two hours with zero contact felt like a lifetime. She'd run more miles than she'd thought possible and had countless therapy sessions with Blue. And even though he was generous with the snuggles, he didn't seem to have any real advice. Today she was even finding it difficult to focus on her scheduled meetup with Dara and Zoey. After Dara texted on Monday following the wedding, they locked in a plan for a casual lunch at one of the local eateries in the park next to her apartment. She checked her phone, telling herself she was curious how much time there was before they arrived, but she knew she was really looking to see if Ashleigh had texted. No such luck. Her stomach twisted into a knot, but she didn't have time to wallow. The apartment intercom system chirped and Sanjay's voice came through announcing her visitors.

"I'll be right down," she said.

Anticipation of this meeting had been building in the days since the wedding, but if she let herself really think about it, she'd been waiting for it for way longer, and Kellan owed it to all of them to be mentally present. But her head was in shambles, her heart on the verge of breaking. Dara might understand why she was distracted if she knew the details. She was an adult, and someone who once upon a time knew her better than anyone else in the world. But Zoey was a different story. First impressions afforded no do-overs, and thirteen-year-old girls were a notoriously tough crowd. She bounced up and down on her toes and shook out her entire body. She needed to bring it.

"Hey, guys," she said, waving from the elevator bank as she strode toward them.

Dara immediately pulled her into a bear hug and Kellan clutched her tightly. She felt Zoey's arms around her back and adjusted her embrace to include her. It was such a simple, small action, but in that instant she felt twelve years of ice completely melt away, and when she pulled pack, it was obvious she wasn't the only one overwhelmed with emotion.

Dara wiped at her eyes. "It has been too long."

"I know." She turned to Zoey. "And you. I haven't seen you since you were a baby." She almost rolled her eyes at how old she sounded. "Mom talks about you all the time. She says I'm just like you."

"Is that right?" She stole a look at Dara who answered with a shrug.

"You're an important person in our lives. Whether we see you or not." Dara took her arm, and she guided them through the lobby and into the park.

Kellan felt the emergence of her first smile in days. "Let's see what we can do to fix that."

Over burgers and milkshakes she learned that Zoey was into photography and played lacrosse. She loved music, but Kellan wasn't familiar with too many of the bands she named. She tried to keep a mental list to look them up later. Zoey bragged that math was her favorite subject, and Kellan kept her composure, even when her first thought went to Ashleigh. When it was her turn to talk, she told them of her plan to work at her parents' resort in Colorado and her Brooklyn summer gig babysitting Blue. She supplemented her story with pictures of the cat and the promise to introduce them when they headed back.

No one seemed in a rush to leave as they relaxed at their outdoor table, nursing their shakes. After a while Zoey left to wander the park, within viewable distance, swinging on a tire swing and taking pics of the scenery. Instinctively, Kellan kept watch along with Dara.

"How is Ronnie with her?" she asked.

"He calls on her birthday. And Christmas." Dara toyed with the edge of her hamburger bun. "Sends her over-the-top gifts, of course."

"Fuck, really? He doesn't even see her?" She knew Ronnie was a selfish jerk, but this seemed a new low even for him. "What happened to wanting a family so bad?"

Dara swallowed a snide laugh. "He has two boys with his new wife. They live up in Yonkers. It's not very far from here, but truthfully Zoey doesn't even ask to see him that much."

"I'm sorry, Dara. That sucks."

"You're sweet." Dara's smile was genuine. "We're better off without him." She rested her chin in the palm of her hand. "Zoey is a great kid. I'm lucky." Her eyes held an unspeakable gratitude, and Kellan was moved by the sentiment.

"Does he at least send child support?" she asked.

"He does. Ronnie was always good with money. Parenting, basic communication skills, genuine feelings on the other hand...eh, not so much. But money, he had that shit locked down."

Kellan felt the significance of the statement in her gut. Dara reached over and touched her forearm. "Kellan, I'm sorry. That was insensitive." She shook her head and licked her lips. "I was so excited to see you that I forgot all about that." Dara made real eye contact and Kellan saw the spirit and kindness she had missed for so many years. She didn't need her to continue, but Dara did anyway. "You have to believe me. I didn't know about the money. What Ronnie offered you to go away. I swear I would have left him right then." She let out a sigh, seeming frustrated. "I wish I had known. In retrospect, it would have saved us both a lot of time. I didn't find out until years later when we were finally getting divorced and he tried to throw it in my face." She shook her head. "At the time, when I stopped hearing from you, I thought, I don't know, maybe all this"—she gestured to Zoey in the distance—"was too much. Then when I realized what had really happened, I tried to find you. Which is a remarkably difficult task. The Army was useless, no surprise. And you're not on any social media." A small laugh escaped her. "How does one even exist like that?"

"I do everything through incognito mode and backdoor channels." She winked.

"You were always so savvy at the tech stuff."

"That's my intel background at work." Kellan smiled. "Don't knock the Army. It wasn't all bad."

"Brought us together." Her smile was magnetic and Kellan felt herself respond in kind. "I missed you, kid," Dara said. "Don't go leaving me again."

"I actually had plans to stay." Kellan rubbed a knot in the wooden picnic table, hoping the rough texture would provide even one second of distraction from the pain she felt in her chest. "Now...I don't know." She looked up at the sky but failed to come up with the right words to continue.

"Trouble in paradise?" Without waiting for an answer, Dara continued. "I could sense something brewing between you and your girlfriend at the wedding. What's her name?"

"Ashleigh."

"Ashleigh. Right," she said, seeming to commit it to memory. "You don't have to tell me the details if you don't want to. But I already know it has everything to do with me and Zoey." Dara stood and extended her hand to help Kellan up. "A dozen years may have passed, but you're still you and I'm still me. Let's walk. We'll put the two halves of our shared brain together and have this romance back on track in no time."

Chapter Twenty-four

The knock on the door was so faint, Ashleigh wasn't sure if it was her imagination or not, but she tiptoed past Granny dozing on the living room couch just to make sure she wasn't losing her mind completely.

She looked through the window and felt a knot in the pit in her stomach at the sight of Kellan facing the street, her perfect square fingertips kneading the base of her buzzed hairline. Ashleigh had avoided her all week, coming up with excuses when Kellan suggested they talk and repeatedly texting to ask for more time. In her heart she knew they needed to have this conversation. Her stall tactics were simply prolonging the inevitable.

"Hi," she said, opening the door and stepping out onto the top step of her parents' stoop.

Kellan turned around at the sound of her voice. "Hey. Hi." She looked stressed and sad, worry lines exaggerated by exhaustion, Ashleigh assumed. "I'm sorry to just show up with no warning. I just…I thought you'd tell me not to come if I asked."

Ashleigh took a step forward and held her waist, touching her forehead to the center of Kellan's chest in a kind of embrace. "You're probably right." She looked up into her gorgeous green eyes, but it was too painful to let her stare linger. "Come. Sit," she said, gently guiding them to the steps.

They were silent for a minute, the raucous sounds of summer spilling over from Prospect Park a block away. Ashleigh's mind went back to the day not so long ago when they'd walked along the edge of the park and professed their feelings. Tumbling in behind that image were memories of holding hands as they debated art, laughing as they explored lower Manhattan, flirting over the best coffee on the planet.

"Do you remember the day we went to Central Park?" Ashleigh asked.

"Of course. It was the first day we spent together."

Kellan was seated a step below her, and Ashleigh rubbed her strong shoulders just to feel them one last time. "You insisted on getting a hot dog." She shook her head in spite of her smile. "You were, like, backpedaling to the vendor with this huge grin, and I thought, Holy Christ, how am I going to spend every day with this person? I was already so far gone. And it was day one."

"You could have fooled me." Kellan pressed her body against her bare calf.

"I couldn't let you know I was falling from the get-go." Ashleigh nudged her with her leg. She still loved how Kellan made it so easy to say exactly what was on her mind. "Where's the fun in that?" She heard the strain in her small chuckle, but it was nice to see Kellan's soft smile at her banter.

"Ash, I'm sorry. About everything. I didn't know how to tell you," Kellan said. "Or if I even should. And then with everything that happened between you and me, plus coping with the Dara situation, it was a lot at once. I messed everything up."

"You didn't." Ashleigh looked across the street at the neighbor's house, remembering Kellan's scheduled lunch plan with Dara and Zoey. She knew she needed to ask, no matter how hard it was to accept. She did her best to keep her voice steady. "How was lunch the other day? Did you all have a nice time?"

"Yes." Kellan looked down, seeming unsure of how much detail to provide. "In time everything would have come out. I just needed to see what the deal was first. Please understand that."

It felt like Kellan was seeking forgiveness, but Ashleigh knew it wasn't hers to give. "You don't have to apologize," she said. "I get your reasoning. Honest. The brain part of me does, anyway." She swallowed hard, knowing the hardest words were ahead of her. "I've been wrestling with this all week. What you did for Dara, the gift you gave her, it was selfless and noble. It was everything you really are. Living proof of the very things that make you such an amazing human being, right there."

She felt her throat scratch and knew the tears were only seconds behind, but she forced herself to continue. "Dara and Zoey—even though you hadn't seen them until the other day, I can't help thinking that whole experience must have shaped so much of your life." She wiped away the first tear before it fell. "What you did for your friend, for her family…you changed their lives forever. It can't have been an easy decision. It had to have an impact on who you are. On your life."

"I mean, yes. Of course." Kellan looked at her, but her expression said she wasn't following her train of thought.

"What I keep coming back to is you didn't want to tell me. Whatever you were feeling, I wasn't important enough to share it with. Which is completely your choice—"

"It wasn't like that," Kellan pleaded.

"It's okay. Look, I know I was fired up the other day in the car coming home." She fought past the awkwardness of her knee-jerk reaction. "The truth of the matter is I'm not mad." What she felt was overwhelming sorrow at the imbalance of their feelings. The disparity was glaring in light of the things they'd each chosen to share and keep hidden. "I'm just sad because what I thought this was…" She stopped to try to collect herself, but it was no use. Her composure was cracking. Her voice shook as she waved between them. "I'm realizing now it wasn't."

"How can you say that?"

"I can hear in your voice that you think I'm put off or angry. But that's not it. I swear." In her heart she felt the tiny fissures starting, the first cracks before it ultimately shattered into pieces. Without even thinking about it, she rubbed Kellan's back, needing the contact for her own comfort. "It's just that I confided so much in you. My marriage, my divorce, how small I feel around Reagan and Josh. I can't help thinking you were going through some massive drama too. Being here. So close to Dara and Zoey and not seeing them. It must have been eating away at you. And you didn't want to share it with me, or talk to me about it, or let me help you. Even if I didn't have answers, I would have listened."

"It's not like you're making it sound. It wasn't on my mind all the time."

"But you *are* in Brooklyn. And you knew Dara was here too. You must have been feeling something. I mean obviously you were. Your mom knew. Your aunt knew."

"They don't know. They think they know something. But they're wrong. They don't have a clue about Zoey. I never told anyone."

"That's not really the point."

"But it is the point." Kellan clenched her jaw, and Ashleigh hated to see her upset and clearly fighting hard to hold it together. "You are the only one I ever even considered confiding in."

"I guess that should make me feel better, but my heart just hurts, and I don't think words can fix that."

"Tell me what can. I will do anything."

"It's just too hard, Kellan. You're leaving—"

"But I'm staying. To be with you."

"And to be with them." Kellan looked like she was going to say something, but Ashleigh stopped her. "I know you'll tell me that's not true, or that it's both. And I should be okay with that. And again, logically, I am. But there's this doubt that creeps in."

"But I don't—"

Kellan's protest was soft, but Ashleigh stopped her with a finger to her lips. It wasn't that she didn't want to hear what she had to say. It was simply that this conversation took every ounce of courage she had in her. If Kellan pushed, she would concede. While she cringed to think of the days ahead without her, experience taught her that a relationship founded on unequal footing would never truly balance out. It would always teeter, threatening to collapse under the slightest pressure.

"What we were planning—long-distance, the back and forth—it would have been a challenge to begin with. But now, I just feel…" After nearly a week of internal debate, she knew what she had to do. But the words were still a struggle. "Whether it's true or not, I feel betrayed." She covered her heart, owning her emotion. "I know those are my feelings and not at all what you intended." She acknowledged her sorrow, the feeling of defeat bursting from every cell in her body. "Still. It's hard to get past that in the best of circumstances."

Kellan looked wounded by her words, and she longed to make it better. Ashleigh touched a hand to the side of her face, her thumb caressing her smooth chiseled jawline.

"Please don't look at me like that," she said, letting her tears come. "This summer will always be special to me. I will always remember it as the season you turned my life around. I'll think of you nonstop. I'll see you everywhere. City landmarks, the park, Liam's, every time I see a mom struggling with a stroller in the subway." She laughed through her sniffle as she wiped the stream of tears steadily falling. "This city is full of you now. And I am so grateful for that. You opened my heart again." She prayed for the will to go on. "You taught me things about myself I didn't know. You made me laugh and smile and feel joy. And I will always love you for that."

Kellan was obviously choked up, but she said nothing, simply leaned forward and placed her head in her lap. Ashleigh thought she might be crying, and she stroked her head delicately.

"Please don't cry," she said through her own muffled sob. It was an unfair request, but Ashleigh only had so much willpower. As it was, she was on the verge of cracking. She bent forward and kissed Kellan's head, as always surprised at the softness of her short hair. "I am so weak for you," she whispered through her tears. "Which is, I guess, poetic because you make me feel strong."

"You are strong." Kellan picked her head up. Her eyes were glassy but she was clearly steeling herself for the moment. "You're strong and brave and kind." She scooted away and stood up, pacing the step she stood on. But like their situation, there was nowhere to go. "I don't want to leave," she said.

"You have to." Ashleigh pulled herself up, and standing a step above Kellan, they were nearly the same height. "It is never going to get easier."

Kellan pulled her in to a hug so tight, Ashleigh thought she could feel their hearts beating together. She buried her face in Kellan's shoulder and let everything out, not caring how disheveled she was going to look. Kellan held her and kissed her face until she found her lips, leaving a touch as soft as a whisper.

"I love you," Kellan said.

Ashleigh could barely breathe. She nodded agreement and swallowed her pain. "Good-bye, Kellan." She pulled away and raced into the house, sinking into a crumpled mess on the tile floor as she wondered if her heart would ever fully recover.

CHAPTER TWENTY-FIVE

Why some people protested so hard against the theory of climate change, Ashleigh would never understand. Regardless of where one fell in the party lines, it was difficult to dispute the mild summer temps that stretched well into October in New York these days. Ashleigh looked out her classroom window at the green leaves of a tall tree, wondering if they'd turn by Christmas. She reached for a stack of projects to grade—her weekend entertainment, as she liked to think of it—and slid them into her oversized bag.

"Knock, knock."

"Not today, Shaun. Not next Friday either."

Since school started back up, Shauna had been on a mission to get her to go out more. The after-school Friday teacher drink-fest was when she laid it on the thickest. Time to restart her engine, Shauna kept saying. At least that was the mantra she'd adopted after she'd finally given up on campaigning for Kellan, anyway. Ashleigh had zero interest. She grabbed her keys and turned to face her oldest friend, doing a literal double-take when it wasn't Shauna in her doorway.

"Sorry to sneak up on you. I don't know if you remember me— I'm Kellan's friend."

"Dara. Of course." Ashleigh doubted she'd ever forget her face. She still saw it in her dreams, not as routinely as Kellan's, but every so often, Dara and Zoey made an appearance too.

"Shauna did tell me where I could find you, though." Dara smiled as she inspected a calculus problem detailed on the whiteboard. "It's funny—I used to babysit for her. Shauna," she said, mostly to herself.

"Really?" Considering that tidbit, Ashleigh was surprised she'd never heard her name before the wedding.

"I doubt she even remembers." Dara addressed her obvious confusion. "She was only a toddler. Then our moms had this big row." She shook her head. "Anyway, it's all sorted now. But being eleven years older than Shauna, and then joining the Army, I missed out on that side of my family. I was thrilled to be invited to her wedding. Gave me a chance to reconnect with some distant relatives. Introduce Zoey to some of my cousins, her tías. And then Kellan." She blew out a long breath. "That blew my mind."

"I'm sure." Nearly two months had passed, but it was still agonizing to think about Kellan. She forced a smile to cover her anguish. "Are you here meeting up with Shauna?" she asked.

"Ha. No." Dara leaned on the door frame as her eyes darted around the classroom. "I came here to see you. To talk some sense into you, hopefully."

"Look." Ashleigh stood next to her desk with no idea what to say. "If you're here to talk about Kellan—"

"Of course I'm here to talk about Kellan."

"There's nothing to say. I haven't even spoken to her since she left."

"I know."

"So then you know there's nothing to say."

Dara held one finger up, punctuating the air. "I'm going to disagree with you on that point. See, I just got back from Colorado."

Ashleigh swallowed hard. She didn't know how to respond or, more importantly, how long she'd be able to keep her emotions in check. Thankfully, Dara filled the silence.

"I took Zoey out there for a visit over Columbus Day weekend. Have you ever been? It's beautiful."

"No." She felt a sharp pain at the thought of Kellan at home in a place she couldn't even picture. Thousands of miles away, surrounded by people she didn't know. How had everything changed so radically in such a short time? Sometimes it seemed like she'd only been gone for days. In the worst moments, it felt like an eternity.

"Kellan showed us around the mountains. Her parents' lodge. The adorable town. When we go back in the winter, she's going to teach Zoey to snowboard."

Ashleigh shrugged. "Sounds like you have it all figured out."

"What I can't wrap my head around is why you're here and she's there." Dara dragged a finger along the tops of the desks as she walked farther into the room. "Makes absolutely no sense to me." She stopped in front of Stef Hengle's workspace and perched on the edge of the table.

Ashleigh sighed. "I don't really know what this is—"

"Oh, this?" Dara pointed dramatically. "This is an intervention."

"Did Kellan send you here?"

Dara laughed out loud and hung her head in dramatic fashion. "I'm pretty sure you know the answer to that. She would kill me if she knew I was here. But I love her too much to see her the way she is, so I'm banking on you being the reasonable one."

Ashleigh stuck her chin out at Dara's presumptive tone but didn't get a chance to refute her.

"See, the thing about Kellan is she's got so much pride. Or maybe it's stubbornness. Is there a difference?" She seemed to contemplate the point before continuing. "And maybe that's a flaw. I don't know." Dara picked up a fidget cube and rolled it between her fingers. "I know how she is from witnessing her in action all those years together in the military. But just in case I forgot, I get to see it in Zoey every day. It's actually amazing how similar they are. Athletic, genius with gadgets, can fix nearly anything techy. They both have these unbelievably huge hearts. So selfless. And so much goddamn pride. Neither will admit when they're hurting." She flicked the cube's switch over and over. "You know, when her father left, Zoey wouldn't even cry. Inside, she was crushed. Six years old and she put on a brave face every day. I think so I wouldn't worry. Sound familiar?"

Ashleigh wondered why Dara thought this would help when it only drew attention to the reason Kellan wasn't here. "Well, I'm glad they have each other now. That you all seem to have…whatever it is you have."

"Don't even with that kind of implication." She turned the device over in her hand, moving one finger over the rollerball. "Kellan is my best friend in the world. And yeah, I love her, but not like that. I'm pretty sure you know that. As far as Zoey goes, her father is a deadbeat. She's curious to learn a little about her genetic makeup from a person who doesn't suck. Don't get all up in your head pretending we're going to be some kind of insta-family now."

"But you just said you're going to visit again this winter."

"Yes. That's what friends do. They visit." She put the stress toy back in its place on Stef's desk. "You know, it's also what girlfriends do."

"We're not—"

"No, I know. I know the whole story." Dara put a hand up to stop her. "I'm divorced too," she said proving that she was up to speed on the details. "I get what it's like to have trust issues, particularly after being in a relationship that didn't work out, whatever the reasons. And having to deal with something as unique as this situation can't be easy."

"Please don't think I'm judging. I can't imagine what you went through trying to have a child. And for Kellan to help you the way she did…" Ashleigh fought the sting in her throat. "I'm hardly surprised. Kellan's an amazing person."

"Do you know what the process is like?"

Ashleigh shook her head. She didn't even know what Dara was asking.

"It's intense. Being someone's egg donor," Dara said. "You have to constantly be on top of your health. Monitor blood pressure, temperature, take medicine, give yourself shots daily. And that's all before you go for the surgical procedure." She inspected her short fingernails. "You get nothing for it. Not in this kind of scenario, anyway. Kellan never complained. Not once."

Did Dara really think she would be surprised by Kellan's selflessness or strength?

"I know you know her," Dara said, clearly reading her face. "I'm sure you're not shocked. I just want you to understand that this wasn't treated like some kind of routine favor. It was very serious business. A huge commitment." She stuffed her hands in the pockets of her slim-cut jeans. "I know you feel betrayed that she didn't tell you. I feel partially responsible on that front. If things hadn't gotten so messed up between me and her, I'm sure you would have known. I'm sure of it." Dara withdrew her hands and folded her arms across her chest. "Maybe she handled it all wrong with you. That's not for me to say." She shrugged. "What I do know, what I'm one hundred percent certain of"—Dara looked right at her—"is her intentions were pure. Her heart was in the right place." She covered her chest as she spoke, and her eyes sparkled with respect. "It always is. That's Kellan. And if you love her half as much as she loves you, you know that too. So quit futzing around and go get her."

"What do you mean go get her?" Ashleigh looked around her classroom in awe of Dara's ridiculous suggestion.

"If she thinks you don't want her in your life, she's not going to force her way back in. I know that firsthand. You're going to have to be the one to make it happen."

It was a lot to process, and Ashleigh's brain felt like scrambled eggs. "First of all, I wouldn't even know where to begin." Her mouth was dry, and she licked her lips, buying a few seconds to compute what was happening here. "Honestly, I don't even know how she feels anymore."

"You don't know how she feels?" Dara laughed in her face. "How she feels?" She gaped. Ashleigh could see her tongue poking the inside of her cheek. "How can I put this in a way you'll understand? She feels…" With one finger, Dara circled the air in the vicinity of Ashleigh's face. "She feels how you look. Completely lost. Heartbroken. That paint a picture for you?"

Ashleigh didn't know what to say or how to feel. The thought of Kellan feeling any kind of pain or sorrow tortured her. She focused on the lines of the square terrazzo floor, unable to make eye contact for fear that Dara would see into her heart and know her feelings for Kellan were as strong as ever. When she finally looked up, Dara was leaving.

"Dara, wait."

"Yeah?" She turned in the doorway.

"Thank you. For coming here. For telling me." Ashleigh wiped an unexpected tear away. "I don't know what I'm going to do. Not really." She swiped a tissue from the box on her desk. "But thank you."

Dara smiled and shrugged. "My motives aren't totally pure. Kellan's my other half. My buddy. The yin to my yang. My ride or die. How can I be totally happy when I know how much she's hurting, ya know?"

Ashleigh breathed out long and hard, half crying, half smiling. "What am I going to do?" She was mostly thinking out loud, but Dara answered.

"You'll figure it out." Dara backed away. "The Desmond," she said, with a final point of her finger. "That's the name of her family's resort in Vail." She tossed a playful smirk and added a wink. "Just in case you wanted to show up on a white horse or something."

❖

Ashleigh dumped the pile of clean laundry on her bed, sorting it into categories before reaching for a shirt to fold. She started with Kellan's worn Army tee that she still slept in every night. Out of habit and longing, she brought it to her face, but any scent of Kellan was long gone, replaced by her mom's detergent and fabric softener.

Dara's words echoed on loop through her mind. Only two days had passed, but she'd replayed the conversation in her head a hundred times. She barely left the house all weekend, spending the forty-eight hours cooped up, analyzing every detail of her decision to end things with Kellan.

Even though nothing had changed, hearing Dara's perspective somehow made her feel different than she had before. For the first time, she put herself in Kellan's shoes and wondered what she might have done if the situation was reversed. It certainly wasn't as cut-and-dried as she wanted it to be, and she allowed herself to own the fact that there probably wasn't one right answer.

She folded a camisole in half and was placing it atop the rest of her shirts when it hit her. The dark truth she'd known all along. Kellan's misstep—if it could even be called that—had given her an escape.

Kellan's feelings for her had been true. Of that she was certain. But what if they faded in time? What if she got bored with her routine life? A high school math teacher who liked to visit museums on the weekend might be a decent summer distraction, but for the long term, Kellan would surely want more. Even Reagan had. The idea of having something real with Kellan and then losing her was a pain she couldn't bear to imagine. In the last two years she'd struggled through her break-up with Reagan, and her feelings weren't even romantic for the last half of that union. A split with Kellan would decimate her. She was sure of it. It was the safer choice to bail out before she was in too deep.

But wasn't she destroyed now? She shook off the thought as she put away a stack of leggings. She fought off tears daily when she looked at pictures of their summer together just to see Kellan's face and remember what it felt like to be in her arms. Didn't that qualify as legit heartbreak? The pain of their dissolution didn't feel more palatable because it had come at her own hand.

Ashleigh closed the drawer with a thud and leaned against the dresser, surveying her bedroom. What the fuck was she doing with her life, besides letting it pass by?

She closed her eyes and watched the reel of her existence play out in her mind. Her friends and her parents were always there, her champions through everything. They'd given comfort, support, encouragement, and advice in the last few years and again in recent weeks. She leaned on them like a crutch.

It was time to lose the training wheels.

She opened her eyes and let herself feel joy and excitement surge through her. Some nerves too, for sure. But suddenly, she knew what she needed to do. What she wanted to do. It came to her out of nowhere, like an epiphany. Her own Angel Gabriel with a ridiculous and crazy premonition of the future.

And even though the idea was wild and essentially went against all the logical, rational bones in her body, she knew she had to follow her heart and go for it. It was time to be spontaneous.

❖

"Liam, I'm about to do something crazy." Ashleigh strode into the bar on a mission.

"Good afternoon to you too," he said with a friendly smile.

"I'm sorry." She leaned over the bar and planted a kiss on his cheek. "Hi," she said, prepared to start over. "How are you?"

"Shut up," he teased. "What's going on?" He placed a seltzer with lime in front of her. "It must be serious to get you in here on a Sunday. He leaned back to assess her. "Fill me in."

Ashleigh leaned on her elbows, covering her mouth and nose with both hands, still reeling over her secret decision. "Do you talk to Kellan at all?"

"Yes."

"Is she…I mean does she…" She didn't know really what she

was trying to get at. There was very little Liam could say that would alter her mind. She supposed she just wanted someone neutral to weigh in. Make sure she hadn't truly gone off the deep end. She already had weeks of Shauna and Granny urging her to contact Kellan—she knew where they stood. Because of his friendships with both her and Kellan, Liam seemed to be her best chance of Switzerland.

"Kellan misses you, if that's what you're asking."

"She told you that?"

He took a long breath, wiping the bar as he seemed to select his words carefully. "Ash, I saw her the day she left. She came in here…" He held his palms up in surrender. "She was wrecked. I've been through actual war with Kellan." He licked his lips, the gesture adding a heaviness to his sentiment. "This was a whole other level. Since then, I talk to her. We text. She won't exactly tell me she misses you. But she asks how you are. If you're okay. I'm no idiot. I can read between the lines."

Ashleigh nodded, taking it all in. She took a sip of the crisp seltzer, the tartness of the lime hitting her as she swallowed. "I'm going to go there."

"To Colorado?" He nodded. "Good. Does Kellan know? Did you talk to her?"

"No."

"Gonna surprise her for the weekend?" His tone didn't sound as though he thought it was a bad idea. "Nice."

"Not for the weekend."

"Huh?"

That detail clearly threw him for a loop, and she knew she needed to explain. "Liam, I made a mess of everything. When I found out about Dara and Zoey—" She stopped herself from saying more, fearing she might have just violated a trust.

"It's okay—I know. I didn't before. Then when everything went south with you two, I was confused. Kellan was devastated. Anyway, she filled me in. I basically had to pull it out of her."

"It's so much worse than that. Kellan wanted to stay. To figure it out. To figure us out. I pushed her away. I mean, hard. And the thing is, I was just scared. I love her. And God, it scares the pants off me."

"Heard all about that too."

"Jerk." She pulled the straw from her drink and threw it at him, stifling a smile the entire time. "Here I am pouring my heart out, and you're making jokes about my sex life."

"Sorry. Sorry." He waved a white towel.

"The point I'm trying to make is that I don't know if a weekend will cut it. I want to show her I'm in it for the long haul. I'm going to go out there and prove it to her. I mean, if she's with someone, I don't know, I guess I'll come home. But barring that, I'm going to stay and fight for her."

"What about school?"

"I just texted my principal on the way over here. We actually have a really good relationship. I was completely honest with her. Told her I need a leave of absence and why. Leaving midsemester isn't ideal, but I've never asked for anything. Not even when I was going through my separation and divorce." She felt her heart swell at the thought she would see Kellan so soon. "As far as Colorado goes, the speck of research I did indicates that with a few small steps my New York teaching license will be eligible for reciprocity. So hopefully I can line up some subbing work. Until then, there's private tutoring. Luckily, thanks to my living sitch the last few years, I have some money saved. That helps."

"Wow. You are doing this."

"I am."

"Fuck, I'm going to miss you."

Ashleigh shrugged. "You never know, I could be back in two weeks, tail between my legs."

"You won't be." Liam shook his head definitively. "She loves you, Ash. I saw it in her. I see it in you." He seemed sentimental but in a supportive way. "When are you going?"

"My flight's on Saturday."

"This Saturday? That's, like, not even a full week from now."

"She's been gone fifty-two days, Liam. It feels like forever." Ashleigh twisted the drink in her hands, knowing the swiftness of her actions was completely based in emotion. "I thought the pain would dull. But it hasn't. Not one bit. I don't want to live without her. Not another week. Not even another day." She shrugged, still a teensy bit shocked at her own bold moves in the past three hours. "Once I realized that, I put the wheels in motion."

"Look at you!"

She smiled at his obvious pride. "It may all blow up in my face. I'm going for it anyway."

"I have to admit, I'm bummed there's not even time for a farewell party."

She huffed out a laugh. "I don't want a party. I just want Kellan. Honestly, the whole time I'd be thinking about her anyway. Wishing she was here."

"I get it." He raised his ginger ale to her seltzer. "To going big or going home."

Ashleigh chewed her bottom lip, considering the poignancy of his words. "It's a crazy thing." She took a second to acknowledge the fullness in her heart and the peaceful calm that came with it before meeting his toast midair. "I kind of think I might be doing both."

CHAPTER TWENTY-SIX

Kellan stood in front of the lobby coffee bar debating her third cup. The French roast was fresh, she'd just watched it brew in the kitchen, and the jolt of caffeine would definitely give her a needed boost. Even though it was only two in the afternoon, she was shot.

An entire morning as the Desmond's makeshift concierge always took its toll, but it usually didn't drain her this much. In all honesty, playing social director was her favorite part of working at the resort. She didn't mind the other assignments—managing the cleaning staff and the grounds crew—plus learning the business end of operations with her brother. But there was something about being the guests' initial ambassador to Vail that made her heart smile.

It was fun seeing the awestruck faces of tourists as they spied the mountains and vistas as she guided them on a small walking excursion through the picturesque streets. Their faces lit up with excitement when she gave the nickel tour and clued them in to the secret gems they passed along the way. The secondhand ski shop in case there were odds and ends they'd forgotten. Doyle's burger joint, an eatery as rustic as it was delicious. She always ended at the Corner Café, a hole-in-the-wall coffee shop that looked like nothing but boasted brews to die for. Their coffee was outrageous.

The only problem was she couldn't look at it without thinking of Ashleigh. But then, she couldn't do anything without thinking of Ashleigh.

Wasn't time supposed to ease the pain?

Almost two months had gone by, and Kellan felt worse than ever.

Ashleigh was still in every thought she had. Sappy songs pumping through the hotel sound system reminded her of quiet times together, sweet and romantic. Poppy hits brought back their playful interchange as they frolicked through New York together, laughing and teasing and touching at every turn.

Vail's local architecture was just math she didn't know the inner workings of. She imagined Ashleigh hooking her arm through hers as she analyzed the angles of the structures and shops, explaining how the geometric patterns harkened back to ancient design. She could hear Ashleigh's voice clear as day. Soft and lyrical with the occasional heaviness of her accent coloring words in the cutest way.

That was what was draining her right now. Ashleigh was always in her heart, her mind, her dreams. But this morning, she'd hosted the Sinclairs, a boisterous family who hailed directly from the Bronx. They were funny and nice and so incredibly New York in every word and gesture. Just being in their presence catapulted her back to square one.

Coffee. She needed it to burst out of her funk. She checked the date on her watch. Only a couple more weeks, she thought, as she filled a recyclable cup. Come December, she would set her plan in motion.

But fuck, could she really make it until then? Some days, she thought she wouldn't survive until the next morning, and she'd whip out her phone to check last-minute flights. But she knew she had to be patient. Christmas break meant Ashleigh would be free from school and on vacation. Kellan was dedicated to winning her back, but the brevity of a weekend didn't show the level of commitment she felt inside. She had botched things with Dara so badly years ago. Giving up and letting her go, not fighting for their friendship. But she'd learned her lesson, and damned if she was going to make that mistake with the love of her life.

Kellan reached for the agave sweetener, letting out an audible sigh that was equal parts optimism and sadness.

"Rough day?"

The familiar accent came from just behind her, and she cursed her entire staff for booking so many New Yorkers at one time. She made a mental note to hide in her suite until they were all gone.

"Something like that."

She turned around to face the source of her torture and was

completely unprepared to see Ashleigh in front of her. She actually did a double take, turning and looking behind her, for what, she wasn't entirely sure.

"Can I get a cup of coffee too? I've been up since before dawn." Ashleigh uprighted her luggage and moved closer, brushing her arm against Kellan's as she reached past for a cup.

"Ash..." Kellan was at a true loss. She stuttered and stammered and felt her eyes welling up. "What are you doing here?"

"Well..." Ashleigh bumped her hip into Kellan playfully as she spoke. "I was sitting at home thinking this whole thing is stupid."

Kellan heard a confidence in her tone that was new and exciting. She felt her blood rush everywhere as Ashleigh depressed the urn's lever and filled her cup.

"Life is just too damn short to not spend it with the person you're crazy about. What we had, the way I feel about you..." Ashleigh looked up, and Kellan saw the spirit in her gorgeous blue eyes. "I'm pretty much madly in love with you." Ashleigh shrugged like it was no big deal, but the rest of her body language said she was dead serious, and it was everything Kellan could do to resist taking her in her arms and kissing her senseless.

"Well, that's a relief," she said, placing her half-made coffee aside. She knew she was beaming, her pulse pounding everywhere. She didn't even try to play it cool.

"I freaked out, Kellan. I don't know what to say except I'm sorry. The whole Dara and Zoey thing was an excuse for me. I was just so scared."

"You don't have to apologize."

"I do. I pushed you away. I was...terrified."

Kellan held a hand up to stop her. She wanted to make sure Ashleigh knew that whatever she thought her transgressions were, all was forgiven. All she wanted was Ashleigh in her arms, in her life. "Ash," she started, but Ashleigh interrupted her.

"Wait." Ashleigh met her palm and laced their fingers together. "I need to say this."

As far as Kellan was concerned, Ashleigh didn't need to say anything. The fact that she had come to Vail was enough. But she gave her the floor just the same.

"I'm organized and nerdy and structured. I like to plan, to schedule." Kellan saw her struggling to reveal her feelings and it melted her on the spot. She held her hand and let her talk.

"What you did for Dara all those years ago, it's incredible. A true act of selflessness. I love you more for it, if that's possible. But because I'm me..." Ashleigh cast her eyes on their linked fingers, giving a gentle caress, and Kellan could feel her energy kick up a notch. "In an ideal world I might have liked a minute to process it all before meeting them. But, honestly, I've given it a lot of thought. I don't have a clue what I would have done in your shoes. All I know is that I don't want to spend another minute without you."

Kellan's heart beat like crazy at the words, and she was dying to interrupt and proclaim she felt the exact same way, but Ashleigh was still talking.

"So I'm here to beg you to forgive me for telling you to leave, to plead with you to take me back, to fight for you if I have to."

"There's going to be no fighting or begging or anything like that." Kellan's body was on fire. Her heart felt like it could burst. She ran her fingers along Ashleigh's forearm, the deliberate touch electrifying her with the mix of desire and familiarity. "Can I kiss you yet?"

Ashleigh looked at her with so much love that she didn't need to verbalize a response, but she did. "You better."

Kellan took her face in her hands, placing a soft, tender kiss on her lips. She repeated the gesture over and over, feeling all her emotions rise to the surface. She pulled Ashleigh into her arms and held her tight. "I love you, Ash. So much. Thank you for coming here."

"Maybe I should have called. I wanted to prove to you that I'm in this for real." When Kellan looked down, she could see that Ashleigh was wiping away tears. "I realize you have a life, that you might not be ready for me to burst right in to it—"

Kellan laughed out loud. "You're kidding, right? You're all I think about. Day and night." It floored her that Ashleigh could even consider that she wouldn't want her twenty-four seven, and she wanted her to know it. "I spend every waking minute trying to fix this, figure out a way to win you back. I had a whole game plan concocted for December."

"You did?"

"Yes." She tamped down the emotions threatening to spill over. "I wanted to show you—you're it for me. Because you are. I figured if I came at Christmas, you'd be off from school and we could spend some real time together."

"We'll have plenty of time together now." Ashleigh giggled, but Kellan didn't get the joke.

"Wait." She assessed the multitude of bags a few feet away. "How long can you stay?"

"Funny story," Ashleigh said. "I was kind of hoping...forever?" She shrugged in the most adorable way, and even though Kellan was confused, she felt her body react with an insane amount of happiness.

"What...what does that mean?"

"This is where your life is. Your family. Your job. Kids need to learn math everywhere. I have a few private tutoring interviews lined up. I'm looking into openings in the high school programs for the fall. I want to be where you are. I need to."

"Are you serious?" she asked, already nervous that it was too good to be true. She must be misunderstanding.

Ashleigh nodded confirmation through an adorable grimace. "Too much?"

"Oh my God, I love you." Kellan held Ashleigh and kissed her face, swaying her in her arms, her tears spilling out into Ashleigh's beautiful blond hair. "I love you. I love you. I love you. You could never be too much." She choked back the rest of her emotions. "Come on, let's get you settled in." Kellan started to guide her down the hall, but she felt Ashleigh's resistance.

"I didn't even check in yet."

"You made a reservation?"

"Not here, actually. There were no vacancies this weekend. And I didn't want to assume anything."

Kellan couldn't fight the laughter in her chest. "I'm confused."

"I did everything last minute. The flights were easy, well, because Granny sends me airline updates twice a week. But lodging, I didn't really plan ahead. There was nothing available here at the Desmond. So I booked the Marriott a few blocks away."

"You did what?" Kellan faked horror. "Unacceptable. Good thing the manager there is a friend of mine. I'll reach out and cancel your room."

"Kellan, I don't want to impose. I realize I just got here, and you might want some time to adjust."

Kellan shook her head, smiling the whole time. "You're here. I don't want to spend another night without you. Ever." She shrugged, knowing her heart was fully on her sleeve. "Plus, how's it going to look if I introduce my parents to my girlfriend and then tell them she's staying with the competition?"

"Your girlfriend, huh?"

"My uber-structured, spontaneous girlfriend who moved to Colorado on a whim. Is that better?"

"I love it. I love you."

"Come on." Kellan picked up her carry-on and draped her arm over Ashleigh's shoulder, then led the way down the corridor to her corner suite. "I'll have one of the guys bring the rest of your bags to my room. We need a minute alone so I can kiss you for real. I missed you like crazy."

Ashleigh didn't wait. She leaned up and planted a kiss on her cheek. "Good news, though. I'm here now. We have all the time in the world."

Kellan stopped in front of her door and opened it. She held out her arm for Ashleigh to step in first when it hit her.

"Wait one sec." She placed Ashleigh's bag to the side of the open doorway. "Let's do this the right way."

Kellan scooped Ashleigh into her arms, leaning in and kissing her with all the love in her body and soul. Without another word, she held her gaze and carried her across the threshold, right into the rest of their lives.

EPILOGUE

Five Years Later

"You know, I never typed up a summer agenda."

Ashleigh stood on the stoop assessing the tree-lined Brooklyn street as Kellan slipped the key into the lock and opened the front door of their temporary abode.

Kellan looked over her shoulder, mouth jokingly agape. "Oh, no. Does that mean…spontaneity is in my future?" She held the door open, and Ashleigh poked her in the abdomen as she walked past. She absolutely adored when Kellan teased her, and she would take any excuse to touch her.

"You like my schedules and you know it." She dropped her luggage on the parquet floor of the sun-filled antechamber. "This is nice."

"I don't like your schedules." Kellan hugged her from behind, clearly not ready to move on. "I love them. I love you." The sincerity in Kellan's voice made her swoon, and it was hardly tempered by the heat she felt when Kellan dropped a few baby kisses while ushering them into the living room. "So much that I might have even made a tiny list of my own."

"I knew I'd win you over eventually."

"As if you didn't have me hook, line, and sinker right from that first super-detailed *spontaneous* email years ago." Ashleigh heard the banter in her tone and knew it was all in good fun, so she let Kellan go on without protest. "I knew right then and there that you were the one for me."

"You did not," she said, calling her bluff. "You thought I was an uptight dork."

"You are." Kellan kissed her generously. "Just so happens that was exactly what I needed in my life."

Ashleigh felt herself getting swept up in the moment, and while she loved every minute of it, she still wanted to see the rest of their summer rental. "So, show me this apartment and tell me what you have planned for us this summer."

"It's interesting," Kellan started as they meandered through the eat-in kitchen. "I made a list, but at this point, we've seen just about everything."

If that wasn't the truth. After five years of summering in Brooklyn, their New York City bucket list was pretty thin. Time had afforded them season after season of wonderful local memories.

For Ashleigh, Vail had been home since the moment she'd touched down in Colorado. Once she'd reunited with Kellan, she was simply unwilling to be apart again. And Kellan, God bless her, without even being asked, found a way to even the scales. All winter, spring, and fall, she more than pulled her weight around the resort, so they were free to spend the entire summer in New York.

Five years in, the gesture still made her heart swell.

"Come on, let's check out the back." She left a sweet kiss on Kellan's cheek and pulled her onward, stealing a glance into two bedrooms before she hit the back door.

"Oh my God, how sweet is this?" she said stepping outside into the privacy of a paved yard. "How did you manage to find this place?"

"Well, while you were busy running the high school math department and coaching the mathletes, I was scouring the internet looking for the perfect place. Last year was great, but it was tiny and kind of out of the way."

"This is perfect. My parents' house is three blocks away. Liam's bar is basically down the street. Shauna and Mike can even walk here with Stephon."

"This is not my first rodeo." Ashleigh adored the pride in Kellan's voice, obviously impressed at her coup. "It'll be nice to have a place to cook out. Let our friends' children run amok." Kellan shrugged. "Since we're essentially surrounded by breeders anyway, might as well make it work to our advantage."

Kellan's words were playful, but like always, the sentiment behind them was thoughtful. In recent years they'd witnessed their New York friends expand their families exponentially. Reagan and Josh had added a little girl to their brood, Shauna and Mike traipsed everywhere with three-year old Stephon. Even both her sisters had gotten married and produced three grandchildren thus far. They were truly outnumbered.

"You're a genius." Ashleigh moved closer and put her arms around Kellan's neck, reaching up to whisper in her ear. "It's nice having all the kiddos around." She nibbled an earlobe. "Best part, though, they go home at the end of the day."

"Right?" Kellan said, obviously aware they shared the sentiment. "Except for Zoey. She can stay over all she wants. I'm guessing that's the idea behind the second bedroom."

Kellan looked at the back of the house. "I wasn't looking for a two bedroom at all. But this outdoor space won me over. And honestly, with her going off to college in the fall, I wouldn't mind maximizing our time together this summer."

Over the years, Ashleigh had formed her own kinship with Zoey and Dara. She loved when they vacationed at the Desmond and found that spending time with the smart, confident teen was like having a window into the past. Zoey was kind and compassionate, funny and sharp, and so much like Kellan, even beyond the obvious physical similarities. Some of her fondest memories came from watching them interact.

"We'll all have plenty of time together in the next two months. And I promise to lock them into a winter trip. Sound good?"

"Sounds perfect." Ashleigh felt Kellan's hands lock behind her back as she pulled her closer. "Just like you." Kellan dropped a kiss, and Ashleigh let herself sink into it, knowing it was the first of so many they would share in this yard, in this apartment, in this season, in this city.

"We should go inside," she whispered. They needed to unpack, unwind, prepare for the days of people and events ahead. She saw a smirk emerge, and her pulse rose at the glimmer in Kellan's eye. "Not what I meant," she said, holding her hand as they made their way back to the house.

"That's not a no," Kellan teased.

"Like I ever say no to you."

Kellan wore a knowing look, her expression loaded with charm. "You love me a little bit?"

Silly words, but they melted her right on the spot. "I love you more than I even knew possible. And you so know it."

It was the truth now, and Ashleigh knew it would be always. Whether they were in the mountains of Colorado or on the streets of New York, their affection for each other was true, their devotion deep, their love strong as ever.

"Come on, we should get ready."

"Who are we seeing tonight?" Kellan asked.

"My parents. Dinner at Liam's place."

"Ooh, that's like two-for-one. But who will be first to take credit," she mused with a finger to her chin.

Ashleigh laughed at Kellan's humor. It was a running joke that all the people in their lives liked to take responsibility for their union. From Kellan's mom to Aunt Holly, Shauna, Granny, Liam, they all shared some pride. She and Kellan allowed each of them to bask in the glory, because in fairness, they'd all been there. Even Blue played a part.

Between them they knew the truth.

Their love was the product of fate, timing, the universe, God. Plain and simple, they owed it all to one perfect Brooklyn summer.

About the Author

Maggie Cummings is the author of five novels, including the Bay West Social series. She hails from Staten Island, NY, where she lives with her wife and their two children. She spends the bulk of her time shuttling kids and procrastinating about writing. To pay the bills, she works as a police captain in Brooklyn commanding a squad of detectives, which sounds way more exciting than it is. She is a complete sucker for indulgent TV, kettle cooked potato chips, and pedestrian chocolate.

Books Available From Bold Strokes Books

Brooklyn Summer by Maggie Cummings. When opposites attract, can a summer of passion and adventure lead to a lifetime of love? (978-1-63555-578-3)

City Kitty and Country Mouse by Alyssa Linn Palmer. Pulled in two different directions, can a city kitty and a country mouse fall in love and make it work? (978-1-63555-553-0)

Elimination by Jackie D. When a dangerous homegrown terrorist seeks refuge with the Russian mafia, the team will be put to the ultimate test. (978-1-63555-570-7)

In the Shadow of Darkness by Nicole Stiling. Angeline Vallencourt is a reluctant vampire who must decide what she wants more—obscurity, revenge, or the woman who makes her feel alive. (978-1-63555-624-7)

On Second Thought by C. Spencer. Madisen is falling hard for Rae. Even single life and co-parenting are beginning to click. At least, that is, until her ex-wife begins to have second thoughts. (978-1-63555-415-1)

Out of Practice by Carsen Taite. When attorney Abby Keane discovers the wedding blogger tormenting her client is the woman she had a passionate, anonymous vacation fling with, sparks and subpoenas fly. Legal Affairs: one law firm, three best friends, three chances to fall in love. (978-1-63555-359-8)

Providence by Leigh Hays. With every click of the shutter, photographer Rebekiah Kearns finds it harder and harder to keep Lindsey Blackwell in focus without getting too close. (978-1-63555-620-9)

Taking a Shot at Love by KC Richardson. When academic and athletic worlds collide, will English professor Celeste Bouchard and basketball coach Lisa Tobias ignore their attraction to achieve their professional goals? (978-1-63555-549-3)

Flight to the Horizon by Julie Tizard. Airline captain Kerri Sullivan and flight attendant Janine Case struggle to survive an emergency water landing and overcome dark secrets to give love a chance to fly. (978-1-63555-331-4)

In Helen's Hands by Nanisi Barrett D'Arnuk. As her mistress, Helen pushes Mickey to her sensual limits, delivering the pleasure only a BDSM lifestyle can provide her. (978-1-63555-639-1)

Jamis Bachman, Ghost Hunter by Jen Jensen. In Sage Creek, Utah, a poltergeist stirs to life and past secrets emerge.(978-1-63555-605-6)

Moon Shadow by Suzie Clarke. Add betrayal, season with survival, then serve revenge smokin' hot with a sharp knife. (978-1-63555-584-4)

Spellbound by Jean Copeland and Jackie D. When the supernatural worlds of good and evil face off, love might be what saves them all. (978-1-63555-564-6)

Temptation by Kris Bryant. Can experienced nanny Cassie Miller deny her growing attraction and keep her relationship with her boss professional? Or will they sidestep propriety and give in to temptation? (978-1-63555-508-0)

The Inheritance by Ali Vali. Family ties bring Tucker Delacroix and Willow Vernon together, but they could also tear them, and any chance they have at love, apart. (978-1-63555-303-1)

Thief of the Heart by MJ Williamz. Kit Hanson makes a living seducing rich women in casinos and relieving them of the expensive jewelry most won't even miss. But her streak ends when she meets beautiful FBI agent Savannah Brown. (978-1-63555-572-1)

Face Off by PJ Trebelhorn. Hockey player Savannah Wells rarely spends more than a night with any one woman, but when photographer Madison Scott buys the house next door, she's forced to rethink what she expects out of life. (978-1-63555-480-9)

Hot Ice by Aurora Rey, Elle Spencer, and Erin Zak. Can falling in love melt the hearts of the iciest ice queens? Join Aurora Rey, Elle Spencer, and Erin Zak to find out! A contemporary romance novella collection. (978-1-63555-513-4)